LITTLE, BROWN
LB
LARGE PRINT

Also by Emma Donoghue

Haven

The Pull of the Stars

Akin

The Wonder

Frog Music

Astray

Room

Inseparable: Desire Between Women in Literature

The Sealed Letter

Landing

Touchy Subjects

Life Mask

The Woman Who Gave Birth to Rabbits

Slammerkin

Kissing the Witch: Old Tales in New Skins

Hood

Stir-Fry

LEARNED BY HEART

EMMA DONOGHUE

LITTLE, BROWN AND COMPANY

LARGE PRINT EDITION

This book is a work of fiction. Names, characters, places, and incidents are either the product of the author's imagination or, if real, are used fictitiously.

Little, Brown and Company
Hachette Book Group
1290 Avenue of the Americas, New York, NY 10104
littlebrown.com

First Edition: August 2023

Little, Brown and Company is a division of Hachette Book Group, Inc. The Little, Brown name and logo are trademarks of Hachette Book Group, Inc.

ISBNs: 9780316564434 (hardcover), 9780316566018 (large print), 9780316564458 (ebook)
LCCN 2023934535

Printing 1, 2023

LSC-C

Printed in the United States of America

For Chris Roulston,
ally in all

LEARNED BY HEART

With this
Diamond I cut
this glass with
this face I kissed
a lass

—Graffiti on window,
Huntingdon Room,
King's Manor, York

CONTENTS

RAINE TO LISTER, 1815

My dear Lister,

Last night I went to the Manor again.

I open the door here — I don't delay even to pick up a cape — and step out across the village green. My shoes write inscrutable, fleeting messages on the dewy grass. When I reach the moon-marked road, all I have to do is follow it. In less than a quarter of an hour, at the walls of York, where Bootham Bar has been arching for eight hundred years, here's that antique hodgepodge, King's Manor, hiding our school behind its redbrick face.

The great medieval door with its lion and unicorn opens at my touch, and I find myself in the scented courtyard. I turn right to enter the Manor School itself, where three generations of one family have watched over the better-born daughters of the North. I walk invisible from one familiar, ramshackle room to the next. Through the kitchen and pantry, refectory and offices, and up the footworn stone stairs I float. Through the classrooms on the first floor. Into the north wing, past the mistresses' chambers, and up again, to the second-floor attic. Past Cook's room, then the one the four maids share, then the box room full of trunks and portmanteaus. The fourth door is the Slope's, and it springs open to my fingertips.

You'll understand my wishful fancy; I pay this visit, in fact all these tender nightly visits, in my mind's eye only. In the flesh, I've not passed the lion and unicorn and entered our school in eight years. These days of course I'm prevented, thwarted by circumstances beyond my control. But last year, or in any of the intervening years since I left, although I often passed the lovely old silhouette of King's Manor, somehow—careless—I never thought to knock on that ancient door. *Eliza,* I ask myself now, *why didn't you go back while you still could?*

You won't be surprised that I so treasure these old haunts. It was in York that I received my education; where I was stamped like warm wax by a seal, formed once and for all. I know you'll recall the song—*where all the joy and mirth made this town heaven on earth.* At the Manor School, I tasted *heaven on earth* even as I toiled to pack my poor skull with the knowledge and wisdom I was told I'd need for life. The joke is, Lister, the only lesson I learned, or at least the only lesson I remember, was you.

We two were so young—had barely seen *the change of fourteen years,* as Capulet says of his daughter. Less than a twelvemonth the pair of us spent under our Slope's slanted ceiling, but there are fleeting times in life, especially in youth, that shine out more strongly than all the rest and will never fade: veins of gold in dull rock. For the rest of my life, I believe, I'll be transported back in dreams to memory's private theatre, where our girl selves still move and chat and laugh.

These days I live on words, since my imagination is starved of other stimuli. Not that I keep a diary. The year we turned seventeen, you did your best to teach me that improving habit, but I always found it hard to pluck details from my daily round that seemed worth recording. Without an interested ear inclined towards me, my words dry up; I lack that bottomless spring that bubbles up behind your clever tongue. It strikes me that your own journal-writing has much in common with your other powers—walking, say. Whatever you like, you do with energy and ambition, almost greedily, and with a vigour that impresses us lesser mortals, even if we sometimes find it exhausting. No, only in letters to one sympathetic listener can I open my bosom and speak my pleasures and pains. So I read all day until my eyes are sore, then write to you, though all too hurriedly—two or three pages' worth, I find, is about as much as I can get out under these conditions—before I'm obliged to lay down my pen.

In the night I send out my mind to roam, and of

all the places I've lived in my almost quarter century (Madras, Tottenham, Doncaster, Halifax, Bristol), the lodestone to which my restless mind is always drawn, as a compass needle to true north, is York—and in particular to our Manor School. Less than a mile in distance from this house where I sit scribbling, but in time, a yawning gulf: ten years back, to when we were fourteen. And not just any ten years, but that vast stretch between raw girlhood and settled womanhood.

Like some old lady, at twenty-four I find most fascination in retrospect. The memories come back to me with the irresistible force of waves striking a shore. It would be absurd to deny how changed I am; in ways I need not list, I am not what I was when we met. But I recall that Eliza so vividly, I only have to close my eyes to slip into her, under her skin. Under the mossy, leaky roof of King's Manor, I was quickened to life from the day I first laid eyes on you, Lister. As the old Roman chiselled on our stone, *Happy the spirit of this place.*

In our Slope I passed my best hours, and sometimes I have to remind myself that they are indeed past. But I tell myself that I'm not dead, not yet. Wilted plants have been known to revive if given just a little water. Could I have you by my side once more, I almost believe

CLOSE QUARTERS, AUGUST 1805

ELIZA'S TRAINED HERSELF to wake at seven, just before the bell.

She sleeps in a garret, too low to allow her to stand up except in the very middle, beside her narrow cot. None of the Manor School's bedrooms have carpets that might trip the girls or hold dust, but this one is the barest; the floor unwaxed. Eliza rooms by herself, since Jane (two years her elder) refuses to board. Among so many pairs and trios of sisters—two Misses Parker, Peirson, Simpson, and Dobson, three Burtons, and a full five Percivals—Eliza is effectively an only child.

Of course having a room to herself could be considered a privilege. No one else's noises or smells to impinge on her; no one to break in on her thoughts or disturb her sleep. It might be a mark of the Head's trust in Eliza's good conduct. Respect for her fortune too? Perhaps her guardian, Dr. Duffin, even pays Miss Hargrave extra for this privacy; Eliza's never mustered the courage to ask.

She catches herself in the mirror on the washstand. Of course she's wondered whether Mrs. Tate—who sees to all housekeeping matters for her sister, the

Head—was made nervous by her first glimpse of Eliza and chose to sequester her far from all the other boarders. *A young lady of colour,* though that common phrase irks Eliza, since everyone's some colour or other. As little girls in India, the Raines rarely gave the matter much thought. But when they lurched off the *King George* in Kent, Eliza, at almost seven, felt transformed by the spell of a wicked fairy; so many English stared, pointed, or sneered, as if the sisters' tint was all they could see.

Years later, Dr. Duffin came all the way south to Tottenham to bring his friend and colleague's orphans back with him to their father's county of Yorkshire. Eliza remembers Miss Hargrave assuring Dr. Duffin that first day, "My sister and I see no colour," which sounded more kindly meant than convincing. Introducing the Raines to some forty pupils at dinner, the Head quoted Moses in her rich, low voice: "*The stranger that dwelleth with you shall be unto you as one born among you, and thou shalt love him as thyself.*" Still, surely the sister proprietors feared some of their less enlightened boarders might be loath to live at close quarters with this particular *stranger,* in case Eliza's difference somehow rubbed off? That would explain why Mrs. Tate tutted over her list, remarked that the south range was overcrowded—quite true—and led

Eliza into the north wing and up to an attic floor occupied only by servants, luggage, and broken furniture.

She reminds herself that it matters very little why she was assigned this room; on the whole she likes it. The one low dormer faces northwest. Eliza dips down now to catch a distorted picture, through its uneven diamonds, of fields stretching away towards Clifton village. Closer, to the left she can just glimpse St. Olave's, which is the Manor's own church and a remnant of its ancient abbey, once the richest in the North.

August, with the summer break behind them, and the grey sky's threatening rain. Eliza steps away, in case any labourer's at work in the grounds so early, since *staring out of the windows while in partial undress* earns an indecorum mark, as does *allowing oneself to be seen.*

She dresses fast, which comes of having had no help since she was six. (At the Tottenham boarding school, Eliza deduced that the rich send their daughters to these establishments to live as if poor; "roughing it" is believed to build character.) She swaps her night shift for a day one and scrubs underneath, using the permitted third of a jugful of water; she dries herself on the limp roller towel. Her short buckram stays hook at the front. The only frock allowed at the Manor is white muslin, which saves the trouble of choosing; she slides her arms into the long sleeves, tugging them down over her shift's linen ones, then contorts herself to button it up at the back. The green ribbon belt that's the sign of the Middle Form (ages fourteen and fifteen) sits high up on her ribs. A lace tucker over her neck and chest, its strings knotted behind, and a cotton shawl on top. After tying on her stockings with garters, she steps into her pointed kidskin slippers and laces them up tight enough so they won't sag over the course of the schoolday.

Pupils are allowed a single flounce at the hem, or a silk shawl instead of cotton, without getting a vanity mark, but Eliza doesn't risk it. It gives her a secret gratification to confound expectations. Restraint in dress is not a virtue looked for in a *little Nabobina,* as she heard Betty Foster call her under her breath, that first week. Their classmates seemed disappointed by the Raines' lack of splendour—no decorated palms, thumb-rings the size of walnuts, ropes of pearls, belled ankles, or gold nose-jewels.

Eliza practises her gleaming smile in the speckled looking glass. The well-mannered call her complexion *foreign-looking* or *tawny;* the insolent, *swarthy, dusky, dingy,* or plain *brown*. She reminds herself that her skin is clear, her features generally thought pleasing. She pulls her pomaded hair into a tight knot. Its straight black silkiness is inconvenient, since fashion requires some ringlets to frame the face, so she has four twists of paper bouncing on her forehead, which she undoes and unrolls now, fingering out the curls that have dried in place overnight. Eliza pulls a baggy white cap over her head and sets the wide band so her ringlets show just beneath its starched frill, and laces the sidepieces under her chin. A guiding principle of British dress is: make something just so, then tuck it almost out of sight.

She checks all yesterday's linen is in her laundry bag, because she once earned an inattention mark when a housemaid (the tall, mean one, no doubt) reported a stocking on the floor. To remember all the rules, Eliza finds it simplest to imagine a great eye ever fixed on her.

Downstairs, she hurries outside through the mild morning air to use the necessary, trying not to think about spiders under the seat.

King's Manor is an irregular quadrangle, of which the School occupies less than half. Where the massive city walls around its grounds have crumbled, in recent centuries they've been patched with narrow stonework. Eliza spots a pair of red-belted Seniors pressed against the iron railings at the ruined gatehouse facing Marygate, in conversation with a weedy youth whom one or the other would, if challenged, likely claim as a cousin, therefore a permitted acquaintance.

When Eliza first came to the dilapidated Manor, she found it a labyrinth and, to her mortification, sometimes blundered in on other tenants: a wood-carver, workshops of comb cutters and glove makers, not to mention the huge boar that occupies a small room on the ground floor.

She squeezes into the refectory by the rear door now. She has to veer around Margaret Burn (dark curls) crushing Betty Foster (a porcelain figurine) to her bosom—"I trust you slept well, dearest?"—because those inseparables always perform ecstasies at meeting, like heroines reunited at the end of the fifth act.

At the disgrace table in the back, which has no benches, two blue-belted Juniors and a Senior stand bent over their bowls of gruel, trying not to splash. Mrs. Tate hovers, gaze flickering over the crowd for any infelicity that might disturb the Head. Eliza glides past, as upright as a lily, on the off chance of picking up a deportment merit, but Mrs. Tate turns away to shush a noisy pair of girls, finger to her lips: *"Piano!"*

A tiny wave from Frances Selby, soft curls of straw-gold fringing her mobcap. Eliza throws her a smile and plants herself in the space Frances has saved on the bench just as Mrs. Tate, behind her sister's carved chair at the top table, jangles the bell. The last girls swarm in, picking at knots in their tucker strings or shoving hair into their caps. Just as the ringing stops, Betty and Margaret land on the bench on either side of Mercy Smith like a pair of trained doves.

Mercy's a stickler, disliked not so much for being a charity case as for her evangelical sternness. Eliza thinks it a shame the girl can't convert some of the merits she earns for accurate memorisation of lessons into more useful coin, such as raspberry acid drops, to buy a little popularity. At school a best pal is as indispensable as a chair or a pen, but somehow Mercy trudges on without one. Though it strikes Eliza that since seven is an odd number, one of the Middles of necessity would have to be left on her own. It reminds her of the game A Trip to Jerusalem—when the fiddler stops, all players grab new seats except one, who's out.

Frances is telling her the entire contents of her father's latest letter from Swansfield, their estate in Northumberland. He's hoping to put up a monument to Peace, to go with the tower and the gothic folly, "the very moment the French surrender."

That first week in Tottenham, Eliza, only seven, learned what it was to have no friend to shield her. The Londoners didn't offer any direct insults, only barbed compliments: "What good English you speak, Miss Raine." Not even the girl from the West Indies would pair up with her.

No one until Frances, years later, here at the Manor. Wealthy, her widowed father's darling, universally liked, Frances is so innocent of bias that she can't seem to recognise it in others. Whenever Eliza senses a flicker of an eye, a stiffening of the back, a drawing up of skirts, Frances frowns in distress and says her friend must be mistaken. And since of course Eliza would prefer that to be true, she does her best to believe it.

Miss Lewin is overseeing the Middle Form this breakfast, wig slightly askew so Eliza's fingers itch to tug it into place; the mistress is all mind, never seeming to care how she looks. The housemaid—the tiny, friendly, hunted-looking one—sets down the jug of water. Eliza fills a glass and tries not to wrinkle her nose.

"Greenish today," Nan Moorsom mutters. "It's sure to make me sick." Always longing to be home in Scarborough, Nan takes pride in the variety of her ailments—sore lips, inflammation of the eyes from weeping, oppression in the head, and that's only the ones above the neck.

"I assure you, Miss Moorsom, our Ouse water is filtered through the purest charcoal, no matter how it may taste." Miss Lewin speaks slightly indistinctly, her hand hovering in front of her teeth in case they slip, but with a South of England diction on which Eliza does her best to model her own.

Mulish, Nan dabs one eye. Across the table, Fanny Peirson tries her own water, and makes a tiny grimace in Nan's direction. Eliza would call Fanny even more of a dimwit than her bosom friend Nan, but a sweet one; all the Seniors make a pet of Fanny, and not just because of her withered arm.

Looking out into the courtyard, Eliza breathes in the traces of honeysuckle and rose. Instead of the sour water, she pours herself a cup of chocolate. "Miss Selby, may I help you to a slice of toast or a roll?" To offer is the only way to ask.

Following the formula, Frances answers, "No thank you, Miss Raine," and passes the platter. Eliza nods her thanks and takes two slices. Three are allowed, but any pupil who sneaks four will get a greed mark, as well as no bread at the next meal. One slice is thought best, since underfeeding strengthens the female constitution (though Eliza's never understood how). She spreads butter on one slice and marmalade on the other, then presses them together and takes a small bite, relishing the compound tang. When she grows up and comes into her money, she means to spread marmalade and butter on every slice, and thickly.

The Middles have most of their lessons in a long upstairs room with windows on both sides and an old plaster frieze just under the ceiling. This morning: History, Grammar and Literature, Accounts, and Geography. Nan earns a lesson card by failing to fit Jamaica into the jigsaw puzzle. Finger on the terrestrial globe,

Miss Lewin prompts them: "King George the Third's Empire has spread order, industry, and civilisation four thousand miles west of here to?"

"Rupert's Land," a few voices chime. Betty, peering out the window in hopes of red uniforms, is not even pretending to move her lips.

"And *ten* thousand miles to the southeast," Miss Lewin goes on, "to?"

Just Mercy this time: "New South Wales."

Dwelling on these distances gives Eliza vertigo. The world's so wide; sailing here around the Cape of Good Hope took a year of her childhood.

"The Empire is made up of?"

They chorus, "Great Britain and Ireland, together with His Majesty's colonies, protectorates, and dominions."

"It is populated by how many Britons?"

Fewer voices: "Sixteen million."

Miss Lewin asks, "And their less fortunate brethren?"

It comes to Eliza, like a drip of rain down her back, that the mistress means *less white*.

Margaret hazards a guess: "Thirty— "

Mercy corrects her, precise as ever: "Forty-four million, madam." Though the charity girl's accent is broad York, she always speaks with stiff correctness, avoiding dialect.

Eliza tells herself that none of them are turning to

look at their *less white* classmate. Could she be counted under both headings? No, that would be bad bookkeeping; as the daughter of a Company surgeon from Scarborough, surely she's a true Briton, no matter her shade?

In the afternoon, masters come in for French, Drawing, Dancing, and Music. (Mercy, who can't afford Accomplishments, swots in the Manor's library.) At the end of today, Nan is downcast, because no one else in the Middle Form made an error substantial enough to earn a lesson card, so she can't get rid of hers. Any girl who hasn't been able to pass her lesson card on to another offender must memorise an assigned piece for that subject, on pain of earning an additional card; Nan and her friend Fanny are often a task or two in arrears.

Dinner's at five. Yorkshire puddings (served first, to fill the girls up), giblet soup, mutton, and beans. The three at the disgrace table lap their soup neatly and eye the delights they're denied. Eliza stood there in her third week; she can't remember what she'd done, but it was nothing dreadful, just some confusion about the rules. She found disgrace so humiliating—all those eyes on her, in pity or perhaps confirmation of what the girls had heard about *Asiatic tendencies* to sloth, slyness, or sensuality—that she barely ate for seven days. That was when Eliza resolved to give no one grounds to suspect her. To be known at this school as impeccable.

There's no teacher at the table this evening, so the Middles may chat if they keep their voices low. Betty praises the local regiment's new uniforms, and Margaret reports on a terrible breach between two close cronies among the Seniors. Eliza nods wisely as if she already knew the tale but was too discreet to repeat it; she doesn't care to admit that her sister, Jane, never tells her anything.

There's Jane's friend Hetty Marr on her own at one end of a Seniors table, taking more beans; she always seems to be eating. Hetty's a day girl but generally stays for dinner, whereas Jane dines where she sleeps, at the Duffins' house on Micklegate. This doesn't seem to conduce to anyone's comfort, since Jane constantly provokes the doctor. Eliza finds this baffling; for all his rough edges, Dr. Duffin's the nearest thing to a father they have left.

Fanny tells the Middles that her big sister has had three teeth pulled and the rest filed smooth so there'll be nowhere for food to get caught, with the unfortunate result that her whole mouth is now painfully sensitive. Nan tops this with a description of a time a dentist broke off a piece of her jawbone, which brought on an abscess, "and I had to be plugged up with cotton soaked in eau de cologne for a month, and Mama feared for my life!"

Nan likes to keep her mother's memory alive by mentioning her, Eliza's noticed—something Frances can hardly do, never having met hers. Fanny, like Eliza, lost hers too young to remember much. That's four of the seven of them at this table who have dead mothers; it strikes Eliza that motherlessness could be considered the natural state of affairs, at least at this school. And Margaret will never speak of her unknown mother, which comes to much the same thing.

Rain's starting to spatter the tall windows now. Giving up on the last tough end of mutton, Eliza hides it in her napkin. (Failure to clear the plate earns a mark.) Beside her, Frances chews on placidly. Eliza's staring up at the rain lashing the windows when there's a stir at the back of the refectory. A new pupil, it looks like, shedding a huge greatcoat.

Not pretty, Eliza decides; soaked front hair escaping from a crushed bonnet. Half-boots and hem rusty with mud. A shrimp of a thing, with neither height nor bosom, but as upright as an officer.

"We expected you in a hack, Miss Lister," Mrs. Tate says fretfully.

The stranger chuckles. "I only walked from the White Swan, not the whole twenty miles over Barmby

Moor, though I daresay I could've managed that, at a pinch—my brothers and I think nothing of going ten miles in three hours." The voice is deep and carrying, the accent rather Yorkshire.

"The young ladies of the Manor School do not stride about town unaccompanied."

The newcomer nods, as if noting that.

"And where's your trunk?" Mrs. Tate asks.

"They're sending it over on a barrow." Miss Lister wipes rain off her spectacles with the dun sleeve of her travelling costume, and shoves them back onto the bridge of her nose. She scans the gleaming phalanx of maidens in white caps and frocks.

Eliza waits for the moment she'll be spotted: the odd one out.

Miss Lister's light blue eyes move on, to the end of the row of Middles, then double back to meet Eliza's; they narrow as if taking aim.

The Head has finished her coffee and is gliding down the middle of the refectory. "I bid you welcome, Miss Lister. You have not been at school before?"

"Haven't needed to be, madam, not since I was ten, and I'm fourteen now."

Miss Hargrave blinks, head tilted. "You... haven't needed to be?"

"I teach myself—with a little help from the Vicar—for ten hours a day, not counting the flute."

This sets off a susurration of whispers.

"You teach yourself what, exactly?"

"Geometry, astronomy, heraldry," Miss Lister throws out, "various modern languages, Latin..."

This last raises gasps.

"Your efforts sound creditable," Miss Hargrave concedes, "but there is so much more to the moulding of a young lady than—"

"Oh, I know."

Has the new girl just cut the Head off, mid-sentence? Eliza's transfixed.

"Really I'm here for a quick polish, and new connections, of course," the Lister girl says, "so I can move up into the realm I was born to occupy."

Titters ripple along the refectory.

She quivers like a deer. Then manages a cocky smile, as if she's made the joke instead of being the joke.

Eyes on the ceiling, Miss Hargrave draws the moral: "Half the miseries of mankind arise from pride."

Her sister spells it out: "Kindly acquire the rudiments of common courtesy, miss, and learn not to interrupt anyone, but especially not your superiors."

The Head murmurs, "The savage must be tamed before being *polished*."

Finally a pinking in the girl's flat cheeks.

"You may join your form." Mrs. Tate gestures, and the Middles squirm along their benches to make room.

The newcomer offers vigorous handshakes all round; she doesn't flinch at Fanny's child-sized right arm. Clearly unaware that the way to get a particular food is to offer it to your neighbour, Miss Lister helps herself to every dish within reach, and piles her plate high with the last of the mackerel. Eliza's never seen anyone but a grown man tuck in like this.

"Any relation to the Listers of Heighholme Hall?" Nan's asking. "My father in Scarborough is to marry one of that family next month."

"The bride's barely twenty," Fanny complains in a mutter, on her friend's behalf.

Miss Lister chews and swallows. "Mine is the Halifax branch of the ancient county lineage. Shibden Hall's been in the family for two centuries—a timber-framed manor house, built five years after Agincourt," she says fondly. "The Listers were once the greatest landowners in the district."

This bit of swank makes eyebrows go up. Margaret exchanges a smirk with Betty and says, in a dangerously civil voice, "As it happens, I went to school in Halifax myself—the Misses Mellin—till my guardian moved me to York to keep me under his nose."

"I've studied with those ladies," Miss Lister says, nodding.

"But I hadn't heard that the master of Shibden Hall had any children," Margaret adds.

Eliza's pulse speeds up; the stranger's been caught out in a lie.

"Also, you said you came by Barmby Moor, and that's not Halifax way."

Miss Lister gives her a candid grin. "What I meant to say was, Shibden belongs to my uncle, but I spend my holidays there. Almost the whole year there when I was eleven. I'm the general favourite."

Betty cuts through that: "So where in fact do your parents live?"

"Ah, at the moment, a farm on the edge of the Wolds—just west of Market Weighton, in the East Riding."

In other words, the middle of nowhere.

Betty probes. "Your father keeps a carriage, does he?" Trying to place this interloper on the Manor School's chessboard, without demanding outright whether Mr. Lister counts as a gentleman.

The newcomer glides past the question: "Being a captain, he's obliged to go about the country a lot, recruiting for the French War."

Eliza tries to think of a friendly remark. "If I may—what's your first name?"

Those disconcerting small eyes turn on her. "Anne."

"Miss Ann Moorsom here goes by Nan," Frances tells Miss Lister, then points at herself and Fanny: "Mercifully you're not another Frances, as we've two of those already!"

Here comes the tiny housemaid with a redcurrant tart. Eliza concentrates on her slice and lets the conversation run on, until she hears Miss Lister quip, "I do hope I haven't fallen in with utter ignoramuses."

The word lands like a great gobbet of horse dung.

Betty and Margaret draw back, readying themselves to strike. Betty looks more outraged, but Margaret's faster: "Shouldn't that be *ignorami,* since you claim to be a Latinist?"

The Lister girl answers easily: "In point of fact, Miss Burn, ignoramus can't take that plural ending, as it was never a noun in Latin, only a verb, first person plural present indicative of *ignorare,* meaning"—her gaze skims the group—"*we do not know.*"

The bell rings, and the Middles leave Miss Lister eating on as if to prove herself unrattled by the skirmish.

There's no going out for Recreation on such a wet evening, even though the August air is soft enough that Eliza would rather like a stroll through the dripping grounds, where the Middles could cut the new girl's character to pieces without being overheard.

There's a rule against idle hands at Recreation. In the classroom, the pupils who are sewing press as close to the lamp as they can get, but those who are reading want the light too. Mercy's working a sampler in cross-stitch.

The busy bee, with ceaseless hum
Morn, noon, and evening, sucks the flowers.
Think you such honey e'er will come
To those who waste their fleeting hours?

Whenever Eliza's eyes fall on the lines, she's tempted to ask, *And what are you doing, Mercy, but wasting hundreds of your fleeting hours on these garish yellow-and-black bees?* Not that her own sketch of the Manor Shore—the public promenade between the school grounds and the river—is a much better use of her time on earth. Eliza's been fiddling with it for a fortnight, but still the strolling ladies and gentlemen look as flat as silhouettes in cut paper.

After a glance at wan Miss Vickers at the top of the room, to make sure she's buried in her magazine, Betty whispers: "Vulgar and horrid."

No one disagrees, not even Mercy.

"Her *ancient county lineage*!" Margaret scoffs.

"*Lister* means *dyer*," Betty points out. "I bet her forefathers sold cloth by the bale."

Fanny surprises Eliza by speaking up with a mild heat. "Well, what if they did? I don't mind admitting we Peirsons were tanners before founding our bank. And didn't your father start off sewing sails, Nan, before he set up his?"

Her pal doesn't look happy to have this brought up. She jerks her head at Betty: "Well, I bet Mr. Foster sawed up trees, in his youth, and built ships with his own two hands."

Betty glares.

"Come now, ladies," Frances protests, "don't we all come from trade, if we look back a few generations? Let's not allow silly prejudice of rank to creep in."

Her friend's liberal spirit touches Eliza. But it's easier to ignore the fact that there's a ladder if you're perched at the top.

Betty hisses, "I wouldn't have let a word pass my lips if the Lister brat hadn't put on such airs."

When Eliza carries the horn lantern into her garret, an hour after the sun goes down, it's all wrong. Another small bed's been wheeled in, and Miss Lister's sitting cross-legged on it, in a welter of books, with her spectacles dangling from the neck of her night shift. A second chest of drawers has been jammed under the slanted ceiling, and another lantern is taking up most of the washstand.

"Good evening, Miss Raine. I imagined you'd rather keep the window side?"

"Miss Lister — "

"Lister, please."

"Isn't that what I said?"

"I like my friends to drop the *Miss*."

Surname only? "Like a boy, you mean?"

"Why not?" She springs to her feet, this young person, this Lister-no-Miss. "And you, your Christian name's Eliza?"

Was that a tiny flicker of hesitation before *Christian*? Eliza's as Christian as anyone here; William Raine drove each of his baby girls to be baptised in Madras's Anglican church. To punish her, Eliza says, "I only like my *friends* to call me that."

"I'll call you Raine, then." Bluff, impudent.

"Miss Lister—"

"Just Lister, if you please."

With an effort, Eliza remembers the point at issue. "What are your things doing in my room?"

"*Our* room now, it seems." The Lister girl starts to stash books in her bottom drawer.

Eliza's face is hot. If this disagreeable rustic has been sent up to share the garret, it's not only inconvenient. It means Eliza's been unwanted all along—stashed up here like some uncouth article of furniture, under a dust sheet—and now two such items have been crammed in together willy-nilly. She'd like to slap this Lister, with her shabby clothes and countryfied manner, her pretensions to intellectual superiority and cravings for social advancement. This awkward hobbledehoy, who can take her lantern downstairs and bed with the pig for all Eliza cares—

Miss Lister turns to her. "I am sorry. That is, I can't regret that I've been sent up here, for you to keep a strict eye on, but I do apologise for the invasion."

Eliza purses her lips. "Are you such a troublemaker that you need to be watched?"

"Born unto it, as the sparks fly upwards." A perverse cockiness in the girl's voice.

Eliza turns her back and pulls the curtains against the summer night. She shakes and thumps her feather bed to smoothen it out under the sheet. Then she pulls the upper sheet and blanket taut. She undresses at speed. She's scrubbing her teeth with a rag, the scent of clove and cinnamon rising, when Lister sniffs appreciatively and asks, "What's your tooth powder?"

"Crushed coral, I believe."

Lister's getting the last specks of food out of her teeth with a steel pick; she licks it clean before putting it away in her etui. (Only a worn green leather cylinder, nothing like Eliza's hinged box of ivory and tortoiseshell with blue velvet compartments for everything from pins and needles to brightening washes.) "I rub plain salt on my gums."

Why does Miss Lister think Eliza cares?

"I like to close my eyes and imagine I'm eating some tasty winkles with a pin."

"Good night, ladies." Mrs. Tate, opening the door. She gives motherly kisses to her favourites, but Eliza's never been one. "Miss Lister, here's your green belt, the sign of the Middle Form. Lights?" She always takes away the lanterns at nine to make sure the pupils don't waste candles, or injure their eyesight or health by staying up late reading, or risk starting a fire.

Eliza wants to pour out her grievance, but to try at this hour would probably earn her a disputatiousness mark. Better to bide her time and wait for this hoyden to commit some grave offence.

"Good night, madam." Lister hands over both lanterns.

In the sudden dark, Eliza's cot creaks as she clambers in. The lumpy feather tick spreads under her weight.

The truckle bed skids on squeaky wheels. "What coarse sheets," Lister remarks. "And could the blanket be any thinner?"

She speaks as if she's used to finer at home, which Eliza doubts very much. Eliza answers, "If they hear you speak that way of the bedding, they'll take it away for a night."

Silence, then, at last.

On Tuesday morning at breakfast, the water's fresh—last night's rain, collected in barrels. Eliza nibbles her hard triangular roll, which tastes faintly of nutmeg. Sitting too close beside her, in the uniform white frock and cap, Lister drains a large glass of milk.

"Tea, coffee, or chocolate, Miss Lister?" Fanny offers.

"No thank you, Miss . . . Pearce, was it?"

"Peirson, of Peirson's Bank in Whitby."

Lister nods, as if recording the detail. "May I ask, your arm . . ."

Nan sucks in her breath. "You may not, if you've any manners at all."

"I don't mind," Fanny assures her friend.

Meeting eyes with Betty, Margaret weighs in. "What an appalling breach of— "

"Truly," Fanny pleads, "I'd rather people ask than always be wondering." She turns back to Lister. "I was only two years old when I shattered it. I tripped on the cliffs and tumbled a little way, and a passing gentleman climbed down at great risk to himself and carried me up." Fanny holds up her short, skinny arm in its taken-in sleeve. "The bone never grew back properly after that. But I thank heaven, because I might have died like my poor nursemaid Meg! Trying to block my fall, you see, she plummeted all the way down and was dashed to pieces on the rocks."

"Miss Peirson, what a tale."

Fanny's glowing in the sunbeam of the newcomer's attention.

"May I help you to a slice of toast, or a roll, Miss Lister?" Mercy holds out the dish of bread.

A shake of the narrow head.

Eliza's disconcerted again: no hot drinks and now no bread, even?

"Care for some gruel?" Nan asks.

Some girls find it comfortingly bland but won't take it, as they're unwilling to be seen eating what's served at the disgrace table.

Lister shakes her head and fills up her glass. "I'll just have more milk."

"You ought to eat some breakfast," Frances advises.

"Milk's very nourishing. Calves live on nothing else."

"But something solid, for your health, surely?"

"I enjoy excellent health, thanks, Miss Selby."

"At times I'm so low-spirited, I've no appetite at all," Nan boasts, "and Dr. Mather has to prescribe me sugared calf's-foot jelly from the chemist."

Fanny and she bicker about whether the jelly is delicious or disgusting, which Eliza considers pointless, since the matter is quite literally a matter of taste.

Lister cuts in: "What depresses your spirits so, Miss Moorsom?"

A blunt question, but it gratifies Nan. "Homesickness. Sometimes I have such heartache, it brings on a nervous debility."

Lister's eyebrows lift. "Scarborough's not that far off."

She remembered the name of Nan's hometown, Eliza notices. Does Lister have a little file in her head for each of the Manor girls already?

"Forty miles," Mercy specifies.

Margaret snorts. "I come from Newcastle, which is twice as far."

"It might as well be four hundred, if I can't get home till Christmas," Nan groans. "Oh, to hear the crash of the waves..."

"Scarborough's genteel enough to have some good schools," Lister says. "Why didn't your father choose one of them?"

Nan huffs. "Not far enough away from home to please his new bride, I suppose."

"You're sure you won't have a small roll, even, Miss Lister?" Frances holds the dish out.

Lister only smiles, as if that was a joke. She leans back, and murmurs in Eliza's ear: "Is bread compulsory in Madras?"

The question throws her, as if the city's name is blazoned on her face. No, clearly Lister's managed to extract Eliza's history from some gossip already. Unable to improvise a rebuff, she says, "We had curry and rice."

The fact is, Eliza's bluffing; she remembers tastes, but not which foods they had at which meals. She pictures Myrtle Grove in a far-off way, like a dollhouse kept behind glass. For eight years she hasn't talked to anyone about home; Jane has no patience for harking back. Eliza has inherited some of their parents' personal effects, but no letters, no drawings, nothing outside herself to prove the existence of Myrtle Grove; she couldn't place it on a map of Madras, if she owned a map.

She does recall running through the villa, anywhere she liked, with her ayah hurrying after. She can conjure up glimpses of Father's apartments and Mother's, the kitchens, the servants' quarters, the verandahs where a visiting Englishman might be found sleeping or a cross-legged tailor sewing shirts. Walls flecked in places with red from spat paan, and the warm scent of joss sticks. In her mind's eye she calls up the shimmer of lacquered brass lamps. Low hum of conversation and snores at night, tom-toms in the distance. The swish of Mother's sari in the passages. Eliza's own room, with the high bed in the middle, canopied with mosquito nets. Bearers dozing in a doorway until you needed them to fold and carry a chair, let the blinds down, take the stinking pot away, massage your head, bring you a cool drink, fan you, carry you to the bazaar in the shaded palanquin. Eliza doesn't remember any rules in Myrtle Grove, though she might have forgotten, of course. Every year since leaving, her untouched memories shrink, flatten, and fade a little more, like pressed flowers.

"Curry for breakfast, really?" Lister murmurs. "Fascinating."

Eliza shrugs.

"Why not, I suppose. How arbitrary these customs are."

"Private whispering earns an indecorum mark," Betty tells the two of them.

"Apologies, *mesdemoiselles*. I'm learning." Lister stands and bows to the whole table before she walks off with her unused plate.

Grammar and Literature. The girl inserts herself on the bench beside Eliza, penning her in.

Miss Lewin tells Lister not to cross her legs.

Lister gives her a rueful smile: "I find it most uncomfortable to keep them straight."

"If that's so, it suggests the error of crossing them has become habitual."

"You're quite right, madam. But until I manage to break the habit..."

Miss Lewin's more interested in their learning than their legs. "Well," she says impatiently, "for now, you may cross them at the ankles, but never higher."

She tests the Middles on yesterday's pieces out of *Elegancies of Poetry by the Most Eminent Authors, Compiled for the Improvement of Young Persons.* Mercy recites "Expelled from Paradise" with leaden rigour. Betty always picks something about lovers, this time "Edwin and Angelina." Eliza manages two verses from "Thoughts on a Tomb" with only a couple of trip-ups.

Lister rattles off twenty lines from "The Deserted Village."

Goggling, Nan asks, "When did you have time to—"

"I knew it already," she said, tapping her temple.

Next Miss Lewin has them open their copies of Mrs. Devis's *The Accidence; or, First Rudiments of English Grammar: Designed for the Use of Young Ladies.* The very sight of the cover makes Eliza yawn behind her teeth. Today's passage starts,

> The Imperfect, or imperfectly past time, is so called, because it imperfectly partakes of both present and past—shows that something was then doing, but not quite finished.

Eliza's stuffed her head with so many dry pieces out of *The Accidence,* the volume has the uncanny familiarity of a dream. She whispers the set paragraph now, ten times through, at which point it means as little to her as when she began. *I was reading;* the reading was happening in the past, and no information is given as to whether it has stopped yet, but shouldn't she assume it has? Surely, if the reading were still going on, the statement would be in the present tense, or the present perfect continuous. So in what sense does the imperfect tense *imperfectly partake of both present and past*? Eliza presses hard between her eyes.

Beside her, book shut, Lister is craning up at the plaster frieze.

"Miss Lister," the mistress asks ironically, "may I presume you're ready to favour us?"

She recites it, word-perfect.

Miss Lewin is taken aback. "Ah... you should correct a slight tendency to gruffness."

Betty lets out a tiny snort. Lister lifts her eyes back to the frieze overhead.

The mistress goes crimson from bosom to forehead, and pulls out her ivory-ribbed gauze fan to flap at herself. Miss Lewin's time of life is known as *dodging,* one of many indignities of the female condition; the word makes Eliza think of ducking to avoid hurled vegetables.

Mercy, called on next, must be rattled by the new girl's powers of memorisation, which rival her own; she somehow leaves out a whole sentence.

Fanny's turn. She dries up at the start of the second clause.

Betty stumbles through the piece; Miss Lewin tells her she's "rather too shrill." Asked to explain a point, Betty can only paraphrase it.

"It's *necessary,* but not *sufficient,* to con the passage by heart," Miss Lewin reminds them as Mercy collects the seven volumes and stacks them on the bureau. Next she sets them to show their understanding of the same loathed section by parsing it, one word to each line.

On Eliza's other side, even Frances lets out a tiny sigh as they reach down for the escritoires at their feet.

"I left my writing-box in my room, madam," Lister tells Miss Lewin.

"Take an inattention mark, then."

Lister cocks her head. "I'd have to be aware of a rule to break it, no? I'm afraid I thought the classroom would have desks and materials."

Is she really sneering at the Manor School's facilities?

"Now I know, I'll be sure to come equipped tomorrow. Or should I fetch it now?"

Her daring makes the air quiver.

Overheating again, Miss Lewin tugs at her fichu. "Share with Miss Raine, then."

Eliza's forced to flip her escritoire open and slide it over so it wobbles on her left knee and Lister's right. It belonged to William Raine—dark teak, with dented brass at the corners and surround—and she'd really rather not have anyone else touch it, let alone use her snowy paper and excellent ink. Teeth set, she lifts the hinged slope and gets out supplies before she fits it back into place and unscrews the ink jar.

It gives Eliza some satisfaction that Lister's writing is awful: a cramped hand full of abbreviations, smudges, and words and phrases inserted as afterthoughts. The two of them have to lean so close together, pressing on the slanted leather surface, that Eliza feels the other's breath hot on her ear, like a dog's.

At lunch Eliza takes some cold ham, pickles, and chutneys from the long sideboard, as well as two slices of wiggs, fresh-baked but so strongly flavoured with caraway that it makes her cough. No sign of Lister, which on the whole is a relief.

Once again, the little Dern at one of the Junior tables is weeping. Not to be unfeeling, but the child (almost twelve) has been at school since the start of Michaelmas term last month, and is no better; her muffled sniffles jar Eliza's nerves.

The Head speaks from the top table, in sweetly

ringing tones. "Miss Dern, do dry your eyes. As the proverb has it, *Time and thinking tame the strongest grief.* The Manor School is a family concern, founded by our grandparents"—a sisterly nod takes in Mrs. Tate. "In time it will become your family too."

A sob bursts from Miss Dern.

"The poor duck just wants her own people," Frances says under her breath. Which counts as a sharp rebuke to the proprietors, coming from her.

It occurs to Eliza that by now Miss Hargrave must have informed the Derns of their daughter's persistent grief. So the only logical explanation is that they don't want her back, or at least not as she is at the moment, with her squeaky voice, spotty chin, and helpless sorrow. If ever Eliza's inclined to bewail her orphan state, she should remember that possessing a pair of parents is no guarantee of a happy home with them.

The Head's lovely face tightens, and she looks to her sister.

Who springs into action: "Off to the storeroom, then, child, until you choose to be quiet." Mrs. Tate hurries to lead her away by the hand.

The thick-doored storeroom off the refectory is used to contain any uncontrolled emotion: fits of rage or laughter, but mostly plain tears. Eliza's never crossed its threshold. She does wonder if little Miss Dern may find it some relief to be left to cry in private, on a sack of flour rather than at table with forty girls giving her irritated stares.

"I'm the same way," Nan murmurs to the Middles, hand on heart. "I can hardly get to sleep without the sound of the sea, it's in my blood so, what with our mother's father having been a ship's captain."

Margaret claps down her knife and fork. "You spend every holiday and half-term in your beloved Scarborough, Nan, so let's hear no more about it."

Fanny begins, "Oh, but— "

Margaret holds up one palm. "Furthermore, that Dern child's sorrow has become a fixed habit, and one she needs to break."

"Surely she would if she could?" Frances asks.

Sometimes it strikes Eliza that the sharp-witted Margaret would be a more entertaining best friend than Frances, who's rather too much of a saint. But of course such a pairing would draw too much attention to the obvious flaw Margaret and Eliza share: having been born to a mother not lawfully married. So Eliza looks away from the dispute, and works the pit out of an olive with her tongue.

There's Jane among the Seniors, making them laugh. Her eyes don't stray in her little sister's direction. The Raines have never been close, but they were once rather closer than this, weren't they? Eliza's sure she remembers Jane braiding her hair. On the *King George* from

Madras, when Eliza was six to Jane's eight, they slept back-to-back in a bunk, shoulder blades like swords in a rack. Then at their first school, in Tottenham, Eliza clung to Jane like a drowner, as long as Jane let her.

Someone hovering. "I'm off to explore—unless you'd care to show me around," Lister says in her ear.

"This is lunch," Mercy says, as if explaining an unfamiliar word.

"I'm rarely hungry in the middle of the day, Miss Smith."

"But we always eat lunch," Nan objects.

A snort from Lister. "What, yet another school rule? The best medical authorities agree that more people die of eating too much than too little."

Eliza swallows her ham fast—a hard lump in her throat—and slips the second slice of wiggs into her pocket. She's on her feet, lifting her dishes. "I suppose one of us had better see she doesn't go astray," she tells the others in a mildly put-upon voice.

"How kind of you," Frances whispers.

First Eliza leads the way upstairs for her umbrella.

"It's a very fine day," Lister points out.

"I need it against the sun." Eliza was raised never to let sunlight touch her face, but she's not going to spell that out.

Ahead of her, Lister takes the steps two or three at a time, as if she were a giant, instead of shorter than

Eliza. Despite her skinniness, she seems awfully strong. A bulky rectangle distorts the line of her frock.

"Is that a book?"

"Oh, I'm never without one. I can't stand to be bored for a moment." Lister lifts her skirt to reveal a pocket sewn onto her petticoat and tugs out the volume, straining the stitches. It's the third part of something called *Clarissa, or, The History of a Young Lady.*

Eliza gestures for her to hide it away again. "If you're caught with a Book Not Approved, they'll confiscate it and give you a deceit mark."

Lister jerks her chin. "Care despised, say I! *Clarissa*'s worth the risk. The part when she loses her mind—it simply harrows me." Out of her tight sleeve she pulls a tiny notebook, with a stub of pencil attached by a string. "I always have this on me, too, for noting down facts of interest. Forbidden?"

"I'm not aware of a rule against notebooks," Eliza concedes. As they go up the next staircase, she lays out the whole system of marks, merits, lesson cards, Judgement and Consequences.

Lister snorts. "This sounds as complicated as the rules of All Fours. At my first school they simply whipped me every day."

"They did *what*?"

"Oh, I deserved it. I've been a great pickle since I

could talk, so when I was seven my mother packed me off to Ripon in the West Riding."

"Whipped at a girls' school? Every day?"

"Almost."

Which Eliza takes as an admission of exaggeration. "Both your parents are still living, are they?"

A nod. "And two brothers, Sam and John, at school near Pickering. Also a sister of eight, Marian, a great annoyance. That makes four of us still standing, out of six—our first John was before my time," Lister adds, "and little Jeremy died when I was eleven, though I barely knew him, as he was put out to nurse ten miles away."

Most families have lost children, but few will offer this private information. Eliza doesn't know what to say.

"I've no grandparents left," Lister goes on, "but a horde of uncles and aunts."

Eliza finds herself volunteering, "My sister, Jane, and I know of only four relatives aboveground."

"Which ones?" Lister asks.

She numbers them on her fingers. "Our father's sick old brother. Their feebleminded sister. Her daughter, who's estranged from a cruel baron husband. And *her* brother, who's so disreputable that no one will pronounce his name."

Lister takes all this in stride. "And on the Indian side?"

All Eliza can do is shrug.

A little stiff: "Pardon my curiosity."

"No," she assures Lister, "I don't mind the question, it's only that . . . I'm not sure whether any of our mother's people are still alive."

Eliza puts it that way to make it sound like an ordinary family. The fact is, she only remembers Mother gliding through the rooms of Myrtle Grove alone, like a ghost attached to its old house. She doesn't recall her ever taking tea with relatives, or friends—only smoking hookah with Father in the evenings, or calling for her little girls for an hour. (Her musical laugh. The tiny, juicy sounds she made when she chewed sweet paan.) Eliza can't remember any Indians at Myrtle Grove, except those who came on business. Did Mother fall completely out of touch with her people when she became an Englishman's wife? (That's the word she used, and Father too: *wife*. A *country marriage,* people sometimes called it; nothing particularly illicit about it.) Or perhaps Mother hadn't lost her relations, they just didn't live near Madras. Or perhaps they did visit Myrtle Grove, but Eliza was so young that she's forgotten. She wishes she had some sense of how much has slipped her mind since she was shipped out at six years old, even if the details are irretrievable.

Lister nods. "Not a full deck of relatives so much as a few dog-eared cards, then. Just as well Dr. Raine left you rich, at least."

Eliza blinks at this candour. Or is it plain rudeness? "One thing can't be set in the scales against the other. I don't suppose you'd swap your family for four thousand pounds." She names the figure deliberately, to show she can guess how much Lister's found out about her already.

The little mouth twitches doubtfully.

"You would not!"

"Don't tempt me," Lister mutters.

Eliza laughs, despite herself, imagining how appalled the family in the Wolds would be to hear this.

She hurries along the creaking passage to the fourth door, their garret room. "We're not allowed to be up here during the day, but if we're seen, I'll explain." She nips in and grabs her green oiled-silk umbrella.

Coming out and past the box room, she glances through the crack and spots a familiar figure, hands knotted, stooped over. She whispers, "Mercy Smith—she holes up in there to pray sometimes, when she can snatch half an hour during the day."

"For what does she pray, do you think?"

"That the Smiths will prosper, and the rest of us will go to hell?"

Lister lets out a cackle.

Eliza tugs her away. Down on the first floor, she says, "Oh, and never knock on a locked door, such as this one, as they're the tenants' rooms."

"What, Miss Hargrave has to let out part of the Manor?"

She keeps her voice low: "I don't believe the family's ever owned an inch of the property. Lord Grantham leases the place from the Crown, you see, and rents most of it to our school, and smaller parcels to various tradesmen. There are woodworkers that way, and a granary through there, in the old ballroom."

"A granary!"

"Well, so I've heard."

On the ground floor, Eliza spots Miss Vickers in conversation with old Mr. Halfpenny; the hollow-eyed mistress never hides the fact that she dislikes her situation, but she seems to have a soft spot for the drawing master. Eliza pivots and hurries out the nearest door, Lister on her heels.

The sun lifts her spirits; she basks in its warmth on her neck through her lace tucker, though she's careful to put up her umbrella to shield her face. She breaks her wiggs into pellets to slip into her mouth as they stroll.

"Is that a crime too?"

Eliza laughs under her breath. "As long as it was in the refectory, the bread was licit— "

"Almost compulsory, as I recall," Lister says.

"But it became contraband as soon as I took it outdoors... for which I blame you." Eliza leads the way around the jagged square building, with its one long block coming off a corner to make the shape of a capital Q. "You can see the plan of the Manor better from outside."

Lister curls the arms of her spectacles around her ears and blinks up at the chimneys. "*Plan* hardly seems the word for it. Not a straight line in sight. Almost every second casement is blocked up too."

True, the stairs and storerooms are always dim. "Perhaps the old glass is cracked?"

"More likely our thrifty Head means to cut the window-tax in half."

Eliza never knew there was a tax on windows.

"Limestone and brick and... is that timber?" Lister asks. "Cobbled together over the centuries into a rambling, crumbling pile. A higgledy-piggledy jumble. But so picturesque, in its decrepit way. That arcaded nave over there with its trefoil traceries." She canters through the long grass towards the most dramatic remains, one long wall with a dozen Gothic windows arching up, far overhead. "How I love to tread in the footsteps of the ancients."

Eliza's never heard anyone their age say such a thing. "Mind you don't tread in the cowpats."

A whoop of merriment.

As Eliza tries to keep up with Lister's stride, the girl fires off a barrage of questions: how many, how high, how old? What's stored in the greened-over ruins under the great alders? "I'm curious where those hundreds of monks went."

"When?" Eliza asks, at a loss.

"When Henry the Eighth came to stay with his fourth queen—or was it his fifth?—and put down the abbey, and seized the estate for himself."

This girl's only just arrived, but she seems to know more about the history of King's Manor than Eliza.

"Did he expel all the monks overnight?" Lister wonders aloud.

"Pensioned them off?" Eliza suggests. Though that may be wishful thinking.

"Back to their families, I suppose."

"Those who still had families living."

"I hadn't considered that," Lister says, chastened.

"And even if they had... how strange it would be, after living in a monastery, to have to go home and put on breeches again," Eliza says.

"Wouldn't it!"

Lister's tone turns practical again as she speculates about how many head of cattle can be grazed among the ruins. She assures Eliza that the prices of hay, flax, coke, and steel are all set by something called *the invisible hand of the market*. This Lister's like some middle-aged man of business in the body of an adolescent female, and very fond of the sound of her own opinions. "What's behind that wall?"

"The river."

"Can we—"

"Not today. Lunch must be nearly over." Eliza steers them back towards the Manor.

Lister checks her watch: "Ten minutes yet." She twirls it on its chain, and whistles.

"Whistling's expressly—"

"Don't tell me." Lister jams her fingers in her ears. "Then I can claim ignorance."

"That trick won't work more than once."

"How's this: I promise I won't do it loudly enough to summon the guards."

"We have no..." Belatedly realising this is a tease, Eliza smiles.

Lister whistles on, like a bird in a bush. Then breaks off and points: "A Roman fortress? This alone was worth the ride from Market Weighton."

"We call it our Multiangular Tower."

"But the upper section, with the *meurtrières,* looks more medieval."

"With the...what?"

"Murderers. That's what the French call the arrow slits." Lister capers around the massive wall. "Can we get inside?"

"We're not supposed to — "

"Oh, it's broken open at the back here." Lister disappears, then calls from within: "*Ten* sides, I believe it used to have. A *decagonal* tower."

The interior's crammed with cracked bedsteads and rotting carts, like a lumber room open to the sky. Eliza finds Lister leaning over a stone, scrubbing at it with her fist. "*Genio lou,* no, *genio loci feliciter,*" Lister reads. "*Happy the genius of this place*? Or *the spirit of this place,* more like."

"We should go back," Eliza pleads.

But Lister insists that at this point it'll be faster to complete their circuit of the Manor. As they hurry along, she comments on the weathercocks, and badgers Eliza with questions about the prevailing winds in York, as well as spandrels and soffits, whatever they are.

Eliza hopes the boar might be showing himself. Yes, by great luck, here he is, in his corner chamber — up on his hind legs with two trotters resting on the sill as he snuffs the August air.

"If the old kings could see swine running amok in their palace," Lister marvels. "Oh, the transience of earthly grandeur."

"Prinny doesn't run amok," Eliza says primly.

"You've named him after the Prince of Wales?"

"Who else is so famously fat?"

"Any bread left, to give him?"

"Sorry, I ate it all."

"Raine and I will bring you a treat tomorrow," Lister promises Prinny. She steps back, then scampers towards the wall; two steps up and she's gripping the sill so she can pat his great bristly snout.

"Get down!" If Lister's spotted practically climbing into Prinny's sty, she could be sent home, and though that prospect would have pleased Eliza this morning, somehow things are different now.

Music is taught in the high-ceilinged room at the front of the Manor with unpapered walls that bear spectral traces of old bricked-up doors. Mr. Camidge isn't come yet, so Eliza slips onto a stool and shakes out her hands to loosen them. Of the square fortepianos, her favourite is this mahogany one on a wobbly trestle stand. (Though why is such an instrument called square, when it has the proportions of a woman's coffin?) She finds her opening chord and launches into "Rondo alla Turca."

Betty and Margaret, behind her, guitars dangling. Betty doesn't bother to keep her voice down: "You seem on very civil terms with that creature."

Eliza's hands freeze. Quietly: "I have to share a room with her, after all."

Margaret surprises her by saying, "Oh, I suppose Miss Lister must have her good points."

Betty looks at her friend sideways. "None that she'll care to display to *ignoramuses*."

Eliza tries diplomacy. "I believe that remark was meant as a joke. Miss Lister must have been nervous, encountering the whole school at dinner."

Betty puffs out her breath. "No wonder. She looks like a stableboy in his sister's petticoats."

"Well, I for one welcome any fresh company to vary our captivity," Margaret says.

Betty's face falls: is her loyal lieutenant abandoning ship?

Margaret forms a chord with her left hand. "Come, my sweet, from the top?"

The pair launch into strumming and picking in unison. Eliza gestures to them to move farther away, but all they do is turn their backs.

Eliza runs through her own piece again, smoothing it a little. Then she notices Lister beside her, wiping her dripping mouthpiece. Of course Lister would have a flute—the instrument many parents won't allow girls, because those jerking movements reveal the elbows in an unladylike way. Lister calls above the clamour, "Utter bedlam!"

"You're just used to practising alone," Eliza answers. "Mr. Camidge says this way cultivates concentration."

Lister shakes her head in disbelief. Then puts the flute to her lips and plays on, with competent vigour, elbows stabbing the air as if defending herself in a crush.

Eliza reaches left to pull out the first two stops of the fortepiano so her notes will sustain longer. But she can still barely hear them. To make matters worse, Nan and Fanny are singing an Irish ballad in the corner.

What was it I wished to see?
What wished to hear?
Where all the joy and mirth
Made this town heaven on earth...

Eliza tries to push that tune to the edge of her mind so she can focus on "Rondo alla Turca." How she'd like to be playing alone, in a quiet apartment of her own.

Leaning over her, flute held up like a spear, Lister improvises in a falsetto:

Where all the noise and din
Made this town hell to live in...

Now Eliza's laughing too much to carry on.

"At home I play the drums too," Lister tells her. "Be thankful I couldn't fit them in my trunk."

In the doorway, Mr. Camidge claps slowly until they all fall silent. "My apologies, young ladies. I was kept late at the Minster."

"He's the music master there, like his father was," Eliza whispers to Lister. Mr. Camidge tends towards the moralistic—his sorrowful homilies about *you young ladies of the modern day* blame them for everything from narrow shoes to sleeping late to fast carriages—but his fervour for music is so genuine, they can't help liking him.

Now, for instance, he gets them all playing a four-part round, "Oh My Love, Lov'st Thou Me," and the mishmash of instruments chimes together quite nicely. Then they try the whole thing in a minor key, which has a certain melancholy Eliza likes even better.

At the end of class they file past the master, who scribbles a letter after each name in the ledger.

"So I earned a... a P?" Lister puzzles over it.

"That means *Pretty Well,*" Eliza tells her. "V would be *Very Well,* but that leads to swelled heads so the masters don't give it often. And they save N—meaning *Not Well*—for when a girl covers herself in shame. Mr. Camidge generally gives us all a P."

This evening, she's getting ready for bed when Lister dashes in, already yanking off her creased cap. "Evening, Raine."

Eliza's startled to see that the girl's back hair is cropped to the nape. "Have you had a bad fever?"

Lister grins under her gaze, and rubs it. "No, I just like it kept neat. It saves time brushing. In Paris it's all the mode—*coiffure à la Titus,* as in the Emperor."

"Bonaparte?" Eliza's bewildered.

"No, Titus of Rome."

"Of course." Not that she's ever heard of Titus. She doesn't suppose her new classmate means to discomfit her; erudition just rises off Lister like smoke. Eliza glimpses tiny patches of pink skin through the girl's brown pelt. She's seen short hair on female heads in the occasional print in a stationer's window, though so bedizened with curls, ribbons, and flowers that the effect had nothing classical about it. It occurs to her that elegant ladies might very well be walking about with cropped hair under their caps and bonnets, and as long as they keep a few ringlets on the forehead, who'd know except their intimates?

"So you've visited Paris?" she asks. Though this must have been a few years ago, before this latest outbreak of hostilities.

A sheepish grimace from Lister. "I've not yet been out of Yorkshire, except by reading and imagination."

Eliza likes her for that admission.

"Whereas you, Raine, must have seen half the world, on your way here."

She's still not sure how she feels about being called that, plain Raine. She supposes Father must have gone by his surname at school in Scarborough. "Well, I was only six when I left."

"But you're a great observer."

"What makes you say that?"

"Those dark eyes of yours, ever watchful."

Dark unsettles Eliza, a little.

"I'm the same. I like to notice things and set them down," Lister tells her. "Knowledge is power, we know from Bacon."

She puzzledly thinks of the meat, before realising that Lister must mean the philosopher.

Lister leans against the sloped ceiling to butt it with her head. "Ugh. I hate a low room."

"It's not as if you're tall," Eliza jokes.

"Not yet, but I'm still growing."

She doubts that.

"I scorn everything mean and confining." Lister steps into the middle and waves an imaginary sword overhead. "What do they call this sky parlour of ours?"

"It's a nameless little hole."

"A cupboard for human odds and ends. Even the floor's askew," Lister observes. "That corner seems inches lower than the rest. The Pit of Hell, we'll call that spot." Reaching through a gap in the curtains, she undoes the latch and shoves the window open.

Eliza doesn't want to be obvious and mention that this is strictly against the rules. She tells herself that nobody's likely to be out in the fields to report them at this hour of the evening.

"The scent of York." Lister smacks her thin lips.

"What's that?"

"Well, there's less in the way of sheep dung than at home. Other forms of filth, though. The river. Chemicals. Something baking?"

Hearing the familiar tread in the passage, Eliza rushes to shut the window and pull the curtain.

After Mrs. Tate's taken away their lantern, Lister throws herself on her back. "We shall dub this the Diagonal Chamber," she announces. "No, the Slanted Chamber, that's more poetic. Or the Slope?"

Eliza lets her eyes adjust to the dark.

Lister murmurs, "We met before this, by the way."

She frowns. "You and I?"

"I mean, *I* saw *you,* though no one thought to introduce us."

"When was this?"

"Over a year ago, now. The fourth of August last, at the Hunters'. My aunt brought me."

Dr. Hunter is the mind-doctor who runs York's lunatic asylum. Eliza dimly remembers that party at his house on Low Petergate. Dr. Duffin likes to be seen with his wards on occasion, though Eliza finds it a trial. "Are you sure it was me? My sister, Jane, would have been there too."

She can hear the tiny squeak of the bed as Lister shakes her head. "You were both pointed out to me, and you're not a bit alike."

Except in the obvious way. "Pointed out?" Eliza echoes coldly.

"Well, of course you were—a pair of mysterious orphan heiresses."

Mysterious makes her giggle.

"You're not like anyone, Raine."

Eliza stiffens. "None of the other Manor pupils, you mean?"

"Not like anyone anywhere, I suspect. You're a *rara avis*."

She goes up on one elbow. "What did you just call me?"

"A rare bird. You really must study Latin."

Her heart thumps painfully. "So you remembered me all year as an oddity."

"No, I remembered you as the most beautiful girl I've ever seen."

Eliza's face scorches. She supposes she should say thank you for the compliment, but instead she drops flat and turns to the wall.

* * *

After dinner on Thursday, the August evening is so mild, even those who have to study come out to join the others among the ruins. They sit on old blankets to keep the long grass from greening their frocks. As ever, Eliza is impressed by Mercy's grim determination to keep up in French without ever having had a lesson, by learning parrot-fashion from Frances's book.

Eliza's trying to complete her weekly letter to her guardian. It contains no news the Duffins didn't hear when she went to dinner last Saturday, but the doctor thinks it a useful exercise, and Mrs. Duffin likes proof that Eliza's handwriting is improving. *In Music I have been practising my Mozart...*

Carrying her writing-box, Lister drops into the narrow space between Eliza and Frances, crossing her legs tailor-style. "What's that, Miss Selby?"

Frances's face lights up. "Have you never tried quilling, Miss Lister? Its proper name is paper filigree, and it's the greatest pleasure in the world."

"I find that hard to believe." Lister catches Eliza's eye.

Eliza looks away, feeling disloyal to her old friend.

Frances shows off her tools. "I use an old quill with the nib cut off and a slit made in the end to hold the paper, see? I cut a long, narrow strip of paper and roll it up into a coil, or a scroll, then I glue it in place."

"You're making a pattern around the head of... Is that Princess Amelia?"

"That's right! On the occasion of her birthday, with velvet for a background, or perhaps crushed shells—I haven't decided yet."

Lister purses her small mouth drolly in Eliza's direction.

Frances is not vapid, Eliza would like to tell her. Where's the harm in crafting something pretty in honour of the King's youngest daughter?

Lister leans left, to study Betty's map. The most meticulous needlewoman in the Middle Form, Betty has been embroidering the world for as long as Eliza's been here. "Remarkable work, Miss Foster. Why's there no land at the bottom of the globe?"

"Because there isn't any." Betty taps the dog-eared engraving from which she's copying.

"No, I mean why do you suppose it formed that way, with nothing but ocean at the Southern Pole?"

Betty gives her a blank look. "How should I know?"

"That's how the Almighty in his infinite wisdom shaped the earth." Mercy speaks without looking up from the French primer.

"But why aren't the continents more evenly distributed?" Lister wonders.

"Curiosity killed the cat," Betty snaps.

If Lister had been in Eden, Eliza thinks, she'd have

bitten into the Fruit before the Serpent ever slithered by to offer it. A gulp of laughter escapes her.

"What's so funny?" Lister asks.

Eliza only shakes her head. "Perhaps there *is* land down there at the Pole, but nobody's sailed far enough to spot it."

Lister makes her a little bow. "Now, there's an explanation that appeals to my venturesome spirit."

Eliza gets up on her knees to squint at Betty's deftly threaded letters: *New Holland, Siam, Chinese Tartary, Ethiopic Ocean, Arabia.* "Madras should go just there," putting her fingernail about two-thirds of the way down the peninsula, on the right.

"I've already put Calcutta and Bombay."

Ah, clearly the vast Subcontinent is only to be allotted two cities, even though Europe's riddled with names.

"And York?" Lister asks.

"I've only room to name London," Betty objects.

Lister tuts. "Isn't this the Second City of Britain?"

"No, Bristol's that," Mercy says.

"Newcastle, surely." Margaret's eyes are still on the comedy she's reading.

"Very well, perhaps York's not quite second in population or industry, but in genteelness," Lister argues.

Margaret murmurs: "Only a Yorkshire girl would claim so."

"I find this rather a sleepy old town, for all its so-called elegance." Betty waves discontentedly at the distant towers of the Minster. "They say its Season's not what it was. If my father meant me to be finished in style, he really might have sent me as far as London, or Bath at least."

Eliza's amused: Betty's hometown, fourteen miles down the Ouse, must be a sight sleepier than York. "We're schoolgirls, Betty. What does it matter to us how faded the fashionable round may be?"

Betty scowls, but Lister gives Eliza one of her unsettling smiles.

"York has none of the sea vistas of my dear Scarborough," Nan sighs.

"Seventeen hundred years of history, you goose." Lister flings out her arms. "Ancient walls to walk on."

"If you want to sprain an ankle," Nan grumbles. "A Junior did that and was put in disgrace for a fortnight."

Lister shakes her head, and starts filling her pen.

Fanny leans over, impressed. "Is that a metal nib?"

"Silver." Lister shows her, nonchalant. "I won it as a prize for writing when I was eight."

Margaret snorts without looking up. "Writing, as in the elegance of your penmanship?"

"As in, fluency of invention and precision of construction, Miss Burn."

A snort. "Was this the same school where you were whipped every day?"

Eliza realises, with an odd sting, that Lister's been telling other girls her stories too.

"I was a notable pupil in several respects," Lister murmurs as she fiddles with some black sealing-wax.

Mercy warns her, "Don't seal your letter yet. The Head has to read them."

Lister curls her lip. "An unenviable task, spying on school-girls."

"It's to preserve us from falling prey to the wolf in the fold," Mercy tells her, "or going astray like silly sheep."

Nan and Fanny giggle at that.

Lister taps her own page. "So does Miss Hargrave strike out whatever words she doesn't approve, before sending it on?"

Mercy shakes her head. "If she doesn't like any part of the letter, she'll give it to her sister to burn."

Lister sits up straighter. (Like a soldier in muslin drapery, Eliza thinks.) "And if I wrote home to complain about this policy of censorship?"

"She'd burn that one too, *and* you'd get a disputatiousness mark *and* lose writing privileges for a week."

"I suppose you could always drop off a letter at the post office yourself," Margaret says, her tone intrigued. "But what if your parents betrayed you to the Head?"

"We've had a Senior expelled for secret correspondence," Betty tells Lister.

"That was with a cadet," Margaret reminds her.

"Well," Lister says grimly. "Good to know the number and thickness of our prison bars."

Eliza notices something. "What on earth is your seal?"

"A pelican feeding her young with blood from her breast." Lister passes it to her. "From my mother's stepmother, whose first husband was a Prussian count."

More boasting; Betty throws Margaret a look.

"What's yours?" Lister asks Eliza.

She gives back the pelican and shows the simple French motto on her own seal: *Pensez à moi.*

"*Think of me.* How perfect for a letter." Lister sits back and studies her own seal again. "When my sister was born, my mother let me nurse a little too. I liked it very well."

Uneasy looks pass between the Middles.

"How can you remember your infancy?" Nan wonders.

"No, I was six years old."

Cries of disgust.

Eliza feels the most curious sensation in her own chest, under all the lace.

"The milk's slightly sweet," Lister says, "like the juice of a pear."

Mercy gets to her feet and stalks off towards the building.

But it's clear to Eliza that Lister's not aiming to offend her schoolmates. It's not even that she doesn't care whether she offends or not; the flow of her thought is as urgent and unstoppable as a spring of water.

Margaret drops her book on the blanket and says, "Let's play something."

"A game!" That's Lister.

"Shop." Betty, decisive, packs up her embroidery in her workbag.

"I don't believe I know that one."

Margaret smirks over Lister's head at Betty. "You'll get the hang of it."

"Shop's not a real game," Eliza objects.

"Not the running around, merry kind." Fanny sounds disappointed.

"You begin, darlingest," Betty tells Margaret.

Eliza wonders how these two came to be crowned queens of the Middle Form, long before she arrived.

Margaret says, "I went to the shop, and bought an elephant's foot umbrella stand."

Betty takes it up. "*I* went to the shop and bought an elephant's foot umbrella stand and... a large blue plate."

Nan jumps in third. "I went to the shop and bought an elephant's foot umbrella stand, a large blue plate, and a..." They all wait as she flails for a word that fits. "An egg."

"My turn?" That's Fanny, never sure of where she is in a game. "I went to the shop and bought an elephant's foot umbrella stand, a blue—no, a *large* blue plate, an egg, and a pewter mug."

Lister's gaze flickers from face to face.

Many parlour games have, as their sole purpose, the mockery of those who don't understand how they're played. Really, Eliza thinks, the people in the know might just as well stand the newcomer in a corner and pelt her with chestnuts. She takes her go: "I went to the shop and bought an elephant's foot umbrella stand, a large blue plate, an egg, a pewter mug, and a *hideous hat*..." Leaning into the double *h*'s just enough, her gaze on Lister.

An answering spark in those penetrating eyes.

"Hints are against the rules."

Eliza gives Betty a blank look. "So are unjust accusations."

"What—was there a hint?" Lister's acting her part well. "Did I miss it?"

Margaret clicks her tongue in annoyance.

Eliza allows the tiniest curl in the side of her mouth nearest to Lister.

Frances contributes *an aspic mould* to the imaginary shopping list, Mercy *a nankeen waistcoat*. So by the time it's Lister's turn, she's ready with something to match the final *t* of the clue word, *elephant*. She overdoes it, though. "...a hideous hat, an aspic mould, a nankeen waistcoat...and *a teeny-tiny tea tray*?"

Betty scowls at Margaret. "Eliza gave it away."

"What?" Eliza asks, as if outraged.

"When?" Lister pantomimes innocence. "I just used my powers of deduction."

"We should have played a real game," Fanny says glumly. "Anyone for Blind Man's Buff?"

At bedtime Eliza finds Lister already in her nightdress, pacing up and down the Slope, eyes half-closed. "What are you doing?" she asks as she starts to shed her clothes.

"Committing girls to memory. Betty *Foster,* I picture running from a great slavering dog, but the dog's *faster*. Margaret *Burn,* I imagine standing too close to the fire, so her hem—"

Eliza holds up a hand to hush her. "No need for forty murderous fantasies, Lister."

Who grins, perhaps because Eliza's addressed her the way she likes.

"They only proposed that game to put you in your place, since you boasted of being related to a Prussian count."

Her mouth twists: "*Distantly* related." Then, ruefully, "If people aren't civil, I am sometimes rather too hasty in ranking them among my sworn enemies."

"Well, I applaud your plan to memorise who's who." Eliza chooses a clean page from her red pocket-case and sets it on the flat leather. She remembers making a list, her first week at the Tottenham school, a map of the social maze. *Yellow Room,* she writes, *Betty Foster.* "Betty's father's another banker—he as good as owns their river port." She jots in the names of the other girls who sleep in the Yellow Room.

Lister points at a name she's read upside down. "Two Simpsons from Whitby? I believe they have brothers at school with mine."

"Then Margaret Burn is next door to the Yellow Room, in the Chapel."

"Pupils sleep in a chapel?"

"Oh, it's just a bedroom, but we like to imagine it was once used for secret worship, as the pointed windows look Gothic." Eliza inks in the names of the other roommates under *Chapel.* "Margaret's the cleverest in the Middle Form." (Well, until Lister came, but no need to admit that.)

"Cleverer than Mercy Smith?"

"Mercy's only the hardest working—tortoise to Margaret's hare. Margaret is the school's greatest fortune."

"How many thousands?" Lister asks.

"Ten." More than twice Eliza's four. Girls here speak plainly or jestingly about what some of them have coming; others have only hopes, or little hope of inheriting anything. Future funds seem rather unreal, as long as the pupils are all obliged to wear the same white frocks and drink the same river water. "But on the other hand..." *Go on, can you match this girl's candour?* Eliza chooses the politest term for the disadvantage she and Margaret both have. "She's a magistrate's natural daughter."

Lister nods neutrally.

Mrs. Tate's light footsteps. Lister whips a tallow taper out of her etui, spikes it on a candleholder, and lights it.

Eliza hisses, "No." Private lights are strictly forbidden; two of the Seniors smuggled in lanterns last year and were reported by a maid.

Lister ducks to set it under her bed, then hurries to meet Mrs. Tate at the door.

"Not in bed yet?"

"I beg pardon, madam. Miss Raine was helping me undo a tangled lace."

What a quick, glib liar.

"Well, you can both finish up in the dark," Mrs. Tate scolds mildly.

"Good night, madam." Lister starts shutting the

door as she hands over the lantern, before Mrs. Tate can catch the leakage of light from the taper under the bed.

The two girls stare at each other in its glimmer. Then Eliza resumes. *Green Room, Nan Moorsom, Fanny Peirson,* and half a dozen other names.

Lister says, "The first list I ever drew up, at eleven, was my pedigree."

This amuses Eliza. "Like a racehorse."

"I've reckoned one hundred and thirty-eight generations from my great-grandfather back to Adam."

She laughs out loud. This grandiosity must come of being a nobody from the Wolds; Lister's clothing herself in tinsel, like some ragged strolling player.

Not that Eliza has any grounds for pride of birth herself. Would she swap half or a quarter of her four thousand pounds for an old county name? On the whole, she thinks not. What good would it do Eliza to be a countess, even, when the prejudiced would still look askance and call her a cuckoo in the nest?

Mid Hall: she lists the Percivals (all the mousy-haired spit of each other) and the other Yorkshire girls who fill that chamber. *Double Room, Frances Selby.* "Now, Frances is probably the most well-born of us Middles. Her father is agent to the Duke of Northumberland, and they have a conservatory full of exotics and a flushing water closet."

"And she's your best friend."

A statement or a question?

"Or not quite?" Lister suggests.

"Frances...was the first girl to show me any kindness."

Lister laughs under her breath.

Eliza's fingers hover near her cheek. "None of them at the Tottenham school seemed able to see past this." *Half-blooded, half-caste:* the unspoken words thrum in her head.

"Nasty little bitches."

Her eyes sting with tears and she nods. It's not shock at the obscenity but relief, to have someone confirm what she's felt.

"I quite see you'd be grateful to Miss Selby, then," Lister says. "But gratitude is not the same as friendship."

To change the subject, Eliza says, "Frances can draw on her skin."

Lister gapes.

"With any point, I mean, such as a pencil—pink lines swell up, and stay for an hour. Oh, I forgot Mercy." She adds the name to the Double Room.

"Is Mercy anyone's best friend?"

"Our Saviour's, I suppose."

Lister snorts. "You sit in a group for long stretches without uttering a word, Miss Mouse, but tête-à-tête, you brandish your blades."

Eliza's face heats at the praise—if Lister means it

as praise. "All I mean is that Mercy's on the path to heaven and won't let anyone stand in her way."

"Mercy the merciless."

"You know Miss Hargrave took her in so we'd get our candles gratis?"

Lister cocks her head.

Eliza nods at the leaking taper. "Mr. Smith is a chandler on the Shambles, you see. She agreed to enrol one of his daughters in lieu of paying a huge bill, or that's the story anyway."

"Very practical on both sides," Lister says.

"Now, who are we missing? Among the Juniors in the Double Room are Mary Swann of the well-known York concern— "

"Friends of my aunts," Lister says with a nod. "This place is riddled with bankers' daughters."

"The Swann girl's boon companion is Mrs. Tate's daughter, little Eliza Ann. Have a care: Eliza Ann sidles about with ears flapping and brings the gossip to her aunt."

"Rather than to her mother?"

"Well, all Mrs. Tate can do is report to Miss Hargrave, who rules supreme, so the child prefers to run directly to the throne."

"The sisters are Martha and Mary, aren't they? One of them fusses over household matters, freeing the other to ponder the higher things." Lister's caressing

Eliza's scarlet pocket-case, with its flaps and fold-out slots that hold her letters and banknotes. "Is this from India?"

Eliza shakes her head. "Moroccan donkey-skin. Concentrate."

"I'm capable of thinking several things at once. I've never seen a lady's pocket-case that wasn't cloth."

She struggles to remember who sleeps in the White Room. The three little Burtons share a chamber with the junior mistress, Miss Robinson; she doesn't know its name.

Lister reaches for the page. "Is that the lot?"

"Almost." Eliza pulls it back and writes in the mistresses at the top, though not the masters, as apart from Mr. Tate (the dancing master) they don't live in. Nor do the day girls, but she puts their surnames at the bottom, for completeness. "Day girls always wear an air of superiority because they come and go in the world," she remarks, "but we rather despise them for being outsiders."

Lister chuckles. "Thanks for this, Raine. Oh, but you must add me."

Slope, Eliza writes in a tiny space, if that's what they're calling their garret now. *Miss Lister, Market Weighton.*

Lister makes a little face, reading that. "It wasn't exactly an untruth, about Shibden Hall. It's the home of my heart." She picks up the list. "Oh, but you've forgotten yourself."

Eliza takes it back and writes *E. Raine*. Then wishes she'd started with *Miss*. She could legitimately put York for her home, she supposes, because of the Duffins. Despite the fact that the doctor's an Irishman who spent his career alongside William Raine in India, and that his wife was born there to English parents, the Duffins give the impression of being as thoroughly English as any other genteelly ageing couple on Micklegate. Eliza finds herself writing *India* in the home column after all—then wavers and adds *in Past*.

Saturday means Judgement and Consequences in the refectory, with all the tables pushed to the sides and the pupils standing. "This Manor has been a place of seclusion and study for seven centuries." Miss Hargrave casts her sonorous voice to the back without effort. "Some eighty years ago, our mother's parents founded the School here to train up wives and mothers worthy of the sacred charge of forming the next generation. How glorious a time this is for the education of girls!" She breaks off to beam at her sister. "So many who used to be kept ignorant at home are now admitted to institutions of learning, of which our Manor is, I believe I may say without vanity, among those of highest repute in the land."

"The very highest in the North," Mrs. Tate murmurs.

Miss Hargrave's tone turns stern. "But when you stoop to behaving in ways unworthy of yourselves and your names, you betray that hallowed tradition. So we must curb your faults, using only gentle methods to teach you control over every passion."

Here the Head always names the prevailing vices she's observed with sorrow; this week they include hilarity, contention, and filthiness. (By that, Eliza can't work out whether she means indecent language or tracking in mud from the Manor Shore.) Miss Hargrave calls the Seniors, then Middles, then Juniors to line up one by one in front of the mistresses' table.

Miss Robinson's holding a nosegay—marigold, it looks like to Eliza, with mallow, scabious, and lady's bedstraw. Infatuated Juniors are always bringing Miss Robinson flowers, simply because she's not old, plain, nor bad-tempered. The junior mistress has to teach everything from Penmanship to Gymnastics, and in whatever moments she can snatch, she's rumoured to write poetry.

Pallid Miss Vickers wears her stiffest look, as if she considers this whole exercise undignified. She's been teaching at the Manor as long as any of the Seniors can remember, and doesn't bother to hide the fact that she'd have left long ago if any other opportunity had presented itself.

"Any marks?" Mrs. Tate asks Jane's friend Hetty in tones of regret.

"One for greed," she admits, cheeks purpling.

Having to confess in front of the school can humiliate even the most confident. Eliza inevitably finds herself on the brink of tears, even if she's only admitting to having dropped a cup or slouched. Today, mercifully, when it's her turn to answer she can say, "None."

It occurs to her to wonder how the mistresses can possibly remember all the marks they've given out over the course of the week. Unless they log them in a private ledger after each class and meal? She can't imagine Miss Vickers, for one, going to such trouble. In which case, it should be possible to underreport your misdeeds...but it would be a roll of the dice, of course, because if challenged, you'd get a deceit mark for each one omitted.

Lister gets four marks today, but chooses to cancel them out with the same number of merits earned in class for feats of memory. Many girls prefer to take their Consequences for marks and then enjoy the treat for merits. It happened to be gravy, one Saturday when Eliza won a merit for deportment, and although not particularly fond of the stuff, she felt a surge of excitement every evening that week when she stood up and, following the formula, called, "I claim gravy."

Today five pupils get barred out—put facing the corners of the refectory, as a sign of ignominy. One of them wears the jingling Fool's Hat, another the Vanity Mask (a painted face with swollen red lips, which gives Eliza the horrors). The middle Miss Burton has been caught bribing the kitchen maids to bring in ginger parkin again, so she gets the Liar's Tongue, a great curling triangle in red cloth hanging down her front. Among the Middles, Nan, to work off five inattentions, has to wear the Ass's Ears as she's sent off to clean every lamp-chimney in the Manor. Betty gets debelted—made to trade her green ribbon for the childish blue of a Junior—for exchanging waves and greetings with officers in the street. Margaret (two disputatiousness marks) wears the black Quarreller's Sash over her green belt, and presents herself to each mistress in turn to hear a remark on her character. She carries it off well, but by the end, her lower lip looks chewed raw. Finally, everyone who isn't still in disgrace receives a half-holiday, and the Middles and Seniors go off into the countryside with no mistress in charge.

Most of the harvest has been put up in great ricks by now, but gangs of men are still stooping over and over with their sickles. Dog roses bloom red in the hedges, and a hare runs across the path in front of Eliza. Lister climbs over a stile and reaches for Eliza's hand to help her. Lister's fingers are a little rough, and very strong. She says, "I'm afraid I'm a desperate walker."

"You walk very well," Eliza says.

"That's what I mean—I need to roam almost as desperately as to read."

Eliza would usually walk arm in arm with Frances, the way Betty and Margaret are now. But Frances is farther back, talking to Nan and Fanny. Has she felt neglected? Eliza and she have seen almost nothing of each other since Lister came to school. *You and the new girl are thick as thieves,* Nan remarked yesterday, and Eliza spent so long wondering if that was a rebuke, she forgot to reply.

Up ahead, she spots her sister, Jane, strolling arm in arm with her pal. Hetty's taken a damson off one tree and a greengage off another, as well as some blue-black bilberries and white currants.

As the Manor girls file past an old couple outside their cottage plaiting straw into broad-brimmed sun hats, Eliza has an impulse to buy one, even though summer is almost over.

"Charmingly rustic," Betty calls as Eliza fits it on over her mobcap.

Eliza pretends not to hear the snide tone. "Thank

you." She collapses her umbrella carefully so as not to crack a whalebone strut, and furls and buttons it up. As she walks, she dangles it by its ribbon, along with her discarded bonnet.

"Let me carry that." Lister snatches the umbrella.

The path ahead is blocked with a flock of slow-moving sheep, so Lister proposes they all turn back and follow the fingerpost towards New Earswick instead. The heather's blazing white where the late summer sun hits it. "At least sheep can eat on the march, whereas cattle drovers have to halt and graze them on the way."

"The things you know," Eliza teases.

"I realise they're not things you want to know." Lister slashes at a yellow-sprinkled whin bush.

Eliza corrects her: "Never *knew* I wanted to know."

The two of them are well ahead of the others now, because Lister moves as if in seven-league boots. "That Judgement, this morning..." she says, with one of her abrupt switches of subject.

"What of it?"

"Whipping might be kinder than such shaming. The aim of the spectacle seems to be to make us small and foul in each other's eyes."

Eliza tries to be fair: "It's not so difficult to avoid breaking the rules."

Lister makes a rude sound that would definitely earn an indecorum mark.

Eliza's remembering the Tottenham school, where permission to rise, speak, eat, relieve herself, sit, walk, or sleep had to be sought, often had to be earned. The child from Madras memorised the routines as a dancer might. The Manor isn't half as bad as that. "There's expulsion, instead, for the worst cases," she teases, "—do you prefer the sound of that? Last year a Senior disappeared overnight."

"Do you suppose the good sisters rolled her up in a rug and threw her in the Ouse?"

Eliza frowns at Lister. "She'd crept out at night and seen a man."

"*Seen* as in spoken to? Or worse?" Lister makes holes in the soft ground with the tip of Eliza's umbrella.

"Stop that."

Lister wipes it on a large leaf. "Was this girl from Yorkshire?"

"London. What difference does that make?"

"Well, a family so far away in the South will have been able to gloss it over," Lister assures her.

"You think so?"

"They'll have told all their acquaintances that her school was closed by an outbreak of something."

"Or else they might have her shut up in an attic to this day," Eliza says grimly. Then adds, "I'd have nowhere to go."

"Oh, but Raine, surely your Dr. Duffin..."

"A guardian's not the same as a father."

Lister scrutinises her face. "Is he harsh?"

"Only a little bad-tempered."

"You're invited to dine every week, aren't you?"

"Once a fortnight." Eliza tries to think how to describe the household on Micklegate. "The Duffins collect strays." She's not sure why, because the presence of the young often seems to wear on the doctor's nerves. "Their Irish nieces visit, and there's a vicar's daughter, a Miss Marsh, who's always bustling in and out, and they used to have another Indian ward..." Dearest Anna Maria Montgomery—no, Mrs. James now, more or less lost to Eliza since she was married from the Duffins' country house last October. Settled five miles away from York, but it might as well be five thousand. Her boy's just been born—mother and child both safe—and according to Mrs. Duffin, *so pale you'd hardly know.*

They must have slowed down, because the rest of the Middles are suddenly on their heels, chattering. Lister spins around. "Frances Selby, I hear you have a secret talent for writing on yourself like paper."

The others burst out laughing. Frances blushes up to the roots of her creamy hair and her eyes slide to Eliza.

Who fears Frances will assume she's been making fun of her.

"It's a curious thing," Frances admits. "My mother had it too, my father says."

Lister demands a demonstration, so Frances pushes up her sleeve to bare one long white forearm and lets Lister try with a fingernail. "Nothing indecent, now."

"Don't move."

Frances cranes to see the weals emerge. Lister releases her wrist. Eliza goes closer to see. The flowing red script says, *The Human Page.*

"You're a marvel," Lister says. "In the Dark Ages, they'd have called this a sign of the devil."

"Or God singling out one of his saints," Eliza puts in, defensive.

"Does it hurt?" Lister asks.

"It only itches a little," Frances assures her.

And then the Middles all insist on writing or drawing something, until both Frances's arms are scribbled like a sailor's.

Waking, on a bright August morning, Eliza watches Lister's small eyelids, not three feet away. She doesn't look like other girls, but Eliza can't quite put her finger on it. Something faintly animal about the narrow face. An otter, a weasel?

Water-blue eyes blink open. "Well, once again, that was horrible. This feather bed!" Lister lurches up, and her truckle bed skews on its wheels. "I've never slept on such a spiky backbreaker. What tattered ducks provided these quills?"

"Chicken, we suspect." Eliza sits up too. "The feathers do get matted and smelly if you don't shake them out well." She shows Lister how to take her tick off the striped under-mattress and give it a good pummelling, breaking up the lumps. "Hang it over the foot of my bed," she offers, because Lister's bed is just a box with no rails.

"That won't do much, surely."

"On the next sunny day, the housemaids will dangle them out of the windows for a proper airing."

When both mattresses are draped over the end of Eliza's bed, Lister gives hers a final punch. Tiny quills emerge from holes in the cloth and waft about, making her sneeze. "This school-of-high-repute is rather a sham."

That makes Eliza stare.

"We're camping in shabby hired rooms that haven't been plastered in two centuries," Lister points out.

"What matters is learning, surely, not *décor*."

A snort. "And there's the real fraud."

The bell sounds, on the floor below.

"The library, so called, is no bigger than the box room"—Lister jerks her thumb at the wall—"with only one bookcase of schoolbooks and sermons, and a century-old, crack-backed run of *The Spectator*! What are we being taught but reading, writing, and reckoning, as in any dame school, topped off with a few frills to help us hook husbands? Haphazard, superficial, and tedious, say I. If they're not drilling random passages of old books into our heads, they're scolding us to keep our legs uncrossed. It's not what I'd call education."

Anxiety comes up like acid in Eliza's throat.

Lister subsides on her cot. "Not that other girls' schools are much better. No wonder so many of us end up with frivolous, footling lives."

Eliza finds herself oddly defensive. The Manor is all she has in the way of a home. "If it's so *tedious,* write to Captain Lister and ask him to take you away."

Lister puffs out her breath. "I gave Father my word I'd try my best, this time, so the thirty guineas won't be thrown away."

Eliza doesn't think Lister realises that this sum covers only bed, board, and basic lessons for the year, not Accomplishments, furnishings, coals and candles, quills and copybooks, washing and mending.

"Besides, when I'm at the farm, I drive my mother to drink."

Delivered in a tone of high-pitched comedy—so Lister can deny it later, Eliza guesses. She's beginning to read between this girl's lines. "Come," she says, "the bell's gone."

They tidy their heads in front of the small mirror. Eliza's front curls are still more or less intact, but Lister has to chivvy hers by twisting them round her forefinger. "Why does custom insist we wrap up our heads as tight as puddings, then persuade half an inch of ringlets to peep out the front?"

"I know," Eliza sighs.

"Shall I button you up behind, Raine?"

"Please."

She can't remember why she ever thought she preferred to room alone.

Going down the back stairs after Dancing, Lister says, "Well, our master seemed to find that as dispiriting as I."

Eliza smiles. "Mr. Tate's like that."

"What, always sitting in the corner with his head in his hands?"

"Not always. On his bad days."

"I thought at first he might be..." Lister tips an invisible glass towards her lips.

Eliza shakes her head. "Just sunken in gloom."

"Any relation to our Mrs. Tate?"

"Her husband." Eliza whispers: "But she doesn't seem like a tyrant, only a worrier, so that can't be such a crippling burden, surely?"

"Married life has its murky mysteries," Lister says with a shiver.

"Their daughter in the Juniors, Eliza Ann, when asked to account for her father, all she'll say is that he's a man of sensibility—painfully sensitive feelings, don't you know."

Lister scoffs. "I've no patience for the weak-minded, with their moods and megrims and blue devils."

"That's harsh," Eliza objects. "Some natures sink where others swim."

"He's had *embarrassments*." Margaret's so close behind them that they both jump. "The Tates used to own various properties about town, but everything had to be sold up, so they lodge here at the Manor now."

"Oh, well, debt," Lister says, "that explains his misery."

Eliza's not sure it does, quite.

After French, Lister comes over to ask Eliza their master's name.

"We've no idea," she admits.

"Not a surname, even?"

Eliza puts on a sepulchral voice: "We presume Monsieur has had to keep his identity a deep, dark secret, ever since he fled France."

"Ah. Some stain on the family escutcheon?"

When Eliza doesn't know a word, she pretends she does. "Or perhaps he's a very great aristocrat who escaped the guillotine."

"If his identity is exposed, might he be assassinated in some dark alley in York?" Lister asks.

"Oh, come, we don't know for sure that he fled," Frances points out deflatingly.

"But so many did," Eliza argues.

Margaret nods: "My cousins say Soho's riddled with refugees."

When Eliza sees new arrivals in the street, marked out by some item of dress as well as a stunned expression, she remembers—with a twinge of fellow feeling—stepping off the ship at seven.

"The poor Frog." As if Lister's reading her mind. "To think, the war's been rumbling on for as long as we've been alive, and Monsieur's still stuck here."

Betty twists her blond front curls round her fingers. "What gives me the shivers is that France practically *touches* England."

"Only twenty miles apart, at Dover," Lister says. "According to yesterday's *Herald,* Boney's army of two hundred thousand is standing by in Boulogne, ready to swarm onto barges."

That prompts squeals.

"In Sheffield," Betty adds, "a brick-kiln fire was mistaken for a beacon, and caused a panic, so my brothers' Volunteer brigade was marched to Doncaster for nothing."

Betty never passes up an opportunity to boast of her brothers, particularly the eldest, a major who advanced his whole company's pay last year rather than have them wait for it.

"But if the French invade, we'll blow them to kingdom come," Lister insists.

Frances whispers, as if spies might be listening in the next room: "My father says they're building a gigantic raft, with windmills to power its paddles."

"Our Navy will make mincemeat of their barges and rafts," Lister assures her. "And as a last resort, we're building eighty-eight mighty towers to guard the coast."

"Boney might *fly* in," Nan moans.

Fanny's eyes are bulging. "However could he do that, Nan?"

"I heard he has a fleet of hot-air balloons carrying baskets of bloodthirsty Frenchmen."

"They'd never float this far," Lister says with authority. "They'd burst their gas-bags on the Peaks in Derbyshire."

"He'd only have to get as far as Windsor to kill the poor King." A tear drops from Nan's left eye.

"Then we'd have to speak French all the time." That's Fanny, practically sobbing.

How these girls can work themselves into a frenzy. "The bell's rung," Eliza points out.

On Sundays the Manor girls may put on finer white frocks—cambric, or silk at a pinch. The whole school's obliged to go to St. Olave's, except for the handful of pupils who aren't Anglicans: the Roman Catholics hear Mass at the Bar Convent, the Methodists go to their fancy new chapel, the Presbyterians to their old one, the pair of Quaker sisters to their Meeting House, and Mercy spends the whole day with the Smiths in a room above a pub where worship is led by a dungboat-man who ships the contents of privies to Hull for some industrial purpose.

After service, the Middles are permitted to go for a walk by themselves. Lister's Sunday frock is identical to her weekday one. Eliza wonders whether Lister genuinely doesn't mind about clothes, or just hides it well, but it's too delicate a subject for Eliza to probe.

The smart houses of Bootham give way to open lots and fields, and in a quarter of an hour the girls have reached Clifton Green.

"Are you waving at someone, Betty?" Lister asks.

"The lunatics on their mound."

"*That way madness lies,*" Margaret quotes, pointing.

Eliza can't tell whether that's the Bard or the Bible.

Lister pulls off her glasses to clean them on her frock.

"Behind that wall is a private asylum," Eliza tells her, nodding at the distant cluster of female heads, in white caps just like the Manor girls. "See, the middle of their garden's been built up, like a hillock, so they can look out without getting close enough to climb over and escape."

A hand goes up like a tiny white flag. Signalling back? The Middles all wave. Eliza tilts her umbrella from side to side to mime a greeting.

"Our own Dr. Mather's one of the proprietors, along with a mad-doctor called Belcombe," Margaret says. (Her guardian, the excise collector, seems to know everyone in town.)

"Such funny little faces they have," Frances murmurs sorrowfully.

"You think nervous conditions alter the features?" Lister asks, squinting into the distance.

"Well... perhaps the patients lose their teeth," Fanny says.

"As a consequence of insanity?" Lister asks, sceptical.

"I expect they neglect to clean them." That's Betty.

Eliza thinks of Mr. Tate at his most torpid.

"Perhaps they can't be allowed toothpicks," Margaret suggests, "in case they prick each other."

Nan says, "Or their keepers pull out their teeth so they can't bite?"

Fanny and Frances wail in protest.

"My cousin Lady Crawfurd has teeth of hippopotamus ivory," Eliza mentions.

"What are they like?" Betty asks.

Eliza hasn't seen her father's niece in years, but she's not going to say so. Besides, she's estranged from her baronet husband, so perhaps she's not the most respectable connection to claim. "They do smell, rather."

"What do you suppose Miss Lewin's are made of?" Margaret wonders.

"Hers must have a spring that's too tight," Lister says, "since they try to leap out of her mouth at every other word."

Fanny's walking backwards, watching the shrinking knot of patients in their garden. "But derangement can be cured, can't it?"

"Very often," Margaret agrees. "These are the milder cases—ladies of means who still have hopes of recovery, like the gentlemen in the house next door. The *raving* patients are kept under strict watch at Mather and Belcombe's other asylum in York."

"Didn't King George lose his mind, before we were even born," Betty remembers, "and a doctor got it back for him?"

"My uncle tells me he's lost it again," Lister says. "These days His poor Majesty is held in seclusion at Windsor Castle. Apparently he talks so much he foams at the mouth, and the pages have to sit on him."

"I've never heard that," Betty says.

"Well, the Government won't admit it, especially in wartime—giving comfort to the Enemy and all that."

"What's that sweet song about a madwoman rattling her chains?" Frances frowns, trying to remember.

Eliza nods back towards Clifton Green. "These unfortunates don't seem to be in chains, only shut in."

"Like us at the Manor, every night, you mean?" Lister asks.

They all burst out laughing at the comparison.

She adds dryly, "So the main difference must be, we have more of our teeth."

RAINE TO LISTER, 1815

My dear Lister,

Pensez à moi. Do you think of me at all, these days?

I keep hunting through my bundle of precious letters for your last, which I believe I received many months ago, but the servants seem to have put them all out of order. (Little they realise the distress they cause me by their thoughtlessness; how the whole story is fractured and jumbled now.) After eight years of constant correspondence, our exchange of letters has been strangely interrupted—on your side, I may say, without imputing blame, since how often in this vale of tears some accident prompts what may seem a long and cruel silence, without any malice being intended. In a spirit not of reproach, then, but of fondest *amitié,* let me hint that I would be ever grateful for a resumption of that correspondence, the slim but strong thread on which this bewildered Ariadne has so often relied to help her fumble through the lightless labyrinth.

I'll be frank, as I can hide nothing from your sharp eyes. Pining to hear from you, I unburden myself on paper. I only hope you'll be able to make out these words, between the crossings out and the blurred, salt traces. I hesitate to alarm you, Lister, but I'm not myself.

Time and thinking tame the strongest grief, I was taught, but many a proverb's promise proves false. I've found that thinking only wears away at grief, grinds it deeper, and time only preserves it, encases it in glass for the ages.

At night, how my heart throbs. Sleep is a distant shore, quite out of reach. I pace, turn, look at my narrow bed. You rise so vividly before my eyes that I can scarce believe you're not here, yet the moment I stretch out my hands you dissolve like some phantom. Memory's pleasures are insidious; its moonlight unfits me for the sunshine of real life, and I fear I've lived too long among its shadows.

By day I'm feverish and low, almost incapable of rising. I have no appetite, and live on water. My wool knots; I lose sewing needles in my skirts. I'm quite unfit for society—were there any real society in this house. I try to laugh at the folly of the more irritating lodgers. (That's what they call us—a genteel euphemism meant to salve our mortification at finding ourselves here.) But it only makes me more melancholy to remember how you used to laugh along with me. There are as many petty rules here as there were at the Manor, and you're not with me to make fun of their absurdity.

Very Well, Pretty Well, Not Well, Not Well At All.

Here comes the tide of gloom creeping in. I've lost the knack of dispelling its clinging vapour with my books, drawing, or even playing on my beloved rosewood piano. I can't rouse myself to open the cage and play with the chaffinches. My mind feels bandaged like one of those mummies in the British Museum. I inch through the marsh but find no firm ground.

I wish I could close my ears to the clock's relentless tick. How can the day's allotted time of writing be almost up already?

Dr. Mather continues to have confidence in my prospects of recovery, and Dr. Belcombe assures me that the regimen here at Clifton is perfectly calculated to conduce to the healing of both body and mind. But my eagerness to hear from you is torture, Lister. I can't understand, or seem to have forgotten, if I ever understood, what parted us. The letter I crave is a smaller boon than a visit, and one you surely won't, can't, deny me? Please, please come and tease me out of my *moods and megrims and blue devils*. Pour down your wise and witty words as balm on my bleak spirit, and then I will attempt to reconcile myself to my sorry state. A single page from you would, like the rays of the rising sun, revive my earth and bring forth buds of the greenest hope.

Here comes Matron Clarkson to collect my pen. I protest, but she insists as ever that more than half an hour would strain my

THE COMPANY OF GIRLS, NOVEMBER 1805

A SMOKY NOVEMBER evening, and Lister's dangling her head out the window of the Green Room.

"Don't," Mercy pleads.

"Tell me truly, Mercy, who down there in the street tonight would tell the Head we were leaning out the window? They're all up to far worse."

Mercy steps back, scowling, arms folded as tight as ropes.

Back in the Michaelmas term, the prig of the Middle Form might very well have reported her classmate for rule-breaking, Eliza thinks; by now no one can resist Lister. Eliza is her best friend, but everyone has caught the habit of calling her Lister.

Mischief Night: the eve of Guy Fawkes Day. Tomorrow York's very own traitor—born around the corner on Stonegate—will be burned in effigy, with fireworks representing the bombs he and his Papist conspirators didn't manage to detonate, exactly two hundred years ago. On this chilly autumn night, dozens of Manor girls have crammed into the one bedroom with a window facing east towards the town, to catch a little of the hullabaloo. They're hopeful that even if Mrs. Tate hears them running about overhead, she won't bother to come upstairs until she collects the lanterns at nine.

Fires billow from tar barrels at crossings, in the streets below, and the clanging of saucepans makes rough music. "Oh, to be down there," Lister groans with longing. "Look, there's a pair of mischief-makers trying to climb up a chimney with a bag, to cover it and smoke the householders out..."

"Dreadful." Margaret sounds thrilled.

"I'd be petrified," Fanny says, coughing into her sleeve. (Even though Nan's always claiming to be ill, it's her pal who has a bad chest every winter.)

"Me too," Eliza admits. "Especially on such a night, with villains chasing cats..."

"And insulting anyone in skirts," Nan adds.

"And a boggart lurking in every shadow, likely," Fanny adds.

"You don't really believe in boggarts, do you, Fanny?" Lister teases.

She doesn't answer, only hides her face.

Nan confesses, "After dark I fall prey to every bugbear. I'd be a martyr to nervous insomnia if I didn't take my sleeping draught."

The first firecrackers go off like gunshots, and Lister whoops.

Mercy warns: "If your noise brings a mistress upstairs, and we get a general punishment—"

"We won't," Margaret reassures her. "Did you smell those wonderful beefsteaks browning? I'd lay a guinea the teachers are all swigging hot punch in the Head's parlour."

Giggles at that. "Not Miss Lewin, surely," Betty says. "She'd stick to healthful broth."

"Or arrowroot."

"Sipped lukewarm, so as not to shock the stomach."

The Misses Parker in their red belts push into the room now, insisting the Middles let them have a turn at the window.

"This time last year," Lister tells Eliza, "I was cantering around Halifax with Sam and John, waving our punkie lanterns, smearing honey on doorknobs, banging on knockers and running away..."

"You expect us to believe that your people let you run wild on Mischief Night, like some..." Betty trails off, as all the epithets she might choose are too offensive to pronounce.

"What's a punkie lantern?" Eliza wants to know.

"Carved from a turnip, or a mangel-wurzel at a pinch," Lister tells her. "Haven't you ever made one?"

Amused, Eliza asks, "Where and when would I have been taught to whittle vegetables?"

Lister's struck by that. "School has been all you've known of England, I suppose."

"Ooo!" the Middles cry out as more fireworks burst, spattering hot orange across the night sky.

Margaret breaks into a song.

The roads they are so muddy
We cannot walk about,
So roll me in your arms, my love,
And blow the candle out...

Eliza wonders what it would be like to be *rolled* in a man's arms. The fresh dark after the light's snuffed; the unspeakable secrets to follow. How does any bride summon nerve enough for the wedding night?

Lister asks, "Who knows the glee 'Miss Bailey's Ghost'? Come, you'll all pick it up as quick as anything." She begins the verse, in her deep alto:

A captain bold in Halifax
Who dwelt in country quarters,
Seduced a maid, who hanged herself
One morning in her garters.

Hisses of disapproval. The Parker girls, Roman Catholics, cross themselves in protest.

"Seduction *and* self-murder, really?" Mercy sounds as if she's about to pop.

Lister thrusts her way back to the window and leans out so far that the other girls have to grab her skirts to make sure she won't tip out. "Tantalising, to glimpse all the fun from up here, like so many Rapunzels..."

An hour later, Eliza and Lister have *sloped off* to their Slope, as Lister puts it, and each is shivering under her blankets. Girls who share a room often bundle together for warmth on a cold night, despite the rule, but somehow Eliza feels that wouldn't do, with Lister.

In the dark, she's still struck by the image of Rapunzels locked in their tower. "My father was a prisoner for four years, in India." (Not even bothering to lower her voice, as the servants are still carousing in the kitchen.)

"Four years!" Lister marvels. "Which war was this?"

Eliza's glad Lister didn't make the mistake of asking for what crime William Raine had been jailed. "Our Company's, against Mysore, a southern kingdom whose ruler was in league with the French."

"The East India Company, this is?"

"Those of us born into it simply call it the Company. The most powerful firm the world's ever known," Eliza boasts, "with its own coinage and taxes." According to Dr. Duffin, the Company's composed of two hundred clerks in a small office in London, backed by a hundred and fifty thousand soldiers abroad: *We hold two-thirds of India already, and rule her better than her princelings ever have.* But she's meant to be telling the story of Father's captivity. "Our forces were facing an appalling new weapon, Mysorean war rockets."

"What on earth are war rockets?"

"Swords, propelled hundreds of yards through the air from exploding iron tubes."

Lister whistles.

"Colonel Baillie's imperial troops were cut to pieces, British and native alike," Eliza tells her. "The Mysoreans dragged the few survivors off to Bangalore Fort, including Father and another injured doctor—he died in a matter of days. It was a medical miracle Father ever got his own wound to close up."

"I *revere* an indomitable spirit," Lister says.

"You really should have been born a boy."

She half laughs at that. "I'm rather an enigma even to myself. Nature was in a funny mood the day she made me. Perhaps I'm the connecting link between the sexes."

That notion makes Eliza blink. Who could think such a thing about herself—say it out loud, even—and not be mortified? It's a sign of how much Lister's come to trust her, she reminds herself.

"Where was your father injured?"

"A place called Pollilur, inland from Madras," Eliza says.

"No, where on his person?"

"Oh, he never said." William Raine was rather a private man, and touchy if questioned. "He nursed the other captives, as well as the family of the Qiladar—the governor of the fort—who was so grateful, he struck off Father's irons." Eliza treasures that detail.

"Until that moment, he must have thought it was all up with him," Lister remarks.

"I suppose so." Eliza considers the matter as she never has before, as if she didn't know the turn his story was about to take. "Past forty, in a filthy dungeon, leaking pus..." Yes, how could Father have warded off despair? Eliza finds it hard enough to keep her spirits up some winter afternoons when the Manor reeks of boiled fish and gloom creeps in like smoke under the door. If she were a shackled prisoner with little hope of ever getting free...well, she could imagine turning her face to the wall and refusing food, even though self-murder is the worst of sins.

"And to think," Lister says, "around a blind corner, he had another whole stretch of life. It all goes to prove, one never knows."

Eliza nods in the dark. "Sixteen more years of health and prosperity, waiting for him." In a lovely villa, with a lovely wife.

"And two daughters! My own father was never captured," Lister says, "but he was wounded, back in the seventies. You've heard of the city of Boston?"

Eliza doesn't want to say she hasn't.

"Well, Ensign Lister wasn't part of a detachment ordered to retrieve a cache of arms, but a certain lieutenant shammed Abraham—pretended to be taken ill—so Father volunteered to go in the coward's place, for the honour of the regiment."

"And there was a battle?"

"Was there! At a place called Concord the brave Redcoats found themselves outnumbered." Lister springs up in her bed now, its wheels squeaking. "They sent for reinforcements but were refused—told there were surely enough of them to defend a bridge. Well, the skulking Rebels harried the British detachment *savagely*. My father proposed to tear down the bridge rather than let the Americans take it. But before he could pull up the first plank, his right elbow was shattered by a bullet."

Eliza flinches.

"Imagine the chaos. The poor Redcoats limping and bleeding all the way back to Boston under a constant hail of gunfire from behind the hedges."

"So they retreated?"

"Those were their orders," Lister says sharply. "My father was feeling faint, so he borrowed a mount, but just when he rode past another horse, with an injured soldier on its back and three more hanging off its sides, he saw a Rebel gun it down. So naturally he handed over his own to the wounded. All told, he marched sixty miles in twenty-four hours, the last thirty-six of them dripping blood."

"And his arm, did he lose it?" Eliza asks.

"He came perilously close. The next half-year he spent in agony—twice the surgeons had to lay it open, taking out pieces of bone the size of hazelnuts—and only Jesuit's powder twice a day prevented mortification." Lister's tone lightens. "Father always says he was in more danger of dying from the invalid diet. Only after he was allowed a morsel of meat and a spoonful of wine did he finally begin to mend. Then he was invalided home to Yorkshire and made a lieutenant."

Silence stretches in the cold, stuffy dark. "And if they hadn't endured, and survived," Eliza says, "they wouldn't have become our fathers. We would never have been . . . begot."

The biblical word makes them both giggle. "No you, nor me," Lister murmurs.

Eliza knows she's lucky, too, that Father didn't leave her and Jane in ignorance of their origins. He gave them his surname, rather than some alias. Really, they can reproach him with nothing. "I hate it when people ask if my father was a nabob, as if every Briton in India pillages every village he enters, and sails home laden with tusks and diamonds."

"So how does a doctor make eight thousand pounds?"

She blinks. But Lister's questions always seem to rouse a similar forthrightness in Eliza. "No one's ever given me any details. I suppose Company men receive gifts, and are in a good position to engage in trading on the side. At any rate," she adds crisply, "he didn't live to enjoy it."

"How old were you when he— "

"Nine."

"I'm sorry you lost him."

The phrase makes it sound as if Eliza mislaid her father somewhere. She supposes the day William Raine was more or less lost to her and Jane was three years earlier, when he took the little girls in a coir-woven skiff across the Madras sandbar, through the terrible breakers where the sharks hung waiting, to deposit them on the *King George*. Like parcels; valuable ones, but parcels nonetheless. His parting words would turn out to be the last Eliza ever had from him—if only she could remember what they were.

There is one thing she'd like to know: was he expecting his daughters to come back to India when quite schooled and grown? Or never—did he consider his job done, once he'd packed them off to be thoroughly Englished? "He took furlough, the year I was nine," she tells Lister. "His ship had almost reached the island of St. Helena, far west of Africa, when he died."

"He was *en voyage* to be reunited with you, then?"

Eliza hesitates. No letters came in response to those the girls, under instruction, sent their father. They'll never know how he meant to settle his affairs, except that his will named them as *beloved Daughters* to the tune of four thousand apiece. Is this a set phrase that the lawyer would have suggested? Or was it William Raine who told him to put *beloved*?

"Buried at sea, then," Lister murmurs. "Something magnificent about that."

What Eliza remembers from her year in mourning, at the Tottenham school, are the clothes: little buckled shoes, black bombazine. "I can really only picture him from the portrait at the Duffins' house," she admits. Much like every other gentleman at half-length: a pale round face above a sombre suit.

Lister's voice deepens as she recites:

Full fathom five thy father lies;
Of his bones are coral made.

Eliza's shaken by the image: a scarlet, coral-boned skeleton.

"*The Tempest,*" Lister adds in explanation. "You've read Shakespeare?"

"Ah . . . some of the sonnets."

"Oh, you must go all the way through the plays. This is from a sprite's song about a drowned man." She bursts into verse again.

Those are pearls that were his eyes:
Nothing of him that doth fade,
But doth suffer a sea-change
Into something rich and strange.

Eliza imagines William Raine in the portrait, but *sea-changed*. This singular young person can take something awful and make a thrilling show of it. Now Eliza will always think of her lost father on the seabed of the South Atlantic, as a bronze carbuncled Neptune glimmering in the dim, a bejewelled nabob of the deeps.

Since winter's drawing in early, modified rules of dress apply at the Manor. Thick stockings are encouraged, and as many extra petticoats as required. The white frock on top may be of bleached calico, holland, or linsey-woolsey (but not pure wool, as that's needed for soldiers' uniforms as long as the War drags on). Eliza likes to add a short Spencer jacket, buttoned up, and on top a Kashmir shawl that still smells of the fragrant oil used to keep off moths on the ship.

The Head and her sister have fires in their own

parlours for the sake of their health, but when it comes to young ladies, frost is believed to make the plant hardier. Lister doesn't feel the cold, even though there's so little flesh on her bones. If the Middles are going to pass their Recreation outside the garden wall, on the Manor Shore, Eliza brings Lister's lined cloak down from the Slope with her own, as otherwise her friend will claim she doesn't need it. Could this be because Lister's always in motion? She stands with arms akimbo, bouncing on the pads of her toes, or twists around in a chair with her elbow lolling over the back; her limbs bend too far. *Unpleasing,* the mistresses call it; what they mean is, mannish.

Lister still whistles, whenever she's out of their earshot. She eats only when she's hungry—hardly at all, at some meals, and at others, as if stoking a fire. If she's reading or sewing, she pulls off her glasses, with the result that faces become blurs to her. Until the moment Mrs. Tate comes up to the Slope for her and Eliza's lantern, Lister darns her stockings by its light and turns up the frayed hems of her frocks, to save her parents the expense of sending the things out for mending.

Also, she's too lively to stay asleep all night. Often Eliza half wakes, hours before dawn, to find the Slope lit by a forbidden taper in a jar, and her roommate engrossed in a volume of exotic travels,or a study of husbandry—which turns out to have nothing to do with husbands—or logic. *If a Cretan philosopher claims all Cretans are liars, must he be lying?* Lister's favourite poet is Virgil, from before the time of Christ, and her favourite line of his is *Fata vocant,* which she translates as *The Fates are calling.*

"So we're in the hands of Dame Destiny, helpless?" Eliza doesn't like the sound of that.

"Not at all," Lister corrects her. "We answer the call or not, don't we? So it could be said that we make our own fate."

Lister likes to be right, a trait Eliza would find unappealing except that Lister generally is. She counts things, even her footsteps; she mutters numbers under her breath as she and Eliza hurry downstairs to breakfast. In the tiny notebook up her sleeve, she keeps a record of how many days a letter's taken in the post, and how many degrees (by the thermometer hanging outside beside the lion-and-unicorn door) the temperature's dropped overnight. She likes to make estimates, too, and later note how accurate she was.

Nor would Lister deny any of this; she takes a peculiar satisfaction in being peculiar. Eliza witnesses her break rules every day but get away with it, whether by evasion of scrutiny, barefaced denial, or lawyerly quibbles over the classification of the fault that go on until the mistress loses patience and lets it drop. Confidence—is that what armours Lister? Eliza's seen her uneasy at the mirror, wrestling with those botched front curls, but as soon as Lister opens her mouth a stream of fluent language buoys her up. She may not be good at everything—her drawing's too fast to be correct, her flute fingering clumsy—but she's interested in everything, and remembers everything. Some of the Seniors (only half mockingly) refer to her as Lexicon Lister, or the school Solomon.

It's become clear to Eliza that she herself is not the *rara avis*. Next to Lister, she's an ordinary little sparrow. She couldn't be more glad of the friendship, but she doesn't feel she deserves it, and at times she's troubled by a question: what can this prodigy possibly want with her?

In Accounts, this chilly morning, the bench is hard under Eliza's bones. The Middles are working on small slates on their laps; just as well white dresses don't show the chalk. Miss Robinson—a few chrysanthemums from her devoted Juniors drooping in a jar beside her—seems harried today. "*A merchant at Amsterdam is indebted to a merchant at London in the amount of six hundred and forty-two pounds*," she reads, "*and would pay it in Spanish guilders at two shillings per piece.* No, perhaps that's beyond us."

Lister finishes flicking through *Arithmetick Made*

Plain and Simple for the Use of the Young and says in Eliza's ear, "There's not a female in this whole book."

At the big slate board, Miss Robinson sets them to reckon how many soldiers of the three hundred and sixty in a foreign outpost will have to be turned out so the half-year's worth of provisions will last the remaining nine months till they're resupplied by the next ship.

"How should I know what a man eats in a day?" Eliza whispers to Lister.

"You don't need the specifics, only the ratio."

"The what?"

Of course Mercy's already halfway through the sum, her slate full of boxy digits.

"Picture each of the three hundred and sixty carrying a sack full of his food for the month," Lister advises.

"Wouldn't it rot?"

"Not salt beef and hardtack. Now each man's holding six sacks."

"He couldn't."

"Strong British Redcoats could," Lister says patriotically.

"Private chatter earns an inattention card," Miss Robinson murmurs.

Mercy corrects her: "An indecorum card, I believe."

"We're talking of nothing but mathematics, madam," Lister assures the mistress. In Eliza's ear: "So how many sacks do you see?"

Eliza multiplies 360 by 6 on her slate: 2,160.

"But the garrison has to hold out for *nine* months now," Lister goes on. "How many of these sacks of food can they use up each month?"

She divides by nine. "Two hundred and forty?"

"That's enough to ration out to how many men?"

One sack per man per month. "Ah... two hundred and forty?"

"So how many soldiers must be let go from the three hundred sixty?"

"One hundred and twenty."

Lister clicks her fingers, which earns a glare from Miss Robinson. "You're ready to be mistress of a whole fort," she whispers to Eliza.

But Eliza's worrying about what those hundred and twenty—stripped to their shirts and cast out—will find to eat, beyond the walls of the fort.

Lister lingers after class, fiddling with the celestial globe, which is shoved into a corner since young ladies are assumed to have no use for stars. Eliza watches her climb up on the teacher's chair to examine the plaster frieze. Someone could walk in on them at any minute. "Get down!"

But Lister still can't quite see the details, so she stacks three copies of *Elegancies of Poetry* and steps on, to compound her crime. "The plaster-carver told me these are the arms of the Earl of Huntingdon, President of the Council of the North in Queen Elizabeth's day."

"What plaster-carver?" Eliza asks, confused.

"Mr. Wolstenholme." Lister jerks her head towards one of the Manor's forbidden areas. She fingers the ornate plaster moulding.

Eliza tugs at Lister's dusty hem. "We'll be late for lunch."

Lister intones, "*Man shall not live on bread alone.* Hm. Here's a bear with a ragged staff, but is that an orange?"

"A pomegranate," Eliza corrects her.

"That's a legendary fruit, isn't it? Something like a unicorn or a griffin?"

She laughs. "It's quite real, you ninny. In Madras we used to eat pomegranate sprinkled on everything—they have these lustrous seeds, like rubies." Oh, the tart-sweet crunch of the seeds' facets between her teeth. More than half Eliza's fourteen years fall away and she's a six-year-old with a red-stained mouth again, in a gauze-draped *dhoolie* swaying from the poles on the shoulders of two bearers.

Lister gazes down enviously. "Really, Raine, how can you bear plain old England?"

"When I came here, it seemed more strange than plain to me."

"But now, when you haven't had a taste of pomegranate in, what, eight years?"

Eliza shrugs. "Give me a fresh-baked cake any day."

Lister lands lightly on the desk, then on the floorboards, like a goat. She brushes her footprint off the top copy of *Elegancies of Poetry*.

"Lunch now?" Eliza asks.

But Lister picks up the chair and plants it by the windows over the courtyard, where generations of Manor girls have made their prisoners' marks on the diamond-shaped panes. "I just want a proper look at some of these scratchings."

"Lister!"

Lister goes up on tiptoe to read the highest one. Haltingly: "*Had I been Paris & Miss Senhouse there, the... the apple had never fell to Venus's share. Signed Nanny Wrightson.* Very romantic," she comments, "though *fell* is ungrammatical."

"This one's touching." Eliza puts her fingers to one she remembers, down at her waist level: "*I hope Dame means to let me go to another play this winter,*" she reads aloud. "Do you suppose they addressed all their mistresses as Dame, in the last century?"

"Why don't we get taken to the theatre?"

"You should propose it to Miss Hargrave."

"Why me?"

"Because there's no one like you for cheek, Lister."

"No one in the school?"

"Perhaps no one in the world."

That makes Lister grin. She taps a pane. "Look, a

title. *Lady Christina Elizabeth Keith came to the Manor, 1786.*"

"Clearly the school's rather slid down in the world since her day." Eliza wonders which pupil was the first bold enough to score her words on the lead-barred cage of glass. "Some were so young," she says, troubled. "Look: *M. Boyes came to the Manor at five years old.* Very creditable handwriting, for such a little girl."

"*I love Miss Parker and Miss Walker,*" Lister reads, "*says A. M. Armytage.* Ah, Miss Armytage must be daughter to one of the baronets—several of that family have been MPs for York, haven't they?"

Eliza wonders if the young Miss Parker of that inscription is now an elderly aunt of the Parker sisters in the Senior Form. And whether she and Miss Walker were Miss Armytage's teachers or her friends. "All this passionate affection!" Judging by these jottings, it's the only thing that seems to have made life at the school endurable.

"*I love Miss Green better than Mi*— That's where this one breaks off. The writer must have been interrupted in her scratching," Lister points out.

"Unless she decided against putting the rejected favourite's name and making an enemy? Oh, I know one that'll amuse you." Eliza squints and bends till she's found the maxim: *"Shun all men. E. T."*

Lister roars with laughter at that, and finally jumps down so they can go to lunch.

In Drawing, another afternoon, Eliza's fingertips grow numb. She enjoys sketching plants or people, but Mr. Halfpenny's set each Middle to fill a whole page with various shades of cross-hatching.

"This must be wasteful of paper," Betty laments, "which seems wrong in wartime."

"I never understand why it's so dear," Nan says. "Won't it grow in England?"

"Won't what grow?" Margaret asks.

"The paper tree." Nan falters, as they stare. "Unless it's a shrub?"

Derision ripples through the class.

Mr. Halfpenny speaks up. "Paper is formed, with considerable trouble, from rags, Miss Moorsom."

"Oh." Nan quavers with embarrassment. "No one ever told me that."

"Nor I, I don't think," Fanny lies loyally.

"And it can't be just any old rags," Betty adds, "only pure white ones, which are in short supply."

"Especially in a girls' school," Margaret murmurs to Lister, too low for the old master to hear.

Lister gives a tiny snort.

Eliza doesn't get the joke. A worry crosses her mind. Might Margaret be considering dropping Betty, with a view to stealing Lister? Margaret's qualities are so much more shining than Eliza's. The notion of having to compete to keep her friend makes Eliza contract like a snail into its shell.

Then she realises the two of them must have been alluding to that business of obscure complaints among Middles and Seniors, rags hung up to dry at wash-stands, hints about *those* and *them* and *my time.* Jane has *her time,* Eliza's deduced, but won't tell her little sister anything about it.

Nan's still frowning. "Why do the rags have to be white?"

Lister bursts out, "So the paper will be white like-wise, you noodle."

Mr. Halfpenny says regretfully, "Take an indeco-rum mark, Miss Lister."

She salutes like a soldier.

The Middles crosshatch on.

Lister stifles a yawn. "I wonder, sir, are you any rela-tion to the Halfpenny who published that collection of the ornaments of York Minster?"

The master blinks, swells with pleasure, and tells them his whole history.

Eliza likes him for volunteering the fact that he was a mere house painter, son of a gardener, until he became clerk to the architect restoring the Minster, and taught himself engraving so he could bring its ancient intricacies to the attention of the public. Lister draws him out on his hobbyhorse at such respectful length that Betty nudges Margaret and winks, as if Lister must be pulling his leg. But Eliza guesses that Gothic stonework really might be one of Lister's arcane interests, which include fossils, steam-powered mills, and human anatomy.

Next day, the Saturday half-holiday, and Eliza and Lister, having each paid off one mark with one merit, are walking into town to order stockings, or rather that's their pretext for roaming through York's tightly knotted lanes. It's such a grey November day, Eliza hasn't bothered with an umbrella to shield her face from the sun, and besides, the half-timbered houses leaning over the alleys shade them.

She and Lister turn a corner and come on the Minster from the side, its one squared-off tower in the middle and two spiked ones at the end. "Like a dragon lying on its back," Lister suggests.

"Just so! With its claws out."

Town's thick with goods being delivered, men making deals. Boys are nailing up posters for a prizefight featuring THE BLACK TERROR BILL RICHMOND, ERSTWHILE SLAVE, NOW CABINETMAKER OF YORK; Eliza's eyes catch the crude woodcut, as they always do the faces of the few people of colour who live here. The wife and light-skinned children of a lascar seaman, who all run a needles and notions stall at the Wednesday market; an African-looking preacher who gives fiery sermons from his crate on Pavement; a prosperous-looking wife Eliza's heard ordering shoes in what she thinks is a Jamaican accent; various servants she's glimpsed bearing messages; and a balladeer who wears a vast model ship glued to his hat, presumably in token of his past at sea.

She looks down at her own flat shoes, strapped into ugly leather clogs. "I'm sick of pattens, and winter's barely begun."

"At least yours don't make as much of a clatter as mine." Lister's pattens are the crude kind, of wood and iron. "In the holidays, I prefer to ramble about in my brother Sam's knee boots."

"Then what does Sam wear?"

Lister chuckles. "Depends whether he's fast enough to catch up and take them back."

They pass the huge Black Swan on Coney Street, where there's always a coach coming or going: Leeds, Carlisle, Hull. "London's only thirty hours away now," Lister says longingly.

"You'll go, when you're grown," Eliza promises, stepping around some fresh horse dung.

"I'll go *everywhere,* when I'm grown."

Yellow hacks are lined up ready for hire, with drivers dressed in the same hue, smoking pipes.

"Bad women," Lister mutters knowledgeably.

"Where?" Eliza turns her head from side to side, and spots the two Lister must mean. "How can you tell—are they wearing paint?"

A shake of the head. "Why else would they be standing about at the inn?"

"They might be waiting for someone off the coach," she objects. But watching the two as they chat, their familiar, businesslike manner...Eliza thinks Lister may be right. Imagine lying down with strangers for a handful of small coin. Why don't they go mad from the daily, hourly, humiliation?

"I used to run away from our nursemaid, of an evening, when I was very small—got out my window and went among the common people. I saw some queer scenes, let me tell you."

The grandiosity of *went among the common people* amuses Eliza: like a king visiting his soldiers incognito.

She has to jump to the side of the street now to avoid a curricle shooting by.

"What a beautifully matched pair." Lister's eyes linger on the horses' glossy rears.

It strikes Eliza that her friend will have to marry very well indeed. She doesn't voice her thought, because it seems unlikely—Lister's not the kind to attract a swarm of suitors—but it would be Lister's only chance of winning the life she wants. Not position so much as possibility: the distant cities, the horseflesh, the liberty...

Eliza spots a pastry stall hanging off a donkey. She nips over to buy some flat Shrewsbury cakes. "Cinnamon or rose-water?" she calls over her shoulder.

"I've no money on me." This is a euphemism; Lister never has more than a shilling or two to her name.

Eliza buys a quarter pound of each flavour, and promises the baker she'll bring back the horn dish on their way home.

By Lister's side again, she nods towards the next alley, so they won't be spotted snacking in the street. Out of sight, they can even take their gloves off. "If you're ever sulking and won't speak to me," Lister remarks, "I'll only have to coax you with confectionery."

Eliza licks a finger. "Not Pomfret cakes—nasty."

"Ah well, the name's a fib, as they're just liquorice."

"The Duffins gave us some, our first week in Yorkshire, and I had great trouble pretending to like them."

Lister asks, straight-faced, "The Duffins, or the Pomfret cakes?"

Eliza laughs, brushing crumbs off her hands. "Likely the fault is mine."

"What fault?"

"The awkwardness I sometimes feel, with them, on Micklegate or in their country house." She makes sure to keep her distance from Jane's squabbles but has a sense that both girls are in the way; even on good days, the Raines and the Duffins seem to be holding one another at arm's length. It's an accidental family, she supposes, formed when William Raine's death foisted two little girls on a childless man of fifty-two. "It's hard to forget that Dr. Duffin's doing Father a very great favour." A tribute to friendship and memory, one that he's been paying for years already; one that will take at least seven more (until Eliza's twenty-one) to work off. "Really, he manages our funds, concerns himself with our health and education...how can I not be grateful for his protection?"

Lister grimaces. "I suppose *guardian* and *ward* mean no more than that: the one who *wards* off danger, and the one he *guards*."

Eliza's never thought about the words.

"Is your sister rather more of a daughter to them, if she's there every evening?"

Eliza shakes her head. "All the more opportunity to quarrel, and—"

She breaks off at the sight of that beggarwoman who staggers like a drunk but never has a bottle, only the sacks she drags everywhere. Eliza tugs at Lister's elbow and leads her out of the alley the other way.

Coins, she could spare, but the creature demands to be heard. Tugging her gloves back on, she whispers: "I think of this one as Mad Margery, like the lunatic in the ballad."

Lister's put her spectacles on to look back at the vagrant. "We don't know that she's lunatic, exactly. Perhaps just poor—I imagine hunger rather scrambles the brains."

Where the most elegant shops cluster on Castlegate, the girls go into a haberdashery, lured by embroidered muslins hanging in the doorway. Eliza lets the assistant shopman show her half a dozen damasks and velvets.

"And Miss Selby," he says, "may I ask, is she, too, in health?"

She nods, remembering coming in here with Frances to order a new frock each for last summer. Guilt, like a snap of a dog; once Lister arrived, Eliza let the old friendship drop as easily as changing her petticoat. She doesn't regret her choice, only the way it happened—so fast, some would say ruthlessly. These rearrangements happen in every school, like swapping partners in a game, but it's an uncomfortable business. These days Frances is friendly with everyone in the Middle Form but has no particular pal. Eliza would apologise, if there were any way to do it without making Frances feel an object of pity. The two of them never had such a closeness as Eliza has with Lister, she tells herself. Does that go any way towards excusing what she's done?

Being with Lister is not what Eliza thought best-friendship would be: a soothing support. Lister unsettles and thrills her as if something's about to topple from a shelf, as if a thunderstorm's on the way.

The assistant drops hints about having some smuggled French lace in a drawer, but Eliza's wasted enough of his time already. She and Lister go off to find the hosier's shop. The woman stands knitting at top speed, barely breaking off to note down their order for stockings.

Passing a hairdresser's, Lister spots a clump of brown on the windowsill. When they peer through the square of glass, the thing turns out to be a fine comb that fits over the arch of the hairline, with two ringlets dangling on each side. "What a convenience!" Lister ducks inside.

The apprentice leans on his broom and says the French call it a frisette, and it's half a crown.

Lister's face falls. "York prices."

"Let me get it." Eliza has her purse open.

"No, no, I don't suppose I really need—"

Eliza cuts in. "To stop your hapless fussing over your front hair in the glass every morning, I'd consider half a crown excellent value."

Lister surrenders gracefully.

"To be sent to the Manor, miss?" the apprentice asks.

"Parcel it up and we'll take it with us," Eliza tells him, in case there's some obscure school rule against false curls.

By the Castle, they pass a long crocodile of Spinning School charity girls in worsted grey cloaks. Eliza shivers. "Imagine spinning all day long, every day."

"They get bed and board, and clothes, and they're taught to read," Lister points out. She's gazing up at the Castle's crumbling keep. "Look, that's where the valiant Jews of York took their own lives."

"What?"

"This was back in the time of the Crusades," Lister tells her, "when a Christian mob burned down the houses of the moneylenders they owed. Hundreds barricaded themselves in there." She gestures up at the massive walls. "Rather than be massacred, or surrender and be baptised by force and perhaps massacred anyway, each man killed his wife and children before himself."

Sometimes Lister's relish for the bloodier passages of the past leaves Eliza at a loss for words. How can she have a head full of such awful stories yet keep so cheerful? "I wonder whether the wives and children had any share in the decision."

"History never stops to consult the children," Lister says grimly.

"Some girls claim Margaret's a Jewess," Eliza mentions.

"But she comes to St. Olave's on Sundays."

"Had a Jewish mother, I mean, whom Mr. Burn couldn't marry."

Lister scoffs. "Men don't need a special reason not to marry the women they've— " She pulls up short, like a horse at a tricky jump.

Eliza fills in the phrase: *The women they've made their whores.* And wants to say, *Mine wasn't my father's whore.* Hard to explain the *custom of the country,* when that country lies so far away.

Instead she stares at a large wooden needle hanging above a door, the sign of a seamstress for hire. Then at a grocery with those new plate-glass windows, displaying bowls of pears and oranges.

"I only mean, the simpler explanation's more likely." Lister hooks Eliza's elbow. "Shall we go down to look at the boats?"

"Gladly, but not by the Water Lanes." The squalid byways between the Castle and the river are out of bounds.

"I know the rule," Lister sighs.

Today there's a two-masted brig on the Ouse, as well as many smaller sailboats. At the muddy wharf on

Skeldergate, a gigantic crane hoists sacks of cargo off a barge. Lister admires the horses towing the huge Hull coal boats. "Mercy tells me sometimes gangs bow-haul them instead, scores of fellows roped together. Wouldn't that be a sight to see?"

"Now you sound like Betty," Eliza mocks her, "always longing to catch a glimpse of handsome man-flesh."

"Ah, the difference is, I'm merely curious about the world, and Betty's a dyed-in-the-wool flirt."

As they turn back, Lister ducks into a stationer's for a newspaper, leaving Eliza waiting on the footpath.

She has a foolish dread of being alone in public. She doesn't suppose people are really staring at her any more than when she's with a friend, but on her own she's twice as aware of her colour; the gaze of every stranger makes her twitch. So she tugs her bonnet forwards now and dips her head. On a pole beside her, she reads posters advertising lectures on astronomy and galvanism, and a bull-baiting at a cockpit.

Lister comes out unfolding the two-page *York Herald*.

"You took an age," Eliza tells her.

"And you call *me* impatient?"

"I hate when people stare."

"Well, can you blame them?"

Eliza bristles.

"Who wouldn't want to look at you? Perhaps it's envy, perhaps plain worship."

"Don't tease."

"Do them that much kindness, let them see." Lister reaches out and pushes Eliza's bonnet back an inch. "It's the closest they'll come to watching a goddess tread the earth."

Eliza dissolves into laughter.

"I need to read now. I only have it for half an hour." Lister's putting away her spectacles in her bag.

"I'd have bought you a copy— "

"Why pay sixpence, when renting's only a halfpenny?"

That's not the real reason, Eliza knows; Lister prefers to pay her own way, if she possibly can.

They walk a little way till they spot a bench to sit on. Head down over the minute, smeary print, Lister reads items aloud. The inevitable advertisement for Cordial Balm of Gilead, as well as something called Gutta Salutaris to cure unmentionable ailments *with the utmost safety and secrecy.* "Oh, this is intriguing: *Lost, a parcel of papers, which can be of no use whatever to anyone but the owner. Was put into a chaise with a lady at the Black Swan.* Or what about this? *At York Academy on Blake Street, by the Theatre Royal, Mr. Williams prepares young gentlemen for universities and professions. French,*

German, Italian, Latin, Greek, Hebrew, botany, chemistry, and fencing." Lister groans. "Hebrew! Fencing! Petticoat slavery, I call it."

It takes Eliza a moment to puzzle this out. "You believe girls are oppressed by *not* studying Hebrew?"

"Quite. Oh, to wrap ourselves in greatcoats, disguise our voices, and enrol at the York Academy..."

"No thank you. I'm far too stupid for six languages."

"Nonsense, Raine. You're clever enough for anything."

Eliza wishes that were true. "I'll stay at the Manor and flutter my handkerchief at you from the window."

"Well, then I won't run away." Lister's nose is practically touching the page. "I'd miss it too much."

Eliza waits. "The Manor?"

"The company."

Does Lister mean Eliza's company? Or more generally, the company of girls? That's one of those unaskable questions.

The next Tuesday, Miss Robinson beckons Eliza up to the desk after Accounts and tells her that she's invited to tea in Miss Hargrave's parlour.

At least Eliza doesn't need to torment herself with wondering what she's done to draw down on herself the Head's Medusa gaze. This invitation is always extended on the second Tuesday of the month to two pupils, as a treat (so called) as well as a lesson in manners.

Today's other guest turns out to be Frances, who musters a timid smile as they meet outside the Head's parlour, Eliza a diffident one. They haven't had a proper conversation since before the half-term break in September. Did Mrs. Tate couple their names as friends on a list back in July? Eliza wonders. Or could it simply be alphabetical, *Raine* with *Selby*?

Hum of women's voices behind the door. Frances taps so lightly it's barely audible.

In the parlour, Eliza's eyes go straight down to the vivid Turkish carpet. Miss Hargrave and Mrs. Tate are across the tea table from the latter's taciturn husband. "Ah, Miss Raine. How is the good doctor?" is the Head's first question.

Grown-ups often call her guardian *good* or *benevolent*—conventional epithets, but Eliza suspects they're praising him for having taken on his foreign wards. "He and Mrs. Duffin are both very well, thank you, madam."

"In town at the moment?"

"No, madam, at their place in Nun Monkton, two hours from here." Was that one *madam* too many? In such company Eliza has an absurd dread of making any tiny slip that might seem to betray her origins. She learned English at William Raine's knee, she reminds herself; it's her father tongue.

The housemaid—the tall, sour-faced one who waits on the mistresses—finally rushes in with the tea. The cups are old-fashioned fluted bowls with no handles. Eliza's distracted by the china pot, the slightly clumsy letters that read,

Health to the Sick,
Honour to the Brave,
Success to the Lover,
Freedom to the Slave.

"Our mother's," Mrs. Tate remarks with a smile.

Eliza's eyes swerve to her. "I beg your pardon?"

"Her Huguenot grandfather came to this country as a refugee from French tyranny, and as a consequence our family has always sympathised with the downtrodden. Around the time Mr. Tate and I were married, Mamma gave up Blood Sugar, in detestation of the Trade." She rotates the pot to show the other side: a chained, ink-black female figure down on one knee.

Eliza's hot, squirming. Is this daub what she looks like to the proprietors? She doesn't glance sideways to see whether Frances is staring at the image too.

"My sister and I are loyal to Mamma's memory,"

Miss Hargrave says, "therefore willing to pay the premium for sugar from *your* homeland instead, Miss Raine, to avoid the taint of West Indian slavery." She tongs a jagged lump into Eliza's cup and trickles the brown liquid over it.

"In the *East* Indies, you see," Mrs. Tate explains to the girls, "the cane is cut by servants who are indentured for a limited time, not sold for life like those poor chattels in Barbados or Antigua. Hence the added expense."

Eliza knows nothing about any of this—neither the lives of those distant figures reaping the canefields of her childhood nor those on Caribbean islands. She must take Mrs. Tate's word for it that there's all the difference in the world between the lot of a bonded labourer and a slave.

"Will you have a queen cake?"

They're small; Eliza wishes Mrs. Tate said *some* rather than *a*. She takes one. When she's swallowed her first bite, she grasps at a new subject. "Cook has been making excellent puddings from those apples Mr. Selby sent down from his orchard," she tries, nodding towards Frances.

But Frances, forehead creased, turns the conversation back into its awful rut. "I must admit, I never thought to worry about where sugar comes from."

"From whence sugar comes," Miss Hargrave corrects her gently.

"Yes, madam, thank you."

"The school puddings are free of the stain of guilt," the Head assures them. "My sister and I feel it our duty to make sure *all* sugar supplied to the Manor's tables is East Indian, no matter the cost."

Eliza lifts her cup to her lips, fingertips burning. Company tea, no doubt. Her eyes are riveted to the kneeling, shackled silhouette on the curve of the creamy teapot. She's trying to call up the name of her father's dead sister's husband—Lascelles, was it?—whose family made their vast fortune in Barbados. Could that awful fact possibly be set to Eliza's account—does it make her a slaver by association? Frantic, she considers how the subject of Mr. Selby's apples might plausibly lead to another, such as the weather's being fine for November.

But Frances harps on. "I believe my father's mentioned that our Member of Parliament here is a fervent abolitionist?"

Mrs. Tate nods fondly. "A shrimp of a man, Mr. Wilberforce, but when he gets up on a trestle in Castle Yard, how his booming voice carries. *God hath made of one blood all nations of men,*" she quotes reverently.

Mr. Tate lets out a sigh.

Eliza wonders why the dancing master is here. Will

his wife and sister-in-law not allow him to take his tea and cakes alone?

"I understand the Lords have defeated Mr. Wilberforce's bill," Miss Hargrave mentions, "on grounds that if Britain withdraws precipitately from the market, our Enemy will engross it. French captains are known to have no compunction, and cram their vessels much more tightly. So perhaps it is better to reform the trade little by little, from within."

"Reform the selling of human beings?"

Eliza jumps at the dancing master's gruff voice.

His wife tilts her head. "What's that, Mr. Tate?"

"Reform it, how?" he growls. "If I chain up my neighbour—surely the chain must be either left on or struck off? There's no halfway."

Squirming, Eliza keeps her gaze on her white holland skirt.

"I believe you may be oversimplifying a very complex problem," Miss Hargrave tells her brother-in-law, "which has puzzled the great minds of our time."

"Then the more fools they."

"Husband, stick to dancing."

Eliza's never heard Mrs. Tate say anything so sharp.

She chokes down the end of her queen cake, so she and Frances can make their excuses and leave. In the passage, she almost trips over Pirate Peg—one of the Manor's cats, missing an eye as well as a foot.

Frances gasps, "Please let them not invite us more than once a year."

"It wasn't worth it, not for two bites of dry cake."

That night, on the way up to bed, Eliza almost bumps into Lister on the stairs, peeping out through a crack in the boards over a window. "What is it?"

"Just the lights," Lister murmurs. "So many."

"Where?" York has no street lamps like the capital.

"In the houses."

Eliza supposes they must seem brightly illuminated compared to a smallholding in the Wolds.

As they go upstairs side by side, Lister turns her eyes on her and asks, "What's the matter?"

"How did you know?"

She touches one narrow fingertip to Eliza's temple. "Our minds chime, Raine. Of course I know."

And when Eliza recounts the terrible tea party, Lister laughs and cringes with her. "No doubt they'll have you painted on their next teapot, and display that to visitors as proof that their noble natures are utterly above prejudice."

"Exactly!" Eliza sobers suddenly. "But I keep thinking of one of my father's sisters—her husband made his money in that vile business. They're both dead now. I never met them."

"Oh come, you're hardly the only one with relatives who've profited from slave labour. Fanny has a planter uncle in South Carolina," Lister tells her. Sheepish, she adds, "My own grandfather's brothers tried to make a go of tobacco in Virginia, but failed."

Eliza frowns and shakes her head, still troubled by that silhouette on the teapot, kneeling in her chains.

When they're in bed in the dark, Lister surprises her by asking, "Will you ever go home to Madras?"

Home—is that the word? "Oh, Lister, I don't know. It's so far."

A thrilled murmur: "So very far."

"The ship Jane and I came on wasn't even a passenger vessel," Eliza explains, "just an East Indiaman loaded with silk and jute and indigo, and a handful of us squeezed on board and ordered to keep out of the way." She remembers scurrying around with the other children. "We stopped at the Cape Colony for Christmas—"

Lister's voice lights up. "Africa?"

"—and the men got so roaring drunk, the second mate punched the captain and spent the rest of the voyage in chains in the hold."

A gasp. "Was he executed for mutiny?"

"Strictly speaking it's only mutiny if it happens on board."

"*The things you know,*" Lister quotes satirically.

"He was committed for two years to the Marshalsea." Though it occurs to Eliza now that such a notorious prison might just have meant a slower death.

"What else?" Lister asks greedily.

"Ah . . . there was a dreadful typhoon. I was sick all down myself, and Jane was convinced we'd be wrecked."

"Why does your sister never say a word to you?"

Eliza forces a laugh. "I suppose she's cast me off along with other childish things."

"Who but a fool would cast you off, Raine?"

The words make her smile in the dark. "I remember a sailor shot a shark, and hauled it in with a net, and we had soup for days on end."

Lister lets out a longing sigh. "The voyage must be shorter these days, surely? Isn't everything getting faster?"

"Unless your ship were to be captured by the French," Eliza suggests.

"I mean to be a very great traveller, you know."

Not just to roam, then, but to become a *traveller,* as if it's a profession; Eliza's never heard anyone declare this ambition, least of all a girl without enough cash to pay her way to Norwich.

Lister breaks into a snatch of song:

I'm going, my Lady Nancy Belle,
Strange countries for to see, see, see,
Strange countries for to see.

A muffled rap on the wall, three rooms away, so Eliza tells her, "Shh!" (Cook and the maids have to get up so early to prepare breakfast for some fifty people.) She goes on in a murmur, "Our fort was known as White Town because it glittered. Great big colonnaded buildings along the seashore, all faced in polished plaster. Our visitors said it looked like Italian marble." But then she's uneasy; were the walls really the reason why that part of Madras was known as White Town?

"Your family lived in the fort?"

"No, a mile to the southwest, across two little rivers, on the Great Choultry Plain, which was a thoroughly English enclave, almost all Company families. We had a garden villa called Myrtle Grove, with views of the hills. Do you know myrtle?"

"I've heard of it," Lister says, uncertain for once.

"Imagine great big bushes covered in white stars, and very fragrant."

"A garden villa—is that like a little teahouse in a garden?"

"No, no, an extensive bungalow with a verandah—" But those are both Indian terms. A *mansion,* Eliza's sometimes called her childhood home, when describing it to haughty girls. "The villa had just one huge storey, raised on a platform with terraces all around to catch the sea breeze."

"A house with no upstairs at all?"

"No need. There was so much space, you see, that the buildings could stretch out, with balconies on all sides." Eliza's not choosing to mention the occasional terrifying floods when monsoon rains broke through the roof, or the smell of dung fires. Nor the white ants that gnawed their way through books and tigerskin rugs, nor the time she almost trod on a cobra curled up under the bath. She wants her friend to picture how airy Myrtle Grove was, with countless rooms opening off the hall through gauze-hung doorways. "We had gardens full of coconuts, mangoes, bananas..."

"I've seen drawings of bananas," Lister says. "They look so unlikely, with their long yellow fingers."

"They grow green. They only yellow in storage. Once peeled, they're white."

"What, like a man's—"

She hisses: "Lister!" Horrified by this bawdiness, but tickled too.

"What does it taste like, a banana?"

"Plain and comforting. Softer than an apple, drier than a plum, sweeter than a gooseberry."

"And were there elephants, really?" Lister sounds like a small child being told a story.

"As real as pomegranates and bananas," Eliza assures her. "The ground shook when they lumbered by." Also garlanded cows—how to explain them? Schools of golden fish belly-up in the river's clouds of blue where dyer-women dipped chintz; vultures clustering over the places where the dead were set out. What would sound exotic but not bizarre? "Macaques, a kind of monkey, screeching in the trees." Those flushed hairless faces, pointed ears, a whorl of hair above. How freely they sprang from tree to tree with a twining tail like a fifth grey limb. They'd snatch any food, scratch themselves, even do their obscene rutting in the middle of the path. "A funny thing about macaques that visitors never know, to their cost, is that their smiles mean rage."

"Hypocrites!"

"I don't believe the creature means to deceive," Eliza tells her. "It's baring its teeth. But travellers inevitably say, 'Look at the charming little monkey!' and try to pick it up, whereupon it bites them to the bone."

Lister laughs under her breath. Then, "Why do you suppose your father didn't marry an Englishwoman?"

Eliza takes a breath to buy her a moment. "There were almost none in Madras." Though Dr. Duffin found one, it occurs to her; an Englishwoman, even if born and raised in India. (Curious to think that Mrs. Duffin spent fifty years on the Subcontinent, to Eliza's six, but nobody would ever call the doctor's pale wife Indian.) Perhaps William Raine didn't look as hard as his friend did—or look at all—for a chalk-white bride. She can hear what Lister's not asking. "It's sometimes known as a country marriage." How to convince her how common these unions were, how respected, how lasting?

"A *left-handed marriage*, I've heard it called," Lister says, nodding. "Or a *wife in watercolours*."

Eliza hasn't heard that phrase. Mother in fading hues, yes, washed away little by little by the passing waves and the passing years, diluted to the faintest trace. But she needs Lister to know that Mother wasn't some cast-off mistress. "After Father's death, we were told she stayed on in our villa for two years. She died when I was eleven."

"Died of what? I presume she was younger than him."

"I don't think the Duffins ever heard. Or if they did, they never told us." She conjures up tiny shards of memory. The elaborate jewelled nosepiece Mother wore on one side, against infection. The padding of her bejewelled slippers, the tinkle of her bangles (glass, silver, and gold), how they chimed for good luck as she walked, *chan-chan, chan-chan*.

Then Eliza recalls something else. The memory, like a hand gripping her throat. "On our ship, Jane got in a spat with an English girl"—one of the whey-faced Cuppage daughters, who'd never seen England either—"and she was the first person who ever called us . . . well, a word that was new to me."

"Ah, so many epithets to choose from," Lister murmurs. "Such an array of insulting terms for those not responsible for the circumstances of their conception."

Her playful tone eases Eliza's tension. She thought the word would stick like a fishbone, but it pops out: "It was *bastard*."

"Charming. Though I prefer *merry-begot*."

Eliza can hardly believe they're managing to make light of such painful matters. "There's always *by-blow*. Or *side-slip*." What else? *"Blunder. Born on the wrong side of the blanket."*

"Chance-child," Lister supplies. *"Cloud-faller. Colt-in-the-woods."*

Eliza's never heard those ones. Their giggles ripple through the room, growing too loud, until three rooms away Cook starts thumping on her wall again.

"If your mother was anything like you," Lister whispers, "I can see why your father couldn't help but fall in love."

At a loss for words, Eliza lies very still in the dark.

Miss Lewin has the Middles memorise a page from *Woodhouselee's General History* and chant it back to her in chorus.

Lister puts her hand up to remark that York is

mentioned surprisingly often, considering the book covers the past of the whole world.

"Why might that be the case?" the mistress asks the class.

Mercy's arm, always up, like a flagpole. "York may not be large, but it is distinguished."

"You would say that, having been born in the Shambles," Betty murmurs.

Mercy adds coldly, "No, as evinced by Constantine the Great being hailed as Emperor here in the year three hundred and six."

Eliza wonders whether *evinced* is the same as *evidenced*.

Miss Lewin nods and fingers her teeth back into place. "Eboracum, the Romans called this town. Constantine had to fight rival claimants for eighteen years to keep his crown, or his laurel wreath, I suppose I mean. But when his mother converted him to Christianity, he told his troops to paint the Cross on their shields, and they triumphed."

"Which proves the rightness of the One True Faith," Mercy insists.

Miss Lewin leaps ahead to the year 866, when the leading citizens of what the Anglo-Saxons were now calling Eoforwic gathered in the Minster to celebrate All Saints' Day, and the heathen Vikings sneaked in and seized the town. They made its streets run with blood and renamed it Jorvik.

Lister, like a fly in Eliza's ear: "Tempting to ask why the True Faithful didn't prevail on that occasion."

Eliza suppresses a smile.

The mistress adds, "The Vikings were led by a villain called Ivar the Boneless."

Lister lets out a snort of hilarity. "I beg your pardon, madam. It's just—the *Boneless*?"

Miss Lewin scratches under the rim of her wig. "Something may have been muddled in the translation from the Old Norse," she admits. "Now, back to our memorised passages. Whom did I hear last?"

Just then the bells of St. Olave's start to ring. All six of them, pealing their different pitches, in a complex sequence that Eliza expects will reach its conclusion in a minute or two, but no.

It goes on. Nan moans, "Is the city being attacked?"

"An alarm would be just one note," Mercy roars back at her.

Yes, this is a festive composition, an extraordinary, deafening celebration.

Lister's on her feet. "We'll find out what's happened, shall we?"

"What?" Miss Lewin's clutching her wig.

"Back in a minute." Lister snatches at Eliza, pulling

her off the bench. The two dash out, the door banging shut behind them. Through the rooms, still hand in hand, down the staircase. Eliza's breathless, her head echoing with the bells' overwhelming resonance.

Out in the damp November, speeding across the grass. Lister pulls her not towards St. Olave's as Eliza expected but down the drive to the Manor's front gate. Bootham's crammed with people, like a fair in the middle of a weekday—whirling, dancing, drinking, embracing, have the citizens gone mad? And behind and above everything, the six great bells of St. Olave's, and all the others across the city, ring out their huge, bewildering music.

Lister shoves open the gate and catapults the pair of them into the street. "What is it?" she demands of the nearest man. "What's the news?"

"We've beat Boney, haven't we?"

Lister lets out a screech that goes higher than all the bells, and flings her arms around Eliza in a hug that robs her breath.

Over a hastily dished-up gala dinner that evening—mock turtle soup made of a calf's head, potted trout, tongue, cold souse with brawn, batter pudding with preserved plums, Wensleydale cheese—the Manor girls get the full story. The Navy's demolished the French fleet at a spot on the Spanish coast called Cape

Trafalgar, even though the British admiral was unfortunately shot dead.

"Twenty-two ships downed on the Enemy's side," Lister gloats, "and not a one on ours."

"So this means we've won the war?" Fanny asks.

"Well... it certainly should do."

Eliza is oddly touched to realise that her friend's at the limit of her knowledge.

"At the very least, the Enemy can't possibly invade now," Lister argues.

"Or only by balloon." Eliza means it as a tease, but Lister's face tenses up again.

"If they try that trick," Betty says, "my brothers' battalions will shoot their gas-bags down."

In French, Monsieur sets the *jeunes filles stupides* a list of proverbs. The Middles whisper over their books, impressing the sayings on their memories.

As rapid as a lizard, he's on his feet. *"Fermez vos livres!"*

They shut their volumes.

He snaps his fingers at Fanny. *"Chacun voit midi..."*

Her mouth opens, fish-like.

He repeats, *"Chacun voit midi!"*

She tries hoarsely, "Ah... *chacun voit midi chaque jour?*"

Eliza bites down on a smile. *Everyone sees noon every*

day, Fanny's said; it sounds almost plausible, one of those wise old saws that means nothing at all.

Monsieur holds up a menacing finger, meaning, mistake number one; three will earn a mark.

Fanny strains for a breath.

Betty supplies the correct proverb in a leaden accent: *"Chacun voit midi à sa porte."*

"*Ce qui veut dire*... One of you," Monsieur commands, "what does this mean?"

Everyone sees noon at their own door? Margaret drawls fluently, "*Ça veut dire, Monsieur, que chaque personne voit les choses différemment.*"

We all see things differently. Margaret's answer seems to bring Monsieur no satisfaction. Eliza supposes every teacher learns, in the first week, who's a fool and who's brilliant, and he'd rather bring the whole class up to the same level, like spreading butter on toast.

"Next, *Le jeu*..." He waits. *"Mademoiselle?"*

Eliza realises it's her turn. *"Le jeu..."* She can't remember this one.

"Le jeu ne vaut pas..."

The game's not worth ... She scrabbles for it in the back of her mind: the candle. *"La chandelle."*

"*Le jeu ne vaut pas la chandelle,*" Monsieur echoes, nodding. *"Ce qui veut dire..."*

Lister supplies the meaning without putting her hand up. *"Pas la peine de s'embêter."*

It's not worth the bother.

The master gives Lister a sharp look. *"Vous vous exprimez trop informellement."*

"Mais j'ai raison? C'est correct?"

Several mouths fall open. Lister's insisting that what she said was right, even if slangy.

Monsieur's moustache twitches. With rage, Eliza wonders, or could it be mirth?

The lesson goes on. At one point he tells Nan she's hardly trying. *"Vous ne vous intéressez guère à la langue française?"*

"Non, Monsieur!"

Has Nan just accidentally agreed that yes, she takes little or no interest in the French language?

She corrects herself desperately: "That's to say . . . *Je veux dire oui, si, tellement, vraiment.*" Weakly: no, yes, she really truly does interest herself in it.

"Eh bien, pourquoi?"

Is his a rhetorical *why*? Eliza wonders.

Nan's eyes cross.

Monsieur gestures impatiently at the next girl, Frances.

"*Le français, c'est une belle langage,*" she offers, an unexceptionable sentiment.

Sometimes Eliza wonders how she bore Frances's blandness so long.

"*Une belle langue,*" Monsieur corrects her. *"Mais pourquoi l'étudier?"* Why study French?

Every civilised person should speak the language of *politesse,* Margaret suggests. *La langue de la littérature, des arts…*

"C'est la langue de nos ennemis."

Monsieur spins around. The language of their enemies—of the Enemy—is that really what Lister just said? Eliza almost giggles. In a class taught by a Frenchman, has Lister broken the unspoken rule and brought up the war?

"Exact." He nods sharply. "It is *très important* to master the language of one's enemies, *n'est-ce pas*?"

Fanny coughs heavily. "Why? In case they invade?"

Monsieur frowns. "Well, we will pray, in our different churches, that this will not come to pass, yes?"

Lister asks why he thinks Boney, spirits unbowed, is now said to be marching on Vienna.

"*Pourquoi,* why demand that of me?" Monsieur protests. *L'Empereur Napoléon, soi-disant* is a deep-dyed, bloody, *monstre sanguinaire,* and he, their unfortunate teacher, is not privy to the man's world-devouring plans.

She pushes: "Have you ever seen him?"

Monsieur chokes. "I would have you know I left *ma patrie* during *la Terreur,* at peril *de ma vie,* and furthermore I spent eleven years toiling as a humble provincial *professeur de jeunes demoiselles stupides…*"

Eliza wouldn't say *humble* is the word for Monsieur.

But she's intrigued by this new information that he really did flee from the Regicides.

"So no, Miss Lister, I did not set eyes on the great barbarian, and if I ever did I would *cracher* upon him!" He spits, dryly but loudly.

Lister's grinning. "You're our friend, then. If you're the enemy of our Enemy."

Surprisingly, Monsieur laughs. "Another excellent proverb to add to our collection. Take dictation, young ladies: *L'ennemi de mon ennemi est mon ami.*"

They write it down.

After lessons, in the twilight of half-past four, Lister has taken to leading the Middles down to the Manor Shore. Mercy won't come because she doesn't believe it's allowed. Yes, the door in the back wall is customarily left unlocked, but she argues that's only so the labourers can get in and out of the grounds with cattle or wheelbarrows.

The great elms and oaks are leafless now. From the Shore, the Ouse looks a hundred feet wide.

"Is that blackened spot at the top of that mound a beacon?" Lister's pointing to the other side of the river.

Margaret nods. "The fire was lit the night the news of Trafalgar came—I saw it from my window."

A pair of swans glide by, giving Eliza disdainful looks.

"Do you know," Lister asks, "all unmarked swans belong by rights to the King?"

A brief pause, then Betty says, unconvincingly, "Who doesn't know that?"

Lister goes right down to the bank, and leans over.

"Don't!" Eliza races to grab her by the elbow.

"I'm just examining the high flood line." Lister slides her chilly fingers into Eliza's and pulls herself back up.

The girls could almost be in the countryside except for the clanking and hissing of the steam pump filling the reservoir in Lendal Tower. The building next to the waterworks is the Baths, where Mrs. Tate leads the Manor pupils every fortnight to bathe in their shifts, *maintaining the highest standard of hygiene with due respect for modesty,* as it says in the school's prospectus. (Eliza likes the hot bath, some prefer the tepid, and Mercy of course chooses the cold, like some martyr of old.)

It's too chilly to sit on the grassy Shore, in the darkening afternoon, so the Middles pace up and down, talking about the youngest princess, the King's granddaughter, Charlotte, who's only nine but lives in a house of her own with dozens of servants.

"I'd hate that," Frances says. "No schoolmates?"

"She's a wilful, wayward thing," Lister says. "I hear she likes whistling and horse riding, going disguised into the streets...even the occasional bout of fisticuffs."

To Eliza, this sounds like a disguised self-portrait. "Oh come, Lister."

"It's as true as holy writ."

"Where's her mother?" Nan wants to know.

"The Prince of Wales banished his wife for being a strumpet," Betty murmurs.

"Don't say that word," Frances begs.

Margaret says, "My cousins in London tell me the Princess of Wales is forbidden to see her little Charlotte—her only child. So she's taken in dozens of fosterlings. Pitiful!"

Several of the Middles complain of being cold to the bone, so Lister proposes a game called Rank and File. She appoints herself captain and lines up all the others in formation. "Twenty paces forward."

They obey.

"Quick march! Now halt. Ten paces back."

"When would soldiers ever be given such an order as *ten paces back*?" Margaret objects.

"Silence in the ranks! You're making a controlled retreat from a great heap of smouldering gunpowder."

They all edge backwards, giggling.

"Now fifteen paces sideways."

"I don't think there's any such thing as a pace sideways," Eliza mentions.

"Like crabs," Lister roars, "on the double!"

They do their best, dishevelled. Nan trips on Fanny's hem and rips it. "I'll mend it so you can't see it before we go to sleep," she swears.

"Now, soldiers— "

"I believe that's enough orders, Captain," Eliza warns.

"One last one. Every private down on one knee."

"We'll green our linen."

"You don't do your own washing," Lister points out. "Come on, kneel!"

So the Middles do, some more willingly than others. Lister strides to the end of the line.

Eliza's beginning to suspect, but she doesn't say a thing.

Their false captain gives Frances a shove so that she tips sideways into Margaret, and Margaret into Betty, and so on, the whole row of them, like dominos, crashing and wailing and laughing themselves sick in a welter of petticoats.

Before dinner Eliza finds Jane in the hall with her pal Hetty, who's looking plumper and prettier than usual.

They're tugging on their kid gloves, and both are in the new poke bonnets called *invisibles* because they hide the face, with a brim that juts so far forwards the wearer might as well be in blinkers.

Hetty smiles at Eliza. "Jane, I believe your little sister wants you."

Jane curls her lip.

"Oh, don't tease the girl."

Jane turns her head towards the hovering Eliza, who gabbles: "If you could bring back that novel I was reading there last Sunday—I believe I left it under a cushion—Miss Edgeworth's *Belinda*?"

Jane scans the hall. "No maids here. To whom are you issuing orders?"

"I mean will you be so kind?" *There's a dear* would only work on a different kind of sister. "Without letting Mrs. Tate see the title, please."

Hetty's holding open the small wooden door cut in the great metal-studded one. She and Jane step out, and Eliza slips after them, onto the drive. "Please, Jane. I promised to lend it to a friend when I'm finished."

"Which friend, that gawky tomboy from the Wolds?"

Eliza decides to ignore that. "Which way do you go to Micklegate, over by the Lendal Ferry?"

"Blake Street, past the Assembly Rooms, then Ouse Bridge, where our ways part," Hetty tells her.

Jane says, with a sudden change of subject, "The subscription balls at the Assembly Rooms start in December."

"Oo!" That's Hetty. She produces from her pocket a long twist of barley sugar in paper and breaks off a piece for Eliza.

Thanks, Eliza mouths, popping it into her mouth.

"I mean to get Duffin to introduce me at the first one," Jane goes on.

Such casual disrespect; she doesn't even grant their guardian a title. Eliza tongues the sweet to the side of her mouth. "Wouldn't that be very... early?"

"Why wait? To marry well requires doing the Season in London, Bath, or York at the very least."

Eliza shrugs. "I'd be terrified, stepping into a ball with all eyes on me."

Hetty murmurs agreement as she crunches.

"And you suppose I won't?" Jane demands. "But there's no catching a deer without going into the woods."

Her friend laughs under her breath.

Jane turns on Eliza. "Pay attention to the lesson, dunce. You and I come into our inheritance the day we turn twenty-one, *or* marry, whichever's first. With our guardian's permission we could have been married as young as twelve—"

Eliza makes a sound of disgust.

"So I ask you," Jane goes on, "since I've already

had to wait for my money four years longer than the law requires, what on earth could possess me to wait another five?"

Silence. Her friend snaps off a longer piece of barley sugar.

"Hetty, not in public!"

She shoves it into her mouth, where it makes an odd shape in her cheek.

They're at the Manor's gate now; Eliza falls back. "Good evening, then."

Jane clangs it shut. Eliza watches the Seniors whisk away, crossing to Bootham Bar.

She's reminded of the occasional time she passes a mirror, glimpses her own face out of the corner of her eye, and for a moment is unnerved, as if she's surprised a burglar. Jane is her closest kin left. *The same brown* (Eliza whispers it in the privacy of her mind), that's what Jane sees when she looks at her sister; that must be why she averts her gaze.

When she goes in to dinner, she finds the post has come, and two of the Juniors have learned that they have new infant brothers.

"Such a happy coincidence," Frances keeps saying.

Eliza would dispute Frances's notion (common among only children) that a brother or a sister is necessarily a source of happiness, but of course she doesn't say that.

Margaret whispers across the table, "Every second baby seems to perish."

The Middles stare.

"Every third, more like?" Lister argues quietly. "I suppose they're so small and frail, anything can carry them off. Cholera and typhoid in the summer."

"Influenza, in the winter," Frances murmurs.

"Funny to think that we were all infants, and we, each of us, might have died as likely as lived," Eliza says with a little shudder.

Her eye falls on little Miss Dern, among the Juniors, who hasn't been weeping for some months now. Have *time and thinking* tamed the eleven-year-old's grief, or has she only learned that there's no point in expressing it to an indifferent world? She seems on amicable terms with the redhead beside her. Eliza chooses to believe that friendship has worked a cure. After all, her own existence at the Manor has been transformed by a wave of Lister's wand.

On the Saturday of Race Week, such excitement. Mary Swann's grandfather being one of the original subscribers to the Knavesmire Grandstand, her father has a silver token of perpetual entry, and he's invited the proprietors of the Manor and a dozen pupils to join him for the afternoon. From the Middle Form, Lister,

Betty, and Eliza are on the list; Eliza can't work out how they were chosen.

The Grandstand is a two-mile walk. Miss Hargrave lectures as they cross Ouse Bridge: "Seventy foot in a single span! This has been described as the greatest bridge in England, but in my view it cannot hold a candle to the Rialto. In Venice," she adds in a raised voice for the benefit of the Juniors at the back. The stones are uneven under Eliza's boots, worn by pattens, horseshoes, and wheels.

The party troops past the Quaker school, where the pupils are clothed even more plainly than the Manor girls, if that's possible—no lace, no coloured belts. "But Quaker families must have bags of gold," Betty argues, "if their principles prevent them from spending any of it on drink, tobacco, or gambling."

"I've heard the pupils are made to recite French verbs on walks," Eliza tells her.

Mrs. Tate turns to remind them: "Two by two, keep in your crocodile. And don't dawdle."

"Remember, to waste time is to steal from oneself." The Head's usual calm seems ruffled by their outing. "At first I demurred," she's telling the Seniors now, "not thinking a sporting arena suitable for females of tender years. Until very recently, criminals used to be hanged at the Racecourse, and left dangling as a horrid warning."

Mrs. Tate pats her sister's arm: "These days that's done more decently at the Castle."

Lister says in Eliza's ear, "I read a girl just got the noose for doing away with her newborn."

Eliza cringes at the thought.

"These days, Mr. Swann assures me every care is taken to make the Races an elegant occasion," Mrs. Tate goes on.

"Look, the cavalry barracks!" Betty points out the handsome building, which has a parade ground and stabling for hundreds of horses. "Lord Grantham could be in there right this minute, carousing with his officers." Betty takes an inordinate interest in the Manor's young landlord, who's a major in the West Riding Yeomanry.

"It's only a part-time regiment," Lister says deflatingly, "so His Lordship will most likely be in London."

"Still, a girl can dream."

"Of what, becoming Lady Grantham?"

Betty smirks. "I give you fair warning, I'll evict the school and do up the whole of King's Manor as my town house. Turn the granary back into a ballroom."

"You won't banish Prinny, though?" Eliza asks.

"No, he can keep his sty, *for auld lang syne*."

They catch sight of the Grandstand from a distance: a classical palace, two storeys tall, rearing up out of the wintry meadows. It turns out none of the pupils but

Mary Swann has ever seen a race. She names legendary horses who've pounded the turf here: Gimcrack, Eclipse.

"May we watch from the upper level?" Lister asks Mrs. Tate.

She dithers. "That depends on the number of racegoers. We would not want to be pressed in the crowd."

"From the balcony, then?"

Mary Swann pipes up: "There's a viewing platform on the roof itself."

"Oh, that sounds rather unsafe," Mrs. Tate says.

"But there's a low wall around it," Betty says, pointing.

Mary's father comes out to greet her schoolmates, hailing them too loudly: "I spotted you near a mile off!"

Eliza and Lister meet eyes: is he halfway to soused?

As a York banker, Mr. Swann seems to know everyone in the Grandstand by name. He leads the Manor party upstairs and orders tea and buns, though they have to wait an age because of the hordes ahead of them. He's sorry they've just missed the six-year-olds' race; Haphazard has triumphed, for the Earl of Darlington. The hundred-guinea plate will be run at the end of the day, by which time the pupils will be tucked up at the Manor. There's a pedestrianism event on, but it won't finish till the middle of night—two footmen are tramping to Sheffield and back, a distance of a hundred miles. "The record from eighty-eight still stands," Mr. Swann crows, "twenty-one hours and thirty-five minutes."

"Keen though I am on walking," Lister murmurs to Eliza, "I can't understand the appeal of waiting up for two footsore footmen to limp into town."

Their host beckons them all onto the crammed roof. Eliza tugs her straw bonnet forwards to keep stray beams of sun off her face.

"There is to be one great novelty this afternoon, which is why the crowd's swelled so," he explains. "A woman is to race!"

"A woman, Mr. Swann?" Miss Hargrave echoes, in stern confusion.

Eliza's picturing one so strong, with such extraordinarily fleet and muscular legs—who's that goddess beginning with an *A*?—that she can pit herself against horses.

"A female jockey, I mean," he says. "It's not one of the subscription purses, of course, just a jollity on the side."

"But in what does the jollity consist, sir?" the Head asks.

"Well, a fellow called Colonel Thornton maintains that his wife rides to hounds as well as any member of the Hunt, so he's put her up against a Captain

Flint—her own brother-in-law— and he's backing her to the tune of a thousand guineas."

"Oh dear," Mrs. Tate frets, "what a considerable sum for this Colonel to lose."

"Here she comes now," Mr. Swann says. "I believe this is the first time such a thing will ever have gone off in the sporting world."

Miss Hargrave begins some statement about heaven and nature, but the spectators are stirring, so the Manor pupils press to the corner of the rooftop, behind the knee-high wall (a mere kerb, really, which seems to Eliza unlikely to save anyone from toppling). They peer down at the spot where the crowd is eddying around a figure in a yellow shirt, a long purple riding habit that sweeps the ground behind her, and—incongruous—a jockey cap of the same shade.

Gripping her hand, Lister's enthralled. "Will Mrs. Thornton ride astride, Mr. Swann?"

Mrs. Tate frowns down at her.

"No, no, sidesaddle of course," Mr. Swann says. "Here's her husband's mount now, Old Vingarillo, very experienced."

Would Lister like to be this Amazon in imperial purple, Eliza wonders, the subject of remarks and quizzing from thousands? Eliza would rather die. Really, the two girls could not be more different, but they fit together like pieces of a puzzle.

The girls gasp as Mrs. Thornton climbs onto Old Vingarillo and trots away to the starting line in the far distance.

"We won't see a thing until it's almost over," Lister complains.

"Betting's six to four on the petticoat," Mr. Swann says jovially.

"That means most of the crowd think she'll win," his daughter Mary informs the older girls over her shoulder.

"Oh! I think they're off," Betty cries.

"I didn't hear a whistle," Eliza objects.

Mary says: "That's because they're four miles away."

"Is the lady ahead, sir?" Lister demands.

Mr. Swann nods. "So far. Mm, well ahead now. Opening quite a gap."

Lister crushes Eliza's hand painfully. "She's going to win."

"Don't speak too soon," Mr. Swann says. "The race could last ten minutes."

Eliza asks Lister, "How can you be sure?"

"Well, any man jack who rides can take part in a race, can't he? But for a female to be put forward, for the first time in history—think how good she must be."

"Do you think he knows?" Eliza murmurs.

Mary Swann overhears that. "My father's a devotee of the turf."

"No, I mean Old Vingarillo—knows a woman's riding him."

Lister squints down at the track, at that flying pennant of purple. "He couldn't fail to feel the sidesaddle, I suppose, and her lighter weight."

"And her signals," Eliza suggests. "The feel of her hands on the reins."

The spectators are roaring.

"She's ahead by a length," Mr. Swann reports.

Lister's nails are digging into Eliza's damp fingers. "Can you believe our luck, to be here on the very day the first ever female jockey triumphs?"

But then something happens; Eliza feels it in the low moan on the rooftop even before she manages to peer through a gap. The rider in purple is pulling up short. Sliding down the horse's left flank. "No!"

Mr. Swann groans. "The saddle-girths have come loose, it looks like."

"Will that stop her?"

"She could be flung. Trampled."

"Shouldn't this Captain Flint wait?" Lister demands. "It's hardly fair play if her saddle's slipped—"

But they can all see that the man's riding on, in a cloud of dust. Alone on the track now, he gallops past the thronged Grandstand. Cheers; boos and hisses as well. Over the chalked line he thunders.

"He's done it," Mr. Swann reports. "Poor Mrs. Thornton. A very spirited performance."

"That wretched sidesaddle!" Lister, too loud.

Mrs. Tate cocks her head.

"It wasn't a fair competition," she argues. "If she'd been allowed to sit astride and grip properly with her legs — "

"*Piano!*" Mrs. Tate hisses, finger to her lips. "And a disputatiousness mark for you."

Eliza presses Lister's hand, willing her to hold her tongue. She can't take her eyes off Mrs. Thornton, who's slid off the horse and is leading it along the final strength, her head high, while the crowd howl for her.

December's upon the Manor now. The sun slips below the horizon before four o'clock, and the rising bell hauls them out of bed. No matter how weary and shaky Eliza is, fumbling her clothes on in the dark, Lister always manages to set her giggling.

It says in the *Herald* that Napoléon's forces, though vastly outnumbered, have crushed the Russians and Austrians at a place called Austerlitz. "There's none but Britain to resist him now," Lister reports grimly. "We're the last skittle standing."

The Seniors are full of boasts about how they mean to enjoy their Christmas holidays. The two who are engaged plan to have their portraits painted in miniature for their fiancés. Not the whole face, just what's called a *lover's eye*—one brow, eye, and a few framing curls—to be set into a snuffbox or locket. This kind of partial portrait's all the rage, since it lets the gentleman show his friends a glimpse of his fiancée's beauty without revealing her full face.

Eliza usually quite looks forward to the festivities, but this year the Duffins are in low spirits, since a nephew—a cornet out in India—has died of a fever. Told there's no question of being brought to any winter balls, Jane is mutinous. She mutters to Eliza, as they walk to the Manor one morning, "If I were a couple of shades lighter, I bet he'd chance it."

Eliza doubts that; to parade a sixteen-year-old of any complexion around town would seem an invitation to every fortune-hunter in the North. But she won't annoy Jane by saying so. And it's possible her sister's right, or partly. Bias rarely declares itself, after all; you have to peer through a veil, strain to hear the faint note, scent the trace lingering on the air.

All she can anticipate with pleasure, during these holidays, is a possible visit to the famous Grimaldi's pantomime. The prospect of a whole month on Micklegate—in that north-facing guest room that never feels like hers—makes her feel as flat as paper. A month without Lister.

Who'll be without Eliza but at home with her family. Will Lister miss her, or will her brothers' company be distraction enough? To ask *Will you miss me?* would be pathetic; would cast Eliza as the kind of feeble, fragile, nervous friend whom Lister would find it a relief to leave behind.

The Juniors have sore fingertips (pricked with red) from forming holly garlands to decorate the school. On breaking-up day, prizes are given out in the refectory. Lister wins a copy of the New Testament in French, and Mercy a little medal inscribed EMULATION REWARDED. Margaret gets nothing this time, and claims not to give a fig.

"Be sure to write to me, over the holidays, dearest pet," Nan—eyes already red-rimmed—is urging Fanny.

"I will, my darling."

"I can't bear neglect, not with my health so fragile."

"I won't neglect you," Fanny says with a spluttering cough.

Listening, Eliza vows not to ask Lister for a single letter.

Now the last dance. Mr. Tate lines up the pairs—taller "gentlemen" facing their "ladies" from four feet away—and barks them through the series of figures as he saws away on his skinny kit fiddle. The merrier the tune, the more hangdog the master's expression.

Only the top couple is in motion at any time, which gives the others plenty of opportunity for chatting. "Why do we have to dance something as disgustingly named as the York Maggot?" Betty wants to know.

Eliza says, "A maggot only means a tune that wriggles into your ear and— "

"I know that! I could shake this one out of my ear easily, if Mr. Tate would just stop playing it."

"Well, at least it's not a rigadoon. I can't stand all that hopping," Margaret sighs.

Betty nods, with a meaningful glance down at her bosom: "Everything heaves and flops."

Across from Eliza, among the nominal *ladies,* Lister seems to be telling some engrossing story. So ungirlish, yet how she relishes their company; like a dog that plays with cats. Eliza sometimes wonders whether Lister would have paired up with any roommate she happened to be assigned on her first night. Is this, the first true and precious friendship of Eliza's life, a mere matter of luck? Could Eliza lose it as easily as she won it, for as little reason?

"No letter W's!" The master jerks his head at any sharp elbows as he moves among the girls, still fiddling. "Serpentine curves if you please, like a swan's neck," he orders without much hope. "Miss Peirson, that last step should have been a *contretemps,* not a sideways chasse."

Fanny's in a sweat of anxiety. "Please, sir, could we stop for breath?"

Mr. Tate gives them a minute's grace. Then strikes up the inevitable "I'll Gang Nae Mair tae Yon Toon," known as the favourite tune of the Prince of Wales.

Eliza says, "I heard it was recently played at the Assembly Rooms for two and a half hours straight."

The girls groan at that.

But when "Gang Nae Mair" is done, Lister persuades the master (on grounds that it's almost Christmas) to let them have "Sir Roger de Coverley" for the last twenty minutes. The festive crowd-pleaser is all dancing, no thinking. Bottom gent and top lady retire and advance; top gent and bottom lady; repeat with linked arms, then corkscrew, then thread the needle. Top couple turns, each party weaves her way in and out of her line, joins up and promenades home. The dance swirls on, until everyone's smiling.

Well, except Mr. Tate. Perhaps, Eliza thinks, it all sounds like devils making pandemonium to him.

As the pupils spill out, Lister catches little Eliza Ann Tate on the stairs. "Here, missy. Whyever did your father go into this line, since he takes no pleasure in it?"

The child juts out her chin. "His father was a dancing master. Just as Mama's mother had the Manor School from her parents, and passed it on to her daughters."

"What, must we all trudge in our forebears' footsteps?"

The Tate girl looks back blankly, as if the answer's self-evident.

Like a dance, Eliza supposes, a prescribed pattern. Do the Duffins tacitly expect Jane and Eliza to marry doctors, or Company men, and have sons who'll be Company men or doctors? Is her course of life written for her already, when she's barely begun?

"Since Aunt Ann has no children," Eliza Ann Tate goes on, "she's promised I'm to be Head after her."

Lister laughs. "Are you indeed, you self-important infant?"

Eliza marvels at how sure of herself the Tate girl is, and how pleased at the prospect of taking her turn in the procession of generations.

After dinner, during the last Recreation before the breakup, Miss Hargrave relaxes so far as to let the Middles and Seniors play Snap Dragon—dropping raisins and almonds in a dish of brandy and lighting it. They crowd around, waiting for the moment the flame goes out, so they can snatch at the delicious fruits and nuts and lick their scorched fingers.

And when, just before bedtime, they hear the piercing pipes of the Waits—the ancient city band that still gathers at Yuletide and on ceremonial occasions—the pupils are allowed to hurry to their rooms for their cloaks and step outside to listen.

"Just for five minutes," Mrs. Tate calls, as if she's regretting this already.

The men are gathered with their droning wooden shawms in the Ropewalk between King's Manor and the city wall. Invisible to the girls behind the old stonework, except where a hole gives glimpses of them in their silver chains of office over their parti-coloured gowns. They sing a carol full of *fal-la-la*s, then lift their long pipes again and play so merrily that Eliza shares all the coins in her purse with Lister to toss over the wall and rain down on them.

RAINE TO LISTER, 1815

My dearest Lister,

I'm happy to report that you'd hardly know me. Dismality is magicked into merrimality! I have resumed my celebrated style of wearing a white satin ribbon in my hair. I sleep much less but feel better rested. Really, I have here everything I need; I am a little world unto myself. My brain teems with maggots of interesting information, and I have questions and speculations and contemplations enough to keep myself diverted till the end of time. Having gained the summit of life, like a mountain-climber I pause for breath, and with a serene and beatific eye, I survey below me all the turmoils and trials of society, and congratulate myself on having withdrawn from it. *Everyone sees noon at their own door,* and I see clear sparkling day on all sides.

On afternoon strolls with my fellow lodgers—well, let's be frank and call them patients, or those among the patients capable of walking in a straight line, rather than galloping, scuttling, creeping, or rolling around on the ground—I can't help but notice that I'm the object of admiring stares. I suppose I stand out from the others, a bird of bright plumage in dun company. Unless I'm flattering myself, the locals here have begun to imitate my manners, remarks, attitudes, and habiliments. In this humble hamlet, my air of metropolitan fashion must make me an uncommon butterfly. I bestow smiles in all directions, and would honour the handful of shops with my generous patronage if Matron Clarkson wouldn't always insist on hurrying us on.

Back at the house—our asylum in the truest sense, our retreat, our refuge, our haven from harassing circumstances—I snatch any chance to play, though those patients plagued by headaches can't seem to bear even the delightful strains of my Purcell, Cramer, Clementi, unless I mean Corelli, and the "Rondo alla Turca," which I've learned to finger with an astounding rapidity. I like to accompany myself as I sing our old favourite, "Che farò": *What shall I do, where will I go without my love?* The other day a lady newly arrived took exception to my music, or perhaps was roused to fiery jealousy by my command of the ivories, and sank her teeth into my shoulder, but I laughed, and played on. See, the mad don't always lose their teeth!

When I'm barred from my instrument, I go into the garden and climb up on Mount Parnassus. Can you guess what I mean by that? The little hillock, the mound that allows a commanding view over the road. I stand like a nightingale, chanting old tunes. If Matron Clarkson insists on leading me inside, I only smile, as nothing can crush my radiant spirits. I devote hours on end to playing quite silently on a desk—"*Piano! Piano!*" as Mrs. Tate used to hiss—and, you'll marvel to hear, I've invented fourteen original tunes in one night, one of them (with eight variations) entitled "Welly's Farewell" as a fond allusion to the nickname I gave you in days gone by, comparing you to our hero Major-General Wellesley, who'd so distinguished himself against the Marathas in India, long before he won the title of Duke of Wellington, which by happy chance sounds like "Welly" too!

Geometry I expect to understand thoroughly in a month—those fascinating angles that call to mind the intricate maze of life. Also you'll approve the fact that I'm reading all of Shakespeare aloud, in the most carrying voice I can muster, to strengthen my lungs. Next I mean to go through the history and geography of Italy, Greece, both parts of Turkey, and all of Asia. *Strange countries for to see, see, see, Strange countries for to see.* I've taken a notion to roam across the whole world this way, on paper, in preparation; since now our Enemy has been toppled by your namesake Welly at Waterloo, I may finally think of voyaging in person.

An impossible ambition, considering my lack of rank or protection? Well, one never knows, and who can tell? Prison doors have sprung open without warning; we must turn our backs on despair's bony frame and cling to the soft, bending limbs of hope. Perhaps I'll persuade you to come travelling with me, Lister, pistols in bag, as my companion and guard? When we were fourteen you vowed to *go everywhere;* I hope you haven't forgotten. Why might you and I not revel and feast on the banks of the fabled Arno, as we dreamed, but also the Danube, the Moskva, even the Indus and the Ganges?

At this moment I see you as clear as the ink on this page. You seem to laugh at me for my too tender memory, but is this not a mighty power, that whether in the midst of bustle or in solitude, I can conjure up the image of my dear one, miraculously unchanged as the corpse of a saint?

If you and I could only meet in person, I could use my tongue instead of my pen, and speak with that warm eloquence that flows but frigidly on paper. Everything lost may be restored. As inevitably as the constellations turn, you must come back to me, Lister—you, the bright star that's guided me along the stormy coasts. Every rap at the front door makes me cock my ear. Could it be

RARITIES, JANUARY 1806

CHRISTMAS. TWELFTH NIGHT. Plough Monday. The days have dragged by at the Duffins' house on Micklegate. Eliza's thought Lister might write. She hasn't dared send the first letter herself, even though there's no reason why it should be Lister who takes the lead. Eliza knows these are cowardly qualms, but school is its own little world, and out of term-time it's hard to trust that a friendship hasn't evaporated like dew.

January's halfway over by the time the Manor opens again. Snow scores the fields, and leaves white touches on the abbey ruins; hoarfrost silvers the grass. In the hack rattling through town at a quarter past eight in the morning, a low red sun rising through the smeary window, Eliza adds to her Lister list. Opposites; paradoxes; impossible combinations.

Precise . . . yet slapdash.
Energetic . . . yet prone to ennui.
Punctual . . . yet devil-may-care.
Tolerant . . . yet irritable.
Grim . . . yet cheerful.

Comical . . . yet heroic.
Courteous . . . yet haughty.
Fantastical . . . yet practical.
Generous . . . yet a hard bargainer.
Honest . . . yet sly.

Can all these contraries be true at the same time? Or is Eliza simply too dull-witted to make sense of the most intriguing person she's ever met?

A worldly wise romantic.
A businesslike daydreamer.
A provincial cosmopolitan.
An awkward charmer.
An ambitious joker.
A serious clown.

At least there are some absolutes:

Lister is quick.
Lister is odd.
Lister is Lister.

No use: the scrap of paper's full and Eliza's no closer to a conclusion. She crumples it up into a little ball and slides down the window an inch to throw it into the flooded gutter before the carriage turns into the loop of gravel driveway to deposit her at the ancient doorway of King's Manor, with its lion and unicorn.

She's hoping to catch Lister upstairs, in their little Slope. *I found I rather missed you,* she's going to say. But all she finds there is Lister's battered trunk and bags.

Her friend is drinking milk in the refectory, her nose and chin sunburned.

"Where were you to get so tanned," Margaret's inquiring, "Gibraltar?"

"Timbuctoo?" Nan's trying to keep the joke up like a shuttlecock.

Lister directs a long grin at Eliza over their heads before she answers. "Just Halifax. Our mother's breeding again, which wears her out, so Sam and John and I spent our holidays with our uncle and aunts at Shibden Hall, and climbed dozens of trees."

"Lovely! Do you hope for a boy or a girl?" Frances asks.

"A newborn's a mere scrap of flesh," Lister tells her. "Do you know the plates of its skull aren't fixed in place, which allows the head to be squeezed, as it comes out, instead of getting wedged tight?"

Groans of protest. Nan clutches her belly.

"She might be pretty, if she's a girl," Fanny says.

Lister raises her eyebrows. "Can't we admit that babies are weird little monkeys, until they fatten up a bit?"

"Now you sound like an ogre," Eliza murmurs.

Eyes twinkling, Lister bares her teeth.

"You'll think your own are ravishing, when you have some," Nan assures Lister.

Who makes a face. "It's a messy business. I like the grapes, but I wouldn't want to be the poor vine." And she mimes being dragged down by the weight of fruit, which makes them all laugh.

Eliza never knows how to talk to Lister in a group; repartee ricochets too fast. Mostly she watches, listens, forms questions for later.

"But really," Margaret wants to know, "would you rather another little sister or little brother?"

"Frankly, I'd rather my parents marshalled their efforts to rear the four of us they have already."

"The half-cracked things you say!"

"I can be odd without being mad, I hope. Unique."

Betty titters at that.

Lister strikes a pose. "*Etiam si omnes, ego non,* as Peter said to Our Lord. Which means— "

"Did we ask?" Margaret protests.

Lister translates anyway: "*Even if all others, not I.* Oh, Betty, I must break it to you, I saw in the paper that our landlord's married."

Betty scowls. "Lord Grantham? Are you sure?"

"I am capable of reading a name, yes. She's an earl's daughter."

"Wouldn't you know it," Betty mutters. "Birds of a feather peck any newcomers who try to join the flock."

The Middles speculate about the death of Prime Minister Pitt, at forty-six, of a burst stomach. "Dr. Duffin called it a consequence of overindulgence in port," Eliza mentions.

Lister makes a sceptical face. "Or overwork, no? It must be rather a strain, running Britain and her Empire, especially in wartime."

"Don't worry, it's not a responsibility that'll ever land on your shoulders," Margaret teases.

"Death just happens." Mercy speaks so sepulchrally, the Middles stare. "I don't suppose it does any good to try to predict the cause, any more than the date. We should live in expectation of our ends."

"It's this kind of cosy, jolly chat I've really missed," Lister murmurs, and they all laugh, even Mercy.

The classroom in which the Middles spend most of their day has a huge Tudor hearth, but with only a tiny fire in it. Eliza's fingers stay numb right through this morning's lessons.

The refectory, likewise. At Recreation, in the evening, Mrs. Tate and Miss Hargrave sit right by the fire with a screen on a stand to shield their faces from the heat.

"They could shift their derrieres and let us warm ourselves for a minute at least," Nan whispers, winding her second shawl around her neck.

At their cold end of the hall, the Middles are playing Conundrums—except Mercy, who's committing to memory French irregular verbs.

"Why, when you're completely stripped, are you the most heavily clad?" Margaret asks.

"But what can you possibly be wearing if you're not wearing anything?" Fanny wonders.

"I expect it'll be a play on words." Mercy's eyes are locked on her page. "Frances, how do you pronounce this?"

Frances leans over. "*Elles paient,* they pay."

"Do you all give up?" Margaret wants to know.

"No!"

"Again: why, when you're completely stripped— "

"Wait," Lister says. "I think I have it. Bare...a bearskin!"

Margaret smiles in congratulation. "Your reward is, you must come up with the next."

Eliza can never invent on demand; she knows hers is an intelligence like a flower that only opens when it's not watched.

Lister snaps her fingers. "Got one. Why is a sash window like a woman in labour?"

The indecent topic makes Fanny wave her hands as

if to banish smoke. "Mrs. Tate will hear, and you'll get us all a mark."

"I'll assure her that the indecorum is all my own," Lister promises. "So. Why is a sash window— "

"Oh, oh," Fanny whispers, "I think I have it. Something about a pane?"

"Very good, pet," Lister says, surprised. "Because it's full of *panes*."

Eliza's reminded of Mrs. Lister, with her growing belly, who's lost two previous babies of her six, and must fear that this one might be snuffed out by the hard winter. Betty's mother too—she's been able to hold on to just five of her nine. Eliza shivers and rubs her arms through the tight sleeves of her Spencer. She can't imagine how these women can go through all that, and feed and lull their infants, only to have to bury them as often as not.

"Mrs. Tate?" Lister calls out.

"Piano!"

Lister goes over to say, in a quieter voice, "We're perishing here. May we play a running game to warm up?"

Mrs. Tate supposes she can make no objection.

Lister gets the Middles to set chairs in a circle. A couple of Juniors petition to join but are herded away. "I'm the Asker, and you're all the Sayers," she begins, in the centre. "Do you love your neighbour, Fanny?"

"Uh..."

"Say yes."

"Yes, I do."

"Margaret, do you love your neighbour?"

"I suppose so."

"Do you love your neighbour?" Lister's fixing Eliza with her gaze. She doesn't call her *Eliza* as any other girl might, but nor does she say *Raine* in public, because the surname is still a private name between them.

"I don't," Eliza says, just to see what happens if she breaks the pattern.

"Then I'll call out, 'Change chairs, the Queen's come,' and all of you except the Naysayer"—pointing at Eliza—"run around the outside of the circle and find a new seat, which may *not* be the one just vacated by your neighbour. Understood?"

They nod.

"So. If you move before I say 'the Queen's come,' or if I say 'the Queen's not come,'" Lister tells Nan, who's hovering over the edge of her seat, "you get a slap."

Nan shrinks back in her chair.

"Perhaps not on the face," Eliza murmurs.

"On the hand, then. A loving pat." Lister demonstrates with her own right hand on her left. It sounds like a stinging blow, but Eliza knows that when you hurt yourself it lacks the element of shock. "So, Miss Raine, do you love your neighbour?"

"I do not."

"Change chairs…" She makes them wait. "…the Queen's come!"

The thunder of feet and whirl of white skirts. Lister drops into the empty seat beside Eliza and beams at her.

"I've no chair," Nan complains, hovering.

"That means you're the Asker now."

As soon as the game starts to flag, Lister introduces a complication: "The Sayer may exempt a particular neighbour from having to give up her chair by saying, 'No, except for her who begins with an…*F*,' say, in the case of Fanny here."

"That would mean Frances too," Betty mentions.

"Then to avoid confusion you'd say, 'Who begins with an *F* and has brown hair.'"

The game goes on until they're all scarlet and panting; warm, at least for the moment.

Before bedtime, the whole school kneels in the refectory. Tonight the psalm is read by Frances, as diffident as ever.

"Miss Selby," the Head sighs, "I always advise my young ladies to cultivate a chest voice and speak in a low register, with moderated tones, but really yours is *too* subdued, as if you dread to annoy your listeners with Holy Scripture."

"I will try harder," Frances says faintly.

Half the Juniors are hiding yawns, so Miss Hargrave dismisses the school at last. The sisters stand at the bottom of the staircase. "On going to bed," the Head says, "ask yourself what you have done this day to satisfy your two great obligations to society: to be useful and to be agreeable." Each pupil in turn makes her curtsey and says good night. "Miss Percival, I am sorry to see you are lifting your skirt higher than required for mounting the stairs."

A gulp of apology from the mortified child, which turns into a cough. In stays already, Eliza notices, which is ludicrous; really some of these children are too young to be boarders, but the five Percivals insist on moving as a pack.

Mrs. Tate gives a kiss to one Senior and promises to come up and dress her chilblains. She tells a Junior that she'll bring her some syrup for her throat, and says the same to Fanny. It's known that Mrs. Tate can't bear to hear a rasping cough, having lost one of her own children that way.

Now, at last. Eliza and Lister on their own in the Slope, for the first time since before the winter break.

Although once the door's closed behind them, and they're unhooking each other's frocks, and swapping day shifts for night ones and bed socks, all Eliza can think to remark on is Lister's fresh haircut, and the harsh weather.

"Eh, it's right parky and I'm fair nithered!" Then, dropping the broad Yorkshire accent, Lister asks, "Were you always shivering, your first winter in England?"

Eliza's realising something: Lister's managed to change the way she speaks, little by little, in less than five months since coming to the Manor. She wonders how much of an effort it's cost. It's rather unnerving to watch someone tinker with herself. She wonders how else Lister could transform, if she set her mind to it. And are there parts of the self that are unalterable?

"Raine?"

"Sorry. It was so long ago, half my life." She strains to call up the year she was seven. "I do remember the meals at the Tottenham school tasted of nothing—pretend food, as when children make mud-pies."

Lister chuckles at that. She scrubs at a few pimples with a mixture of sand and soap. Eliza can feel a hair coming on her upper lip, so she takes out her tweezers and peers into the glass to pluck it out.

"Did you have some fun over the holidays, after all?"

"Well..." Eliza tries to think of something. "We saw a longsword dance."

Lister snorts. "I saw three. You can't take a step in Yorkshire at Yuletide without tripping over a long-sword. The last performance was so interminable, I was longing for a dancer to lose his grip and sever a finger." She nibbles at her thumb and pulls off a bit of dead skin. She holds it to the candle, scrutinising it. "Look at that. The print goes all the way through."

"Ugh, throw it away," Eliza orders.

"Don't disturb me at my prayers. I'm marvelling at the wonders of Creation." Lister often uses a flippant tone when she's more than half serious. "I'd like to know exactly how many layers we have. And every time we lose a piece of skin, how does it grow a perfect patch to mend it?"

Eliza's busy dampening her front hair at the washstand and working on her four obligatory curls. She wraps a curling paper around each section of sleek black hair and coils it up on a pencil, then secures the strip by knotting it.

Lister jumps in between her sheets. The blanket heaves as she moves her legs like a galloping pony, to take the chill off the sheets.

"I bet Mrs. Tate has put a stone bottle to warm Miss Hargrave's bed already," Eliza says.

"Yes! Why do mistresses always consider that having the smallest of fires in their bedrooms would corrupt the temperament of schoolgirls?"

Eliza laughs under her breath. "As if austerity forms the character, like setting a jelly." She unrolls the last, botched twist and remakes it. If they had even a tiny fire, she could use curling tongs instead, though she did once burn herself that way at the Duffins'. She feels an impulse to confess something of how dreary the long time apart has been. "You know, holidays are rather a trial to me."

"Whyever— "

"Oh, I hardly know." She can't say, *Did you never think to write?* "Without classes, the day seems to have no shape, and Jane keeps stalking out of the room as if I'm an irksome kitten at her heels. Dr. Duffin beats me at chess, every day, and scolds me for my lack of application."

"It sounds miserable. You should have come to Shibden. My brothers and I shake off school discipline there and do as we please."

Neither of them mentions the fact that Eliza wasn't invited.

"I don't think you have any cousins to entertain you?" she asks.

"Oh, my uncle and aunts are brother and sisters, all unmarried," Lister explains. "We're not a family much given to wedlock. Father's the only Lister who's produced any progeny."

"Ah." Eliza grasps what this could mean. "So your uncle's estate..."

"Will likely go to Father, or Sam, in the end. I'd make a much better master of Shibden, but Uncle James doesn't believe in female inheritance," Lister says with bitter humour.

It strikes Eliza that if she and Jane had been unlucky enough to have a brother, he'd likely have inherited most or all of the eight thousand pounds.

"Still, I hope to end up there with Sam and John, quite comfortable."

How odd to think of Lister as a spinster perching on the lives of her brothers like a bird on a fence. "Unless you were to marry."

"Raine. Really. Can you picture that?"

Eliza tries it, then shakes her head.

Lister speaks quite plainly: "It would be against my nature."

But it's for marriage that they're being trained, Eliza thinks, so what have their natures to do with it? And how else is a female to spend her life?

Lister lies watching Eliza brush out her long hair. "I must admit, my holidays were rather too long, like yours."

"What, even with all that tree-climbing at Shibden?"

"Now I'm growing up, I find I require a mind in unison with my own. Without it, all the world's a desert, and I feel alone in a crowd."

Eliza's suddenly warmed, as if a great invisible log is flaming and crackling between them.

Sunday afternoon. St. Olave's is just across the long grass from the Manor, but the proprietors always walk their pupils around the long way, by Marygate, to make a respectable showing to the rest of the congregation.

As the crocodile of girls turns the corner, Lister hangs back and points out the ragged round wall of St. Mary's Tower. "Guess who blew this up with a mine?"

"What kind of mine? A coal mine?" Fanny asks.

"Oh, you dear noodle," Margaret says. "All these years of schooling, and haven't you learned anything?"

Nan snaps back in defence of her pal: "All these years, and you still have the sharpest tongue in the Manor."

Margaret blows her a scornful kiss.

"A mine is a tunnel dug under a fortification to blow it up with gunpowder," Lister tells Fanny. "Well, it was Oliver Cromwell! Or his Roundheads, at least."

"I used to think the Parliamentarians had unusually round heads," Eliza confesses.

This raises a laugh, though Fanny looks a little nervous, as if she thought that too, until just now.

"I got the whole story out of the animal-doctor who came to dose the cows," Lister tells them. "The brave Cavaliers were holding our Manor for its King, when *boom!*—the walls were breached, close combat"—she slashes and stabs the air—"till the orchard and the bowling green were *strewn* with bodies."

Eliza rather wishes the Manor still had an orchard and a bowling green.

Halfway down Marygate, the Head and her sister look back and beckon crossly.

"You'll be put in disgrace if you're reported for talking to strange men," Betty tells Lister.

A snort. "I like that, from you!"

"What *can* you mean?"

"Admit it, my love, you're the greatest flirt in the school." Margaret's the only one who could get away with this.

Betty smirks and tucks her hand through her inseparable's arm.

At the medieval church doors, the proprietors stand waiting. "Take an indecorum mark, Miss Lister," Mrs. Tate hisses.

"I will, thank you, madam."

For a moment it seems to Eliza that this pert response will earn Lister another mark, but which would it be? Not disputatiousness so much as cheerful cheek.

With a pained face, Miss Hargrave gestures for them to hurry into the church.

Really, Eliza decides, the system doesn't work for geniuses. Lister can earn any number of marks for bad behaviour in full confidence of wiping them out by as many memory merits. Perhaps there should be two categories of punishment and reward, one moral and one intellectual, but the whole thing already seems absurdly complicated. Perhaps that's Lister's influence; so many aspects of life that Eliza never thought to question till Lister came.

"Remember," Miss Hargrave whispers in the aisle, "we expect every young lady to join in the psalm, singing no more loudly or softly than her neighbours, and maintaining due reverence of the eyes."

St. Olave's has a peculiarly dank sort of cold. The hangings are dirty baize, and the hassocks (embroidered canvas work, fraying) are almost as hard as the flagstones. The reason service is so late in the afternoon is that this old abbey church has only a part claim on Reverend Worsley, who spends his Sabbaths scurrying among four York congregations. Most of the Manor School's teachers prefer the town's great Minster, with its glorious high nave and Mr. Camidge's virtuosic organ-playing, but the proprietors won't stray from the Manor's own church.

Reverend Worsley's sermons, not improvised but out of his book, are so dull that once Eliza's made a note of the subject—this week it seems to be *civility*—she casts about for something to read. She finds the Bible slightly more entertaining than the prayer book.

Lister cranes her neck to scan the wall monuments, then the gravestones set into the floor. She nudges Eliza and nods at one beside them with a winged hourglass. "*Tempus fugit,*" she mutters. "I prefer Virgil's version, *Fugit inreparabile tempus,* meaning, *It flees, irretrievable time.*"

"Shh." Eliza's eye falls on a broken marble plaque in memory of a wife. The folded hands are still visible but the head's gone.

> She was, but words are wanting to say what,
> Think what a woman should be and she was that.

Nineteen words, and the widower's managed to say nothing about her. It fills Eliza with gloom to think that the best the Manor girls can hope for is to be described in such terms someday—the pristine blankness of a good woman's life.

Well, any of them except Lister. What on earth would her plaque say?

Lister huffs out her breath. "Such a waste to have that huge organ and no one touching it. I'd love to have a go at a simple tune. 'Now Thank We All Our God,' perhaps, since the first line only has two notes—"

Eliza steps hard on the edge of Lister's shoe, to hush her.

The two of them are nothing alike, but every day Eliza finds another respect in which she and Lister are like-minded. Kindred sympathy grows between them like a flowering weed.

Even though the two indulge in none of the showing-off of bosom friends—never a *dearest* or a *darling*—the other Middles have noticed. Eliza has overheard references to her and Lister as *confederates, familiars,* or *shadows, always at each other's elbows, hand in glove.* Why does the language of affection have something so secretive about it, as if a pair of girls amounts to a conspiracy?

One morning Eliza wakes and hears a faint squeaking from the other bed. She lies puzzling over the sound. Could Lister be shaking with laughter? Sobbing silently? Rocking back and forwards, as she sometimes does at dull moments when her energies have no outlet?

Eliza heaves over in bed to face the hard curve of Lister's shoulder. Studies the back of her head, the cropped hair sticking out in all directions. It strikes her that from behind, you'd never take her for a girl.

The squeaking has stopped. Unless Eliza imagined it?

"Awake?" she whispers.

"Barely." Listers offers a great yawn, stretching her arms wide. There's a book in her left hand.

"What are you reading?"

"Just the dictionary."

Eliza's unconvinced. Once they've dressed, she finds an excuse to stay behind while Lister hurries down to breakfast. She looks through the *Pronouncing and Explanatory Dictionary,* wondering whether Lister was studying the meaning of words or their correct pronunciation.

She spots a faint pencil dot beside certain entries. She flicks through the pages, hunting the mark.

Virgin, n., a woman unacquainted with men.
Scrat, n., a goblin, monster, devil, hermaphrodite.
Love, n., the passion between the sexes.
Grubble, v., to feel in the dark.

She's blushing, obscurely troubled. She supposes it serves her right for prying. She closes the book and tucks it back under Lister's pillow.

In French class Monsieur is setting them still more proverbs to get by heart. *Il y a anguille sous roche. There's an eel under the rock,* an image Eliza finds somehow more repulsive than the English equivalent, *A snake in the grass.*

Ce n'est pas la mer à boire. (Eliza likes that cold comfort: *It's no great matter—you don't have to drink the whole sea.*)

Qui n'avance pas, recule. (*To not move forwards is to fall back.*)

Petit à petit, l'oiseau fait son nid. (*Little by little, the bird makes her nest.*)

Qui vivra verra means *If you live, you'll see.* This one's sharper than *Time will tell;* it reminds Eliza of the guillotine that Monsieur somehow evaded. She seems to remember an Indian saying along the lines of *No hand can catch time.*

Monsieur goes on a rant about girls who believe "*Quel temps est-il?*" is the way to ask the time. "*L'heure* means counted time, as I have told you before, whereas *le temps* is used for uncountable time or weather."

Uncountable time: Eliza tries to commit that phrase to memory.

Lister mentions an English proverb, *Time flies among friends*—do the French say that?

The master shakes his head. "We have a different one. *L'amour fait passer le temps, le temps fait passer l'amour.*"

Lister's face falls. *"Mais c'est si cynique, Monsieur."*

"What's so cynical?" Fanny whispers.

"Love passes the time?" That's Nan.

Eliza shakes her head and translates under her breath: *"Love kills time, time kills love."* Neatly phrased—the French have a knack for these jokes—but how it stings.

She wonders whether Monsieur believes this sad creed. He looks like a man who's lost a great deal already.

That Friday, the Manor girls line up for the lancet. They try not to look at Dr. Mather's little blade, with its tortoiseshell handle. Instead they trade cases. "My aunt is stone blind, since she had it as a child," Nan volunteers.

Betty's brother's wife's brother is quite disfigured—one great pucker of scars.

The doctor scrapes Fanny's full-grown arm above the elbow, making her squeal.

"Does it hurt terribly?" Nan asks in sympathy.

He cuts in before Fanny can answer: "It does not. A mere scratch."

Fanny blinks back a tear. "It's just the fright of it."

With the tip of his finger Dr. Mather takes up a little matter from the jar and rubs it into Fanny's arm.

Nan moans. "A stranger's pustules, ground up!"

"As I explained to the whole school, Miss Moorsom, I use the modern process. This is only lymph from milkmaids with cowpox, a much milder infection than smallpox."

"Hence *vaccination,* from *vacca,* a cow," Lister says at the back of the line.

"Will that braggart never cease showing off?" That's Jane, among the Seniors.

Eliza's face scalds on Lister's behalf.

"How's your cough, at night?" Dr. Mather's asking Fanny.

"Much the same."

"I'll stop in next week and try leeches on your chest."

"Thank you, sir," Fanny says fearfully.

"Mercy won't come down from the library," Margaret's telling Betty, "because her parents say it's unchristian to take part of an animal into yourself."

Lister snorts. "What does she think she's doing when she tucks into a plate of beef?"

Nan is examining her own tiny reddened spot. "So I'm going to catch cowpox now?"

Dr. Mather shakes his head. "Some get a little scab, some a slight malaise, that's all. And some fret themselves into a high fever," he adds with a smile, "especially silly schoolgirls who suffer from suggestibility and morbid imagination."

That makes them all laugh.

In *Woodhouselee's General History,* Miss Lewin's class has reached India, which merits a whole two pages. One phrase lodges in Eliza's head—how the Company *conquered and obtained possession of the Subcontinent,* which sounds oddly like a man on his wedding night.

Lister mentions something about Bonaparte's recent march into Naples to put his own brother on the throne.

"That's quite a different thing," Miss Lewin reproves her. "The French Enemy is brutally invading the kingdoms of Europe, rather than winning them over by patent superiority of leadership as the British have done across the Empire."

Eliza's favourite line in Woodhouselee is *There is a high probability that India was the great school from which the most early polished nations of Europe derived their knowledge of arts, sciences, and literature.* But then she reflects that if India is a school, Eliza was expelled at six years old, so it's far from clear what she could have learned.

"Tell me more about Madras, to warm me up," Lister orders from her chilly cot that night.

Eliza smiles as she rubs at her little burning vaccination spot. She tries to conjure it up, that perfumed lost domain of Myrtle Grove. "I remember swinging."

"On what?"

"I couldn't sleep without being rocked in my cradle, so my ayah had a bed made for me in a . . ." She fumbles for the word, moves her hand back and forth in the faint moonlight that leaks through the curtains.

"A hammock?"

"But made of wood. And in the gardens, too, there was a great banyan tree, and hanging from it, a swing we used to ride on." Jane and Eliza broke off the leaves and used the milky juice on their teeth to keep their breath sweet, and it was said to ward off bad dreams too.

"Sitting down?"

She shakes her head. "Standing on the board. Like an equestrienne, upright on a horse." She knows Lister longs to visit a circus.

"Riding the air!"

"*Jhoola,*" Eliza remembers. "That was what the swinging bed was called." Unless her memory's playing tricks. "And at night the servants would capture us fireflies in a jar."

"What are fireflies?"

"Like glowworms, but they fly around."

Lister marvels at that.

In his next class, Mr. Halfpenny sets the Middles to drawing from life—just faces, to avoid any impropriety. They set two benches arm's length apart and the girls sit in pairs, sketching on their escritoires.

Eliza's gaze locks onto Lister's. "Don't make me laugh."

"I wouldn't dream of such a thing."

After a minute, she hisses, "Stop it."

"What am I doing?"

"Being... yourself." Keen blue eyes; small, firm mouth, a little pursed. Not beautiful. No one has ever described Miss Anne Lister as a beauty.

On both sides of them, Eliza's aware of amiable bickering. "Look up, Nan?"

"Hold that expression."

"What expression?"

"Betty! Put your lips back the way they were."

"Just so. Face me head-on."

"Chin up again?"

Eliza's remembering when her form was set this same exercise at the Tottenham school. The London girl who was told to draw Eliza filled in the whole face with the side of the charcoal. When challenged by the master, she muttered, *Well, Miss Raine is hardly paper coloured.*

Nasty little bitch, Eliza mouths to herself with a silent satisfaction.

Already the models are peering at the drawings and raising objections. "Is my nose really so big?"

"I look as if I have moustaches!"

"My ear is a cabbage."

"Beg pardon, the charcoal skidded."

Eliza draws on. It's a curious sensation, tracing the

lines of Lister's face and neck and shoulders. Touching them, but at a remove.

Lister won't let Eliza see her sketch. "It's all wrong. It doesn't capture a tenth of your..." She circles her hand as if trying to paint on the air.

Mr. Halfpenny hums and haws over their sketches; Eliza can tell he doesn't want to be unkind. Next he sets them all to draw themselves, in the hope that they'll be more used to their own features, so will capture them more accurately.

The Middles queue up two by two, to take a minute at the overmantel mirror and copy their features with a fine stick of charcoal. Then they return to their seats to work up their drawings. This is even harder, somehow.

Lister's done hers in a tearing hurry, and smeared it with the heel of her hand already.

"You've made yourself a curly-haired Roman," Eliza observes. "A young soldier."

Lister likes that. She appraises Eliza's drawing. "Well...your left eye's not bad. The way the curve of the eyebrow frames it."

"No flattery, please," Eliza says, sardonic. She studies her own imperfect features in the drawing. *The most beautiful girl I've ever seen,* Lister said. Eliza can't find it, not today; beauty seems to leak away from every inch of her face.

On the other side, Lister and Margaret are having an animated conversation about Newcastle mine-leases, whatever they are.

The most beautiful girl. Is Lister just a dissembler and romancer, a teller of tall tales? *All Cretans are liars.* Eliza feels shame rise in her like water in a gutter. She rips up her drawing.

The sound draws glances.

"Miss Raine?"

"I spoiled it, sir. I beg pardon. I'll do another."

She gathers the curling pieces and brings them over to the wastepaper basket.

At dinner, Eliza carries over her plate of toad-in-the-hole with onions, to find Lister interrogating Fanny. "I know that's the story you were told, but it makes no sense. Your nursemaid let a child of two run along the edge of a precipice?"

Fanny is blinking in perplexity. "Whitby West Cliff, between the flagstaff and the battery."

"The ground's all worn away and frayed there, like the hem of a petticoat," Nan puts in, "but I'm sure this Meg had Fanny by the leading strings."

Lister shakes her head. "If she had, you wouldn't have gone over, would you, Fanny?"

She frowns, rubbing her smaller arm. "Perhaps she was holding my hand? Or I was in her arms?"

"In either of those cases, the two of you would have fallen together, all the way down."

"No need to badger the girl so," Betty murmurs.

Lister slouches back in her chair, and makes a face at Eliza, to drag her into the argument.

"Could the wind have pulled you away from your Meg, before it bowled you both over the edge?" Eliza's trying to remember whether heavier objects fall faster than lighter ones.

Nan nods. "In Scarborough we get terrible gusts—though our cliffs are rather higher, of course."

Margaret swallows her last bite of sausage and says, "If you toppled over together, and were caught on a slight ledge, perhaps, but your nursemaid rolled off…"

"Too many ifs." Lister shakes her head. "It allows of only one logical explanation, Fanny: this Meg threw herself off the cliff—"

Gasps of protest.

"—leaving you to your own devices, whereupon you tripped and broke your arm."

Shoving away her cleared plate, Mercy tells Lister, "Suicide is a *heinous* sin."

"I only named it, not recommended it."

"This is not some gory tale," Margaret snaps. "It's Fanny's own history."

"All the more reason for her to know the true version," Lister argues. "Was your nursemaid unhappy? Or disturbed in her wits?"

"Nobody ever said!"

"Fanny was only two," Nan reminds them.

"I heard of a groom who made away with himself with a pistol," Betty mentions, "and the inquest found it to have been an accident. Everyone knew, but no one would— "

"Piano!" Mrs. Tate appeared beside them, furious.

An icy afternoon, but Miss Robinson insists they do their Gymnastics in the courtyard, draped in extra shawls. As they hoist and lower their dumbbells in the glittering winter sun, Eliza wonders how this can possibly *beautify the figure,* as the prospectus promises.

"We used to perform our exercises on the front lawn," Betty tells Lister, "until some young gentlemen of my acquaintance started gathering to watch through the fence."

Eliza's amused. "They were only passing by."

Betty fixes her with a stony stare. "They were so inflamed by the elegance of our movements, the Head feared they'd make an attempt to abduct one of us."

"It would have been you, if anyone," Margaret assures her.

"No, you, my lovely."

"Are you featherbrains really arguing over which of you would be an abductor's choice?" Lister asks.

"No!"

"Yes, they are," Mercy agrees.

"I don't quite follow," Lister says. "Do you *hope* to be ravished?"

That makes Betty and Margaret howl.

"Young ladies!" Miss Robinson demonstrates a new move, clinking two dumbbells overhead. "Miss Peirson, you may use just one."

"Thank you, madam," Fanny says.

The Middles all shuffle into line to copy the mistress.

There's a new game that Eliza finds very irksome. It'll start out of nowhere, for instance this evening, at Recreation in the draughty refectory. Bent over her embroidery frame, Betty lifts her head and complains, "Ah! *J'ai perdu la partie.*"

"You've lost what?" Eliza wants to know.

Margaret sighs. "And I."

Lister complains, "Now you two have made me lose it too."

Margaret smirks. "Well, that's the game."

Eliza forgets to ask Lister about it, later, when they're in the Slope and chattering about the best books they've ever read.

But the very next day, at breakfast, Fanny suddenly puts her hand to her temple as if she's in pain. *"J'ai perdu la partie."*

Groans from Nan and Margaret.

"What is this game?" Eliza demands.

"It's the game," Fanny says in an innocent voice.

"The *J'ai perdu la partie* game," Nan adds smugly.

"How do you play it?"

"I'm afraid you've already lost," Nan tells Eliza.

"That's nonsense. I haven't even begun."

Betty and Margaret shake their heads.

"I'm not playing your stupid game," Eliza informs them.

"Ah, but everyone's playing it, all the time."

That night, brushing her hair, she remembers to say to Lister, "Explain that game to me."

"Oh, hang it!"

Eliza's eyebrows go up at the curse.

"You've just made me lose, Raine."

"What did I do?"

"You mentioned the game."

"Is it like the Scottish play—it mustn't be named aloud?"

Lister shakes her head. "Even if you don't name it, I'm afraid you've lost."

"How so?"

"On that point, I'm sworn to secrecy."

Eliza grits her teeth. "Who made you swear not to tell me? Margaret? Betty?"

"No, no, don't take offence. It's simply the rule."

"What *is* this wretched game?"

"I'm forbidden to say." Lister leaps onto Eliza's bed, making the boards creak. She leans in very close and murmurs, "I *really* wouldn't recommend giving it too much thought."

"But if you lot are all playing it all the time... you must think about it."

Lister nods. "And you've seen how often we lose."

Eliza tries to shake off her anger and think this through. Her brows knit. "So... if you find yourself thinking about the game, you lose?"

A broad grin.

"It's a game of forgetting, then?"

Lister presses a finger to her own lips.

"So the way to win the game would..."

"Oh, no one can win, in the end, only postpone losing."

"By what, not thinking about the game, for a long stretch?"

Lister doffs an imaginary cap in congratulation.

"As long as you don't think about it, you're winning?" Eliza asks. "But the moment you become aware of that fact, you've lost?"

"There's a certain satisfaction in announcing it, though," Lister tells her, "because then everyone who hears you loses too. A trouble shared is a trouble halved, and all that."

Eliza bursts out laughing. "Who invented this? It's the silliest thing I've ever heard."

Lister shrugs. "Winter's long."

Snow quilts the ground in all directions. Eliza simply can't see how having numb hands is edifying or educational.

In Grammar and Literature class, some of the Middles tuck their fingers into their armpits under their arms. Eliza studies the couplet:

Hence vain deluding Joys,
The brood of Folly without father bred...

"What does Mr. Milton mean by that, *without father bred*?" Miss Lewin asks.

A silence; is Eliza alone in finding it awkward?

Mercy's hand is up, of course, like a lone sapling on

the moor. "It's a figure of speech, madam. Joys are personified as the illegitimate children of Folly."

Illegitimate seems to hang on the air like a smell. Eliza glances under her eyelashes at Margaret, whose face is blank.

The mistress nods. "And why, in later lines, does the poet describe Melancholy's face as *o'er-laid with black*?"

"It's so bright, it would dazzle us," Lister says, "so the goddess has had to shade herself with the colour of wisdom."

Betty puts her hand up. "He just means a black veil, though, doesn't he?"

Miss Lewin tilts her head, which makes her wig slide half an inch.

"She can't actually be dark-skinned, no?"

Eliza wills herself to be part of the furniture, invisible.

"It says so right here, Betty." Lister punches the page with her finger. "The poet compares Melancholy to an *Ethiop queen*."

"But—"

"He could hardly have made it any clearer for readers slow of understanding."

Betty's eyes bulge with rage.

Miss Lewin raises her voice. "Please ask for permission to speak rather than indulging in bickering amongst yourselves."

Lister's lips press together hard.

"Beg pardon, madam, I don't understand." Fanny has her shorter arm half up. "Isn't it an illness?"

Dark skin? Eliza keeps her head down. Could the girl in all seriousness believe it spreads like leprosy?

"Melancholy is more properly defined as a mood," Miss Lewin explains, "which, if too much indulged, can develop into a persistent affliction of mind. But Mr. Milton is using the word here to suggest a serious disposition—hence his elaborate praise of the beauties of Melancholy. Now, each of you learn a dozen lines of *Il Penseroso,* any dozen of your own choosing."

Ugh. That's like allowing the prisoner to pick the whip. Eliza finds a passage that doesn't seem to contain any unpronounceable words, and reminds her of King's Manor. She reads it to herself, doggedly, over and over:

But let my due feet never fail
To walk the studious cloister's pale,
And love the high embowed roof,
With antique pillars massy proof...

On their way to lunch, Lister leads her into the rear courtyard, which is lightly fleeced with snow.

"This is the wrong way."

"Just let me show you something, Raine." She pulls Eliza up the great stone outdoor staircase and unlatches a pair of doors.

"I don't suppose we're meant to— "

"It's not barred, though, is it?" Lister asks.

The granary is enormous, and almost entirely filled with sacks, stuffed fat and tight and piled high on one another in a messy pyramid. Lit by thin wintry sun, it's a heap of cushions for giants. Eliza's mouth falls open. "Lister! Have you ever seen the like?"

"Reminds me of last Sunday's verse from Genesis, about Joseph's dream," Lister says. *"And let them gather all the food of those good years that are coming, and store up grain under the authority of Pharaoh."*

This confirms a suspicion of Eliza's, that while she retains only random lines from the passages they're forced to memorise, Lister keeps it all locked away in her head.

Lister sniffs the air. "I wonder what kind of corn it is. Smells more like oats than wheat, unless there's barley too?"

With the yellow day slicing in, making sundust of the chaff that speckles the air, the granary seems otherworldly to Eliza. Like that old tale about the girl who had to spin a roomful of straw into gold.

She crosses to peek out the window, which looks

down on the Ropewalk between the Manor's wall and the old city wall. The workmen have their dusty fibres stretched out as far as she can see in both directions; they're twisting and winding them, wrapping them around their waists, faces running with sweat despite the cold.

At her side, Lister says: "A thousand feet."

"What?"

"Ropes for the Navy—a thousand is the regulation length."

"*The things you know,*" Eliza murmurs automatically.

Lister moves back into the room and scrambles onto a grain sack. Then the next.

"Don't you dare!"

"Oh, don't I, though?" Lister grins down at her like a monkey from a tree. "Come on up. Unless you're scared?"

Eliza sets her jaw, lifts her hem, and climbs the first sack. Her cold muscles protest.

Lister retreats upwards, giggling. Not looking where she's going.

Eliza puts her arms out for balance. So high, already. She thinks of the *Ethiop queen* in the old poem.

Lister points up at a pierced feature in the ceiling: "That must be the ventilator, for cooling the place down when they had dances here."

Eliza imagines the room full of whirling revellers

instead of bagged grain. She tugs herself up, closer to Lister.

"Catch me if you can." Then Lister tips over, askew. Her leg's gone right down between two sacks.

The two of them might start a landslide; they could be crushed to death like the wilful children in so many storybooks. Eliza calls, "Are you trapped?"

"Not a bit. Give me a pull, will you?"

Eliza climbs up and squats to get hold of Lister by the elbow. She's aware of skitterings and squeaking in the unstable pile; she can't stand rats.

Lister's helpless with laughter.

"Push yourself up," Eliza orders. Something moves in the corner of her eye and she jumps, but it's only Pirate Peg, who'll see to the rats, surely?

On the next pull, Lister rears up, triumphant, and hugs her so hard that Eliza can hear her own ribs creak. Dizzy, Eliza slips onto the next sack, and before she knows it, her right stocking's laid bare. "Oh no, where's my shoe?"

"Where did it come off?"

"How should I know?"

The shoe—one of a dark green nankeen pair—is lost utterly. Lister laughs and laughs.

Eliza has to scurry upstairs to the Slope to change into a lace-up pair, and she gets an inattention mark for being late to lunch.

* * *

Tonight she's first in the Slope. Looking out at the pewter fields gives her a shiver, before she pulls the curtains. That luxurious feeling of indulging in soft sadness for no good reason, like a girl in a romance.

Eliza gets ready for bed, setting her front curls by the lantern light; the papers are worn and brittle from being wetted and dried so many times. A little bored, and unused to being alone in this little garret where until August she was always alone, she looks through the treasures she keeps hidden in her bottom drawer: William Raine's gold locket (empty), knee buckles, epaulets, a silver bell. A small domed birdcage in ivory and brass wire, full of fistfuls of coins: silver fanams and rupees, gold mohurs, pagodas. (When Jane shook her off, at the Tottenham school, Eliza took to playing with these coins, ascribing different characters to the images in low relief.) Folded fancy cloths: a painted chintz, a wavy striped *alacha,* a peacock-and-elephant palampore bedspread. Bengali muslin too fancy for a schoolgirl to wear, worked in gold and silver, with iridescent beetle-wing embroidery.

She looks through Lister's bottom drawer for something new to read. *The Pleasures of Hope,* in heroic couplets; a history of the Roman Empire in six volumes;

a Mr. Emerson on something called mechanics (with diagrams of a vehicle powered by the wind—could that be right?). *Poems from the Portuguese of Luis de Camoens;* Eliza reads a poignant one. She's amused to see that Lister's disguised several books to avoid detection by the proprietors; a French novel called *Julie* wears the cover of *The Universal Preceptor.*

From the poems of Ovid in Latin, a scrap of paper zigzags to the floor. When Eliza picks it up, she's confused. A sketch of an eye?

Eliza's eye. Lister must have rescued it from the wastepaper basket, in Drawing class.

Footsteps in the passage. She tucks the tiny picture back into Ovid, though she's not sure she has the right page, and shoves the book into the drawer.

Lister rushes in.

"What kept you?"

"Cook let me practise jointing a brace of rabbits sent by Frances's father."

If given a week, Eliza would never have guessed that. "Is it one of your secret ambitions to be a butcher?"

Lister scrambles into her night shift. "They're surprisingly like us, you know."

"Butchers?"

"All creatures of the class Mammalia. Four limbs, the same organs..."

That makes Eliza a little queasy.

Mrs. Tate is only a few minutes behind Lister. She says good night and takes away their lantern.

In the dark, Eliza finds she's still mulling over her paper eye. "Tell me a story, Lister."

"Let me sleep, can't you?"

"Why should you sleep if I can't?"

"Oh, you nuisance, you pest, you lovely vexation!"

"One little tale," she wheedles. "Something out of one of your books?"

"I give in. Let's see." Lister takes a long breath. "There's an old legend about the gods creating the first human beings—will that do?"

"It'll do very well."

"Each one of these beings had two arms, and two feet—"

"Like any of us," Eliza objects, thinking of the rabbits.

"But two heads also."

She tries to picture that.

"The Children of the Earth was the name for double females," Lister goes on, "and the Children of the Sun, for double males. The Children of the Moon had both male and female parts."

Eliza's startled by that notion.

Lister's voice changes. "But Zeus feared these new creatures were too wonderful, too powerful, and might rise up against the Gods of Olympus. So he split each of them into two half-persons."

"This is a strange story."

"A Child of the Moon became a male and a female, a Child of the Sun, two males, and a Child of the Earth, two females. Each one stumbled away on two legs, on its own. Imagine the pain of being split from your twin self, Raine."

Eliza nods in the thick darkness.

"So lonely, always longing," Lister says, "they couldn't eat or drink or sleep. They searched the world for what they'd lost, what had been robbed from them. And if two of them were lucky enough to find their missing matches—of course the two halves would press together and hold on tight in the vain hope of being made whole again."

"Why *vain*?"

"Well, because they could only be close," Lister says sensibly, "not one double person, not anymore. Not ever again."

Eliza lets that sink in. "Still, they must have been glad."

"Indeed. It was the nearest thing to happiness. So that, my dear Raine, is the story of the invention of love."

She lies puzzling over that; listens to Lister's breathing until it's as softly regular as the tick of a clock.

* * *

On the first day of February, the Middles race one another to the top of Ouse Bridge's great slippery span. Eliza staggers, almost trips. "I felt a stone lurch!"

Lister taps the chiselled figures: *1566*. "Since this bridge has stood for two and a half centuries, I say it'll stand for ever."

"Since it's stood for two and a half centuries," Margaret pants, "it could be considered more likely to fall down every day."

The Middles lean over the parapet to look for faces at the barred windows of the City Gaol. None today. "It must be so damp in there," Frances says in a troubled tone.

Lister proposes ducks and drakes. She's the only one who manages more than two skips, though a boatman moving downriver roars when her stone glances off his hull, and she has to shout an apology.

"I wonder if he's going through my family's port," Betty says. "Foster boats work the whole Ouse, you know. We have a sloop, and a great brig, and Papa's having another one built of upwards of three hundred tons."

The Middles get to talking about Saint Valentine, and the pleasant superstition that the first girl on whom a young man's eyes fall, on the saint's day, is his true love. "It won't count if she schemes to make it happen—lingers outside his door before sun-up, say," Margaret teases Betty.

Who protests, "She never would!"

"Hey, I spy oyster shells. They'd work better for skimming." Lister's off, galloping down the slope of the bridge.

Eliza rushes to the parapet to watch her pick her way to the edge. Lister's kidskin half-boots are dark at the toes already.

"Strictly forbidden," Mercy calls.

Eliza surprises herself by saying, "Oh, hold your tongue, you killjoy."

Mercy blinks, abashed.

Lister rushes back up with a dozen shells, and it turns out they do fly better than stones. The Middles play ducks and drakes till they've lost them all.

Next morning Miss Lewin sets the Middles a particularly long paragraph out of *The Accidence; or, First Rudiments of English Grammar* that starts, *A subordinate clause is dependent on the main clause, as an inferior in rank is subordinate to the authority of his superior.*

Lister lets out a grunt.

"Do you mean to be *in*subordinate, Miss Lister?"

They look around; was that the mistress's attempt at a joke?

Lister grins. "Aren't we rather too old for so much rote learning, madam?"

In one of her sudden heats, Miss Lewin flaps her red cheeks with her fan. "To commit improving material to memory is a cornerstone of learning."

"Not just a corner, here," Lister mutters, "but the whole edifice, it seems."

"Our aim is to stock the mind with knowledge and wisdom."

The corners of Lister's mouth turn down. "Stored supplies can moulder, no? If we were to study more varied and difficult—"

"I can't agree."

Everyone looks at Eliza, who's spoken without putting her hand up, and contradicted her friend. She feels hot in the face.

Miss Lewin surprises her by gesturing for her to go on.

She stammers, looking only at Lister, "All I mean is—perhaps *you* can afford to scorn memorisation because your head is a treasury already, and never too full to fit more. You skim a book once and you possess it!" That's a compliment, so why does it come out like an accusation?

"True," Nan sighs.

"The rest of us"—no, Eliza can't speak for the class—"many of us have to work hard to retain even a fraction of what we read, and we can't determine which passage or line we may happen to recall. So learning things by heart..." She trails off, losing the thread of her argument.

Head leaning to one side, Lister smiles at her. "But if the mind's constantly trained to remember rather than to reason, won't the faculty of memory become overdeveloped and the mind be left lopsided?"

Miss Levin lets out a little snort. "I'm not unduly troubled by the prospect of any of you *over*developing your minds. Back to the task now, young ladies."

As a very great treat, Miss Hargrave's brought the Middles to the Sycamore Tree in Minster Yard. She's dubious about the prospect of entering a public house, but Mr. Black hurries over, wiping his hands on a cloth.

"I've been given to understand that your Rarities are educational?"

"Couldn't be more so, madam! Marvellous objects, curiosities natural *and* artificial from divers parts of the known world," he assures her.

"You've gathered them yourself, Mr. Black?"

His mouth twists. "Never having the opportunity to go nowhere, I rely on my agents who traverse the globe."

Mrs. Tate negotiates sixpence per girl, though Black

jokes a little coarsely that some of them look like grown women to him.

The Middles hurry through the beer-stinking common room, past long benches with wooden dividers. A limp maid is swiping at one end of the table while at the other a man sleeps with his face pressed to the board. *Drunk,* Nan mouths excitedly at the others.

Upstairs, the girls scatter to examine glass-topped cabinets. "Touch nowt on the shelves, if you please," Black calls out. "Fragile and precious."

Lister asks, "Is everything here dead?"

"Not at all," the publican says. "That turtle...and the insects in that jar, they're alive."

"They're not moving."

"Asleep. Or possibly hibernating," he pronounces.

"My brother's school visited a collection of live beasts at Pickering," Lister tells him.

"On trips to London I've seen a hippopotamus and a Bengal tiger," Margaret says, not to be outdone.

"Well, but a menagerie's a different thing, and right noisome," Black argues. "This here's a *wunderkammer,* a wonder-room. And this fine crocodile was alive and well when I got it," he adds, pointing. "Used to walk around the room as gentle as a lamb."

"What happened to it?" Frances asks.

"Went off its tuck. Couldn't seem to take to our Yorkshire winters."

Is he eyeing Eliza? Does she seem an exotic species to him? She looks away.

"Here, lassies," Black calls, "have a gander at this chimpanzee posed alongside an eleven-foot boa constrictor."

Propped up, wired to an armature of rods, the ape has an unfortunate resemblance to the crucified Christ.

The Middles mill about among the preserved specimens. Eliza's attention is caught by the great jaw of a walrus; a little stuffed animal called a chipmunk; a bird of implausible size labelled THE GREAT CASSOWARY, which sounds like the stage name of a magician. Anne Boleyn's straw hat (which Margaret longs to try on); the armour of a Japanese warrior (Lister, ditto); a pair of shoes from China, where women have weirdly tiny feet; and a vial of blood said to have rained down from the sky on the Isle of Wight. Shells, minerals, intricate boxwood carvings. *How soon variety begins to blunt the observer's appetite,* Eliza thinks. In a section labelled NATURAL ODDITIES, she peers at a five-legged calf in a jar, and a purported unicorn's horn.

Lister's examining something labelled (Eliza hopes falsely) TWO-HEADED SKULL OF A BOY. "I'd like to dissect a corpse one day."

"You only say these things to torment me," Eliza murmurs.

Mr. Black must have overheard, because he laughs and tells Lister, "I applaud your scientific spirit, miss."

Men can't help but like Lister, Eliza's noticed.

When the girls start getting restless, Black demonstrates a new kind of match that only needs dipping into a little bottle to make it burst into flame. Then an invention called a shearing frame, which allows one man turning a crank to cut as much fabric as eight using hand shears.

"Where do they go, the others?" Eliza wants to know.

"The other what, now?"

"The other seven men. Do they, ah, starve?" She can't think of a politer word for it.

Black shrugs. "I suppose they must make their bread another way."

Miss Hargrave says, "The tide of progress is impossible to hold back."

Next Black makes electricity by linking two pieces of metal with a dead frog's leg, so it leaps to life; that conjuring trick earns him a round of applause.

"There's a man in London who does this on hanged criminals," Lister whispers to Eliza. "Makes the cadavers blink and clench their fists."

Eliza gives her a little shove.

Black gets the girls to hold hands in a ring and sends

a shock right through them. Fanny giggles so much she squirms as if she's about to wet herself.

The Head tells her that immoderate laughter is never in good taste.

With a great flourish, Black pulls a dust sheet off a bulky object in the corner. A beautiful blond girl doll, life-sized, leans over a desk.

"Mirabile dictu!" That's Lister.

Eliza cranes to see past her classmates. At a touch from Black, the automaton moves the feather pen in her hand and writes on the page. "There's ink coming out!"

Betty reads aloud, "*Dear—*"

"Her head follows the writing," Eliza says. "Look."

"So do her eyes." Mercy sounds appalled.

Eliza reads, "*Dear Young Ladies of...*"

"Don't touch, now," Black warns. "She's more than forty years old, the jewel of my collection. Made of six thousand different pieces by a Swiss watchmaker."

"Where does one wind the thing up?" Miss Hargrave asks.

"No need, she powers herself."

The Head nods warily, to give the impression she understands.

The automaton writes on. *Dear Young Ladies of the Manor School—*

They scream at that.

"But how does she know us?" Eliza worries.

Black shrugs, smirks.

Lister says in her ear, "He must have told her, somehow."

That's just as unnerving. Eliza would almost prefer a doll that moves on her own than one carrying out the secret orders of her master.

As the machine finishes, and comes to a stop, pen held in midair as if she's considering her next thought, Black whips out the page and holds it up. *Dear Young Ladies of the Manor School, am I not a rarity?*

And even though after that the man draws blinds down over the windows so he can scare the girls with his finale, a magic-lantern show—ghosts hovering in midair, shrinking and looming by turn, skeletons opening their own coffins—Eliza remains unnerved by the writing doll, and keeps sneaking looks at where she sits in the darkest corner of the room.

Next morning, Betty's gone missing.

All Margaret's able to report is that her friend was called into Miss Hargrave's parlour. In whispers, the Middles debate what Betty's transgression could be.

At lunch, she's there with a black ribbon tacked a little unevenly onto the edge of her mobcap, her lovely face as puffy as rising dough. Barely touching her boiled eggs and pickled cabbage. She gives her news stonily.

It shocks them all, though it shouldn't.

"How old was he?" Nan asks.

"Fifty-eight."

"My father was that exact age." Margaret grips Betty by the upper arm, as a guard might a prisoner.

"Had the poor man been ill?" is all Eliza can think to ask.

"Not that I was told."

None of them want to be the one who starts Betty crying again.

"You should eat something, my sweet," Margaret tells her.

Betty turns a piece of cabbage with her fork. "I must go and pack."

"Will you stay long after the funeral?" Fanny wants to know.

Betty's voice is faint. "I had a letter from Mother. I'm not to come back at all."

Stares all round.

"*No,*" Margaret growls.

It's Lister who puts the question: "Can't you afford the fees now?"

"Of course she can," Margaret barks. "She's still a Foster. The bank, the shipyard, the shop—her brothers will keep the whole concern running."

Quite flatly, Betty tells them: "Mother says she'll need me at home. I'm the only unmarried girl."

How long will Betty be needed? Eliza wonders with a sort of dread. She pictures the lovely girl, *not* making her début in a place of fashionable resort, *not* plucking the suitor of her choice from a buzzing throng. Stuck in her small town, making herself *useful, agreeable,* or at the very least decorative, for the rest of her life.

"Tell your mother—ask her, beg her—"

Betty silences Margaret with a hard embrace. Then pulls herself away.

In the Slope that evening, Lister's polishing her shoes with hard strokes. "I've no particular penchant for Betty Foster, who thinks far too well of herself—"

"We shouldn't speak ill of her." And who can match Lister for self-satisfaction, anyway?

"—but it does give me the shivers to see a hole torn in our numbers. Like losing a man in battle."

"Come, Lister, she's not dead." Just bereaved and banished.

"Dead to *us.* Betty's education over like so"—Lister clicks her fingers—"and all because her father's heart gave out at fifty-eight, and her mother requires a crutch, or has a fancy for one. Are we girls sent to school just to keep us out of the way until our services are required, Raine? Don't our lives belong to us at all?"

Eliza has no answer. "Are you afraid it could happen to you?"

Lister chuckles. "What, that our mother will insist I stay and grow mouldy at home, as her prop and comfort? Marian can be that—or the one on the way, if it's a sister. No, I have great plans."

"Of living at Shibden with Sam and John?"

"So much more than that." Lister's voice goes lower, conspiratorial. "I want to be my own master and see the world. Who knows how far I could get? Sail to America. Or overland to Denmark, Russia, Persia, Mesopotamia... even India."

Eliza's blunt: "But how could you ever afford such travels?"

Lister shrugs magnificently. "I fancy I could raise a few hundred pounds at the gaming tables."

"Lister!"

"I mean to make a name for myself. Perhaps I'll win distinction and earn my bread by my pen."

"You'd write? For publication?"

"Some women do. I've thought of trying accounts of travels, as well as translations from the classics. My nom de plume would be Viator." She pronounces the name with relish. "Imagine if the King conferred a barony on me in the end!"

Ignoring this touch of fantasy, Eliza says, "I like that: Viator."

"It's Latin for *wayfarer*. My first destination will be Florence, in the little realm of Etruria."

"Why Florence?"

"It's a cultured place full of artists and foreigners, with ancient ruins, clean streets, even a queen. Or a regent, rather, holding the throne for her little boy. I can picture myself there, on the banks of the Arno, walking in the footsteps of Michelangelo and Galileo, living at liberty."

And Eliza grasps it: what draws Lister so strongly to that particular spot on the globe may be the impossibility of getting there. As long as Boney guards the Continent like a great spider, Florence might as well be the mythical Land of Cockaigne.

After History, on the next wet afternoon, the two of them linger to read the old graffiti on the windows. Dancing is next, but Lister happens to know that Mr. Tate won't be turning up; she overheard his little girl confiding in Mary Swann that her father couldn't get out of bed this morning.

"Perhaps the weather depresses his spirits," Eliza says.

"I like the rain, myself. It seems to say, *Rain, rain*."

She frowns, confused.

"Your name." Lister points straight up. "The sky's calling out, *Raine!*"

Eliza feels a glow at that. A drip on her wrist makes her jump; the old roof hasn't been mended since King Henry came with his fourth or fifth wife. She moves to one side and squints at a small lozenge of glass. "*I love Miss Violet,*" she reads.

"*S Carville loves Miss Nelson best in the house by far,*" Lister contributes.

"This girl here names her two favourites, *Richardson & Duncombe.* Hey, some of them used surnames like you and I do! And here's more love avowed for *Wood & Collins.*" But Eliza's thinking she wouldn't want to be named alongside another girl, in a bland trio.

"Look," Lister says, "*Catherine Fisher loves somebody.* That's as much as Miss Fisher was willing to specify."

"Well, would you dare write more?"

"Watch me!" Then Lister frowns. "I wish I had a diamond. They're said to be the most precise for writing on glass."

Eliza doubts that these generations of Manor girls had diamonds to hand; they must have made do with steel knife tips, files, or nails. But she finds herself saying, quite casually, "I have one. Shall I fetch it?"

Lister, for once, is lost for words.

They run upstairs hand in hand, making sure not

to be seen. In the distance they hear the scraping of a fiddle; clearly some Senior's been pressed into service as an accompanist for the Dancing class. Past Cook's room and the maids' (empty at this time of day), the silent box room.

In the Slope, Eliza opens her bottom drawer, lifts out the birdcage, and finds the fat roll of silk under the coins. The jewels spill out.

Lister whistles at the dazzling array.

"My mother gave me these, when I was leaving Madras."

"Mine's never given me anything but a box on the ears," Lister jokes.

Sun and stars hair ornaments; birds and flowers in enamel. Necklaces, clasp bracelets, toe-rings, earrings with bunched pearls and suspended fish. Jade, tourmaline, topaz. Only one finger-ring: two large diamonds surrounded by a ring of brilliant chips. "This is a Golconda stone, Mughal cut," Eliza says, "the finest kind."

Lister rotates the ring in wonder. "The inside is almost as beautiful as the outside."

Eliza nods, fingering the foliate engraving on the gold. "Shall we go?" Oddly shy.

They find their way back to the classroom, careful not to be intercepted. Lister finds a clear space inside a tiny pane, low down.

(So as not to attract attention, Eliza thinks.)

She sets the diamond ring to the glass.

"You wouldn't put"—*my name,* Eliza almost says—"names?" She doesn't know if she's more appalled or thrilled at the idea.

Lister grimaces. "I suppose it would seem a little vulgar to spell them out on the glass, to be gaped at for centuries."

Them. Does that mean that Lister wants to write *Lister loves,* and then add several names? "What are you going to put?"

"You really don't want to be immortalised?" Lister's half laughing.

Eliza does but is terrified. "No names," she whispers.

"As you please, my lady." Lister crouches, leans on the leading, and sets to work, scoring neat little lines to form her letters.

With—is that the first word? Eliza stoops near, only inches away. Impatience cramps her. *With this.* On the next line: *Diamond.* Oh, she sees it's not about her at all; the gem seems to be speaking of itself. She swallows her disappointment. She reads a word at a time. *With this Diamond I cut this glass.*

"Wait for it," Lister murmurs.

"If we're here much longer we'll be caught." Leaving another unfinished message preserved for the centuries.

"Don't rush me, or I'll make a mistake that can never be erased."

Eliza forces herself to be patient. *With this Diamond I cut this glass,* she reads again. Waits for the next words. *With this face—*

What, the diamond's face? Or Lister's face?

Suddenly Lister's head turns and she's kissing Eliza, claiming her mouth like a low-hanging fruit.

And afterwards (if a kiss can be said to have a beginning or end, when it makes such a strange, lasting lull in the spinning of the world), Lister returns to her work as if nothing's happened.

Blinking, Eliza stares at the verse until Lister's completed it.

With this
Diamond I cut
this glass with
this face I kissed
a lass

"No names, as requested." Lister makes a little bow. "But it says for all to see, if only they've wit to read it."

Eliza nods, unable to speak. Will any of the other pupils spot it? Will they think it an old message—maybe a boy's message—they never noticed before?

"Here." Lister's holding out the ring on her flat palm, its hard gem unharmed.

For a moment Eliza thinks Lister's asking her to

write something too. But the kiss has left her dumbstruck, feeling too much for words. Besides, Lister's the writer, the doer, the darer.

"It's yours."

Oh, Lister's only returning the ring. "No," Eliza breathes.

"Go on."

"No. What I give, I don't take back."

Lister's face lights up, and she closes her fist around the diamond.

RAINE TO LISTER, 1815

Dear Lister,

It has been impressed upon me that I have been more than a little deranged of late. I must apologise for whatever I may have written.

Though on reflection, I realise that you're not likely to have received any of my recent letters. Since I can't bear to submit the expressions of my heart to Matron Clarkson's scrutiny, I've formed the habit of writing *Miss Anne Lister, perhaps at Halifax* on each folded, sealed packet, and dropping it out of my bedroom window in hopes that some passing Good Samaritan will pick it up and take the trouble to send it on. But now I've come back to my senses, it's clear to me that my letters are very probably piling up in the gutter below, made illegible by rain. *A parcel of papers, which can be of no use whatever to anyone but the owner.* I should do you the justice of believing that, had you received even one, you'd have replied, if only out of compassion.

Now I am calm, I'm attempting to form a clear narrative of events in my mind. Matron Clarkson tells me that I came here to the Clifton House Asylum on the final day of October, last year, which was 1814. I must take her word for it; I find it difficult to sort the tangled silks of memory.

I do remember moments, but out of order. I have a vivid recollection of slamming the Duffins' door and fleeing down Micklegate in a pair of silk slippers, in a state of utter dishevelment. I can picture myself thundering along Petergate to the Belcombes' house, to throw myself on the mercy of Mariana, being unable to think of anywhere else I might take refuge. (Her father, Dr. Belcombe, has her eyes; I think of her every time he feels my pulse.) I call it one of Dame Destiny's cruellest jokes, Lister, that your beloved Mariana was kind to me when you—but no, I'll make no accusations. I am quite tranquil today.

What I can't remember is whether I asked Dr. Belcombe or Mather to admit me to their asylum, but I do know I begged them for help. So now I'm here, am kept here. Whenever I express any restlessness, Matron Clarkson persuades me of the need to stay a while longer until my malady be perfectly cured.

She tells me that persons in all walks of life can be struck by lunacy—a hereditary taint in one case, a sharp grief in another. Among the patients next door in the men's house is one young fellow here for his fourth stay, whose madness is always brought on by drink. In my case, the cause is not clear. (*Some natures swim,* I remember telling you, *and some sink.*) My sister's wild and disgraceful behaviour, since she came back from India without her husband, inclines Dr. Belcombe to think it may lie in our blood. Our father's sister (Lady Crawfurd's mother) is of course feebleminded, but Dr. Mather suspects some deeper strain of frailty on the Indian side, about which I can tell them nothing. Neither of them can account for my malady coming on all at once like a storm last autumn (making me lash out at all my nearest connections), except it be by act of God.

Dr. Duffin must have let slip to his colleagues that I came near to being engaged to Captain Alexander two summers back, since they've repeatedly asked me about any "disappointment in love." I give them only blank looks. The truth is, I do believe the start of my undoing was love, Lister, but it's a precious secret I don't mean to spoil by sharing. I was only fourteen when I first tasted that intoxicating draught, and I must have drunk too deep.

But no, you'll hear no more sad music from my quill. *What's done is done,* and no good can come of brooding over it. Recollection is an insidiously rising tide around me. *Qui n'avance pas, recule;* even by standing still I risk slipping backwards, drowning in time past. I must exert myself to shake off morbid preoccupations, and hold tight to my newfound calm.

Dr. Mather has been trying nervous mixtures on me: hartshorn, calomel, digitalis, lavender water. Matron Clarkson gives me shower-baths, warm, to stimulate, or cold, to quell. The regimen here at Clifton is a gentle one, of which no patient can reasonably complain. We rise early (except those unfit for company, one of whom moans unceasingly in her room). New milk in the morning, tea cakes in the afternoon, sago in the evening. There are no mirrors here, since they're thought to have a disturbing effect. We go up on the mound in the garden when we crave a wider view. I always hope to see the Manor girls go by, but haven't yet. We attend church on Sundays and take walks in the countryside every afternoon. Today Matron Clarkson brought us right down Water End to where the ferry crosses the Ouse, and I looked down the river and glimpsed the towers of York on the horizon. There was a pair of swans, and I wondered if they could possibly be the same ones.

The old song rings in my head: *Oh my love, lov'st thou me? Oh my love, lov'st thou me?*

Newspapers are denied us, as upsetting, but from conversation with the matron and the doctors I am quite conversant with the facts of the present day. The Earl of Liverpool is Prime Minister. Mr. Wilberforce has managed to ban the selling, though not the keeping, of slaves. The poor King has lost his mind again, and his quondam piglet rules over us now as Prince Regent. The motherless wildcat Princess Charlotte grew up and broke off her match with the Prince of Orange, ran away in a hack and was dragged back and locked up by the Prince Regent her father, but she'll have satisfaction once he's in the ground: she'll be queen of the whole Empire. The French War is finally won, and Boney exiled to St. Helena, of all places—that baked rock at the end of the world I remember well, where our ship stopped when I was seven years old, and off whose shores our father's body was slipped into the blue waters two years after that.

Better not to harp on what's lost. I remind myself that by following the rules of a well-regulated life, I may fully recover my sanity. I picture the great bulging eye in the ceiling fixed on me, following me everywhere. I know that all here is done with a view to restoring patients and returning them to the bosom of family and friends.

Not that I have any left—friends or family, I mean. Time, *le temps,* uncountable time. *Imperfectly past* time. Its great scythe cuts down all before it. My childhood is a distant country that no ship can reach. I had a sister—have one still, on paper—but we are nothing akin, quite lost to each other. I once had a father, but *full fathom five* he lies. I once had a mother; how long since I forgot how to speak her tongue. Dearer than all these, I once had a friend who was far more than that; a beloved whose name will ever be graven on my heart.

Matron Clarkson came, just now. I begged her for five minutes more with my pen, since I'm thoroughly serene. She said that too much writing could rob me of that serenity but allowed me one more minute.

What to say, when time's so short? Not that you'll read these words, of course. Much as I long for you to read my words, I can't bring myself to submit them to the censors' gaze. These pages, like the others, I'll drop out my window; let the wind take them.

My taper's dying. There's a lesson: we are as grass.

Time's up and here comes Matron, so I'll sign myself,

once your own

Raine

P.S. Do you only frown now, when the rain says my name? Or does it not say it anymore?

P.P.S. I still have my teeth.

CHILDREN OF THE EARTH, MARCH 1806

SINCE THE DIAMOND, since the kiss, what's between them is a stone rolling down a hill.

Fondness, except pricklier. Warmth, though it makes Eliza shake. A pull between the two of them that's almost painful, like a fishhook.

Lister helps her on with her Spencer, in the mornings, and Eliza makes both their beds. If ever Lister has a stomachache, Eliza goes to ask Mrs. Tate for a hot brick. Lister lays a snowdrop on Eliza's washstand one day, a primrose the next. She proposes a ramble whenever they have half an hour of the afternoon free. Eliza's never walked so much in her life. Out by Gillygate and north as far as the first turnpike; by Monkgate, and around the city walls; over Ouse Bridge and back by the Lendal Ferry to the Manor Shore. The two of them watch farmers sow spring fields with barley and wheat. They seem to be in conversation even when they're silent. Rain doesn't stop them. (*Raine,* it says, *Raine!*) Lister has a gentleman's umbrella she carries by a leather strap through the handle, huge enough to cover them both.

They sing together as they walk, softly enough not to be heard and reported for *caterwauling in the street.*

Fare thee well the love I bear thee,
Hopeless yet shall true remain,
Never one I loved before thee,
Ne'er thy like shall see again.

Some of their other favourites are "Abroad as I Was Walking," "Black-Eyed Susan," "Loose Every Sail to the Breeze." Eliza finds a sheet of music on her pillow, "Je suis Lindor," with a message pencilled at the top: *Sung by the Count in disguise as a poor man, not to be played too often for fear of catching the infection of love!*

The weather gets bitter again as March goes on. Eliza wears a pelisse to the knees now, and gathers its loose sleeves in her hands; she adds another flannel petticoat, and fingerless mittens up to her elbows. But still she trembles, sitting still in class, and when called on to repeat the lesson, her teeth chatter.

Miss Lewin seems to suffer less from her flushes, but she wipes the end of her dripping nose a lot. "These long winters!"

"From whereabouts in the South do you hail, madam, may I ask?" That's Frances.

"Hammersmith, Miss Selby. A delightful little town to the west of the capital. Among our neighbours were counted poets, painters, musicians..." Miss Lewin sounds rather peeved to be in Yorkshire.

Everyone seems irritable these days, except Eliza and Lister. What's between them grows like a creeper that covers the ugliest bricks and drainpipes in living green.

Margaret hasn't heard from Betty, and hasn't written. A jerky shrug, when Eliza asks at lunch one day. "Our paths are unlikely to cross again."

"Oh, Margaret, whyever not?"

"Don't be naive. School friendships are just that."

For you, Eliza wants to say. She won't believe this time at the Manor is a childish approximation of real life. Friendship, true and living friendship, has proved to be a bottomless well of surprise. Lister kissed her, and what's more, etched it on glass for ever; will always prize Eliza and care for her more than anyone else in the world. Now Eliza will never be alone.

Across the table, Nan looks up from her letter. "I have a brother. Well, a half-brother."

The Middles congratulate her.

"So, just six months after the wedding," Lister comments.

Nan grimaces. "Almost seven months. I'm told he's very small."

"The infants who come so, ah, early, shall we say, are generally described so."

"Leave her alone, Lister." Fanny with unusual firmness.

"It's all right," Nan tells Fanny. In a baleful whisper: "I'm not one bit surprised about the timing. Really, my father's new bride is nothing more nor less than a dirty har—"

"Nan!" Mercy interrupts the offensive word.

"Don't you dare report her," Margaret warns Mercy. "Hasn't Nan enough to bear?"

Eliza picks the last of her roast gudgeon off the bones. Having wedded this woman of barely twenty, in the nick of time, Mr. Moorsom seems to have saved her reputation, just about. But people will still talk; people can't be stopped from talking.

"I had a letter from Sam," Lister says that night in the Slope, yanking off her false curls. "Our progenitrix continues to embarrass us."

Eliza doesn't know the word but guesses: "Your mother?"

"I suppose I should admire her for being spirited, and going her own way, but she *will* make a pet of a young man and fawn over him, and she drinks a deal too much too."

Eliza's found that Lister is even more frank with her, since the kiss. "How does your father bear it?"

"Oh, the Captain drinks just as much as she does, but no one judges a man for that," she snaps. "He stays out in low taverns, running up bills he can't pay. Really there's little to choose between the two in point of vulgarity."

Eliza slides her hand into the crook of Lister's elbow.

Lister presses her arm to her side, trapping Eliza's fingers warmly. "They're an insufferably vulgar pair, and I wish my uncle and aunts at Shibden would adopt me outright."

"But your parents must be very fond of you, at least. They're surely proud of your talents?"

Lister snorts.

"If they understood your nature—"

"Who does, Raine? Except for you." Lister's eyes latch onto Eliza's so hard that she has trouble catching a breath. "I've never had anyone I could tell these dreadful things."

"Nor I."

"To unburden, and consign my troubles to a bosom where I know they'll be kept as safe as treasure... to spill myself like ink onto your paper..."

All Eliza can do is nod.

"The relief, it makes my heart race. Feel." Lister lifts Eliza's hand, setting her hard-knobbed wrist in its curve.

Eliza tightens her fingers; Lister's narrow wristbones roll. "I can't tell whether it's racing. I think it may be my own I'm feeling," she confesses.

That makes them both laugh.

Next Wednesday, as a very great treat, the young ladies are to go to the Theatre Royal around the corner in Mint Yard.

"It testifies to the dull tenor of our routines that this announcement has caused such a stir," Lister points out.

"Oh, shush," Eliza tells her. "It's the most exciting news of the term."

"Mr. Butler's company does a circuit of the North Riding every winter," Nan says. "I've seen *Inkle and Yarico* and all sorts."

"The Kembles came up as far as Newcastle when I was a child," Margaret says. "Mrs. Siddons played a rather antique Ophelia one night, and a buxom Hamlet the next."

"Oh, my father brought me to those performances," Frances remembers, smiling. "I couldn't be convinced that she wasn't two different persons, an actress and an actor."

Lister says, "All I've seen are fantoccini booths—puppets on strings, you know—and a harlequinade at a fair."

Eliza's never been to the theatre either, but wouldn't admit it in company. She's rather braver than she used to be, but still not half as brave as Lister.

According to the bills nailed up, the famous comedienne Mrs. Jordan is to give *As You Like It*. In class, Lister manages to persuade Miss Lewin that they should read it aloud in preparation for the outing. "And I'll be Rosalind, if you please, madam."

She shakes her head. "I want you for the melancholy Jaques."

Lister groans.

The mistress pretends to misunderstand. "Exactly—he's prey to all the sorrows of the world. Miss Smith, as you read with great correctness, you may take on the role of Rosalind."

"Is she the one who wears men's clothes?" Mercy asks warily.

"Yes, but you'll stay in your own."

"I won't be going to any theatre." The ring of a boast.

Miss Lewin is steadfast. "All the more important for you to develop an appreciation of our national poet in the classroom, then."

Eliza is assigned the role of Celia—the daughter of one duke and the niece of another, confusingly.

Lister groans again.

"Is it so far beyond my capacities?" Eliza whispers.

Lister shakes her head, as if unable to explain.

The play is in the eighth of twenty-one volumes of Shakespeare's works; the seven girls pass the tome among them as they read aloud.

By the time they've gone through the first few scenes, Eliza understands Lister's discontent: clearly she's longing to read Rosalind to Eliza's Celia, because it sounds as if the cousins are more than cousins. Intimates, in fact, in the extraordinary way Lister and Eliza are. If Celia's father means to banish Rosalind from court as a traitor, Celia dares him to also exile her (his own daughter): *I cannot live out of her company.* With an extraordinary confidence, Celia declares to the world what Eliza would have expected her to keep private:

We still have slept together,
Rose at an instant, learned, played, eat together,
And, wheresoe'er we went, like Juno's swans,
Still we went coupled, and inseparable.

This play from two hundred years ago is somehow blabbing their secrets.

Under the curving wave of her skirt on the classroom bench, Eliza grips Lister's hand, feeling for the mingled percussion of their pulses. She thinks of the proud swans on the river, *coupled, and inseparable.*

She soon decides Rosalind is a thrilling character, even with Mercy doing her best to flatten the lines. Especially in the next act when she swaps her skirts for breeches—oh, Lister adores this bit—and calls herself Ganymede. Far from being awkward in her disguise, Rosalind seems set free. Another girl (a silly shepherdess called Phoebe, read by Frances) starts flirting with Rosalind-as-Ganymede, who warns her, *Do not fall in love with me, for I am falser than vows made in wine.*

Miss Lewin comes down on Frances hard for failing to stress any word in particular. "*It is a pretty youth—not very pretty.* That line makes no sense unless you stress the word *very.*"

Frances tries the line again, blushing, a great weal rising on her neck where she's scratched it. Eliza hopes Miss Lewin will know better than to make this mortification, too, the subject of rebuke, plunging Frances into a vortex of self-consciousness about her self-consciousness.

The scene goes on.

These late March evenings, the refectory fire is so ineffective that the Middles send Lister up to charm the proprietors, and she comes back with permission for them to play any games that will warm them up "without making *too* much noise."

For Squeak Piggy Squeak, the Farmer's blindfolded and spun three times in the Pen (a circle of chairs) till she's dizzy, then given a pillow. She chooses a Piggy by pointing at random, places the pillow on the Piggy's lap, and sits on it. From the Piggy's squeak the Farmer must guess her name, whereupon that Piggy becomes the next Farmer. But if she guesses wrong, she stays trapped in the Pen and must be spun again, over and over, as many times as it takes. One evening Fanny has to stagger dizzily out to the necessary to throw up, and it takes all the rest of the Middles to persuade Mercy that it's not her duty to make a report to Mrs. Tate.

Eliza likes Here I Bake, which starts with all the girls taking hands to form a circle. In the middle, the Bride touches one pair of hands, "Here I bake," then another, "here I brew," then, "here I make my wedding cake." Finally, she dives at a pair of hands with "Here I mean to break *through*"—and pushes hard and fast enough to part them. Most girls claim they dread being the Bride, but Eliza finds it rather exciting: the slow pacing around the circle, then the glorious licence to be violent. If the Bride escapes, the girl whose hand first gave way has to take her place, but if the escape fails, the Bride must try again. If she fails three times, she pays a Forfeit, such as having to tell a grave secret, or stand up on a stool as a Statue and let the others place her limbs in any grotesque positions they fancy.

In the Slope, that evening, Lister asks Eliza to trim her hair with her nail scissors. Perhaps it's to save the expense of a hairdresser, but Eliza feels honoured. She's nervous at first, then starts to enjoy herself as she crops her way around Lister's head.

"Take off my front hair too."

"Oh, but surely— "

"I have my artificial curls. Go on!"

Snip, snip. Done. Startlingly short. Lister's whole face, like a flame suddenly uncovered.

Hearing Mrs. Tate's steps in the passage, Eliza snatches up the fallen strands to put in the basket. Lister pulls on her nightcap to cover her bare head.

Once Mrs. Tate's taken away the lantern, Lister produces her hidden taper, and the eighth volume of Shakespeare, which is too big for any pocket.

"How did you smuggle that out of class?" Eliza asks.

"Between my thighs, squeezed tight," Lister boasts. "The tricky part was getting up all those stairs."

They turn straight to *As You Like It,* and the cousins' scenes. When the duke calls his daughter's bluff, Celia doesn't quail: *Shall we be sunder'd? Shall we part, sweet girl? No; let my father seek another heir.*

Lister plays Rosalind like she was born to the role: *"O how full of briars is this working-day world!"* When she hatches the disguise plan, she leaps to her feet to act it out:

Were it not better,
Because that I am more than common tall,
That I did suit me all points like a man?
A gallant curtle-axe upon my thigh,
A boar-spear in my hand—

"What's a curtle-axe?" Eliza wants to know.

Lister shrugs. "Sounds like a cutlass." She snatches up Eliza's hairbrush; slashes, feints, and parries.

Eliza's glad that Celia's not all talk, like some girls. *I'll go along with thee,* she promises, and that's just what she does, leaving everything behind as the two run into the woods.

Now go we in content
To liberty, and not to banishment.

Wednesday at last. The theatre's packed like a barrel of salt beef. Eliza's never been in such a throng; the auditorium seats more than five hundred, according to Miss Lewin, who's sitting with a friend but close enough to keep an eye on the pupils. Every Middle and Senior except Mercy is there, on two benches in the pit, very near the stage. Frances and Margaret are side by side, and chattering away, Eliza notices; could the two, bereft of their former friends, be palling up? Sensible of them, she supposes; a second choice is better than none.

The theatre's so bright and noisy, Eliza finds it hard to concentrate on the performers. A military band plays, which goes down very well with the crowd, and a fat man comes out to lead them in "Rule, Britannia!" Next up is a shrimp of a boy called Master Betty who swaps hats and turbans to perform speeches from various plays, comic and tragic, all with the same grandiose waving of his arms.

"He's only thirteen," Nan reports. "When he came on at Covent Garden last year, people were trampled."

"What, you mean to death?" Lister asks, dubious.

Nan shrugs as if that's a mere detail.

The people of York don't seem half as impressed by Master Betty; they talk so loudly that Eliza can hardly hear him. Up in the gallery, the working folk start thundering with their heels to encourage the boy off the stage. Eliza's boiling hot and fears she needs the pot already; she crosses her legs and puts it out of her mind. When she feels something burning on her neck, she jumps, thinking someone's thrown something at her—but it's only wax from a candelabra overhead.

The main piece begins, and Eliza's glad to have read *As You Like It,* as otherwise she'd have trouble following in all this hubbub. The famous Mrs. Jordan is awfully natural and pretty, with a plump girlishness and warmth. She comes on all hangdog as Rosalind, pretending to be down in the dumps—"*Dear Celia, I show more mirth than I am mistress of, and would you yet I were merrier?*"—and the audience applauds and stamps because yes, merrier is exactly what they demand. Mrs. Jordan winks; she strikes a playful pose; she makes them hoot and roar. "*What shall be our sport, then?*" she asks her *coz,* but her flirtatious gaze takes in the whole crowd.

Eliza likes her even better in the second act when she swaggers on in ribboned pantaloons and the action has to stop for her to take several bows. You really wouldn't know she is Irish, from her accent. Or past forty, from her face, and her light-footed gait.

"Apparently she's had *dozens* of children for the Duke of Clarence," Lister says in Eliza's ear, which she finds hard to believe; wouldn't it leave some trace? She wonders where they are now, these royal *cloud-fallers,* these *colts-in-the-woods.*

So this must be what it is to be a star. Mrs. Jordan's genius is a sort of generosity, Eliza decides; she lavishes her looks, gestures, and words on five hundred people.

(And not just tonight but every night.) She makes almost every line funny, except for the ones she delivers like urgent messages. "*Love is merely a madness,*" she throws straight out at the pit, as if to Eliza alone, "*and, I tell you, deserves as well a dark house and a whip as madmen do.*" She's teasing the Orlando fellow, but she sounds as if she means it too. As if love is a nonsensical derangement, and also the only thing in this world that makes a tittle of sense. It's a cruel line, though. Eliza supposes madmen might require darkness and even whipping, at a pinch, to subdue the most violent cases, but—*deserve*?

The wrestling scene has been swapped for a fencing match, which does seem more genteel. Touchstone the Fool seizes every chance for acrobatic tricks, dropping through a trapdoor or being catapulted on or off stage. Eliza's disconcerted when the whole play halts in the middle for a pantomime called *Robin Goodfellow.* There are thrilling effects: fires, explosions, trees suddenly growing out of rocks. What surprises her most is when Oliver drops dead at the end, and Celia marries Jaques instead. "They've changed the story," she protests in a whisper to Lister.

"Oh well, Shakespeare's in his grave so long, I doubt he'll mind."

A farce with songs is announced, but Miss Hargrave

rises to her feet. Mrs. Tate jumps up at the other end of the row and beckons to the pupils, as if the late hour is somehow their fault. They all squeeze out, past a mob of newcomers pushing in to take their seats at half price for the rest of the evening's entertainment.

Outside in the chill and the dark, Mrs. Tate summons a tiny link-boy to light their way to the Manor with a reeking torch. He leads them home like a line of ants.

At the back, Lister struts and strikes poses. Just before they pass under Bootham Bar, she points up at its three half-size stone figures and remarks, "They always look to me as if they're contemplating taking a great leap and doing away with themselves."

"What a morbid notion," Eliza says.

Lister grabs her hand, winds her up like a top, and sets her spinning across the cobbles.

Mrs. Tate calls, "Miss Raine!"

"Beg pardon, madam," so helpless with laughter she can barely form the words.

It's so late now, but Eliza and Lister have never been this wide-awake in their lives, and the Slope, with its curtains drawn wide, is bright with starlight. They talk in whispers, not to disturb the maids who lie sleeping on the other side of the box room.

The question Eliza's been needing to ask swells like a great berry in her mouth, and all at once she's not scared to let it out, not scared at all, not scared of anything. "Lister, do you think you and I might be... like in your story?"

"Which story?"

"The one from olden days, about the people the gods split." Eliza waits, pulse banging in her chest. "The double-female ones, parted from their missing halves—what were they called?"

"Children of the Earth." Lister's tone is thoughtful.

"You don't believe we are?"

"We can't know for sure."

Eliza's spirits sink. "I suppose not."

"Not unless we try."

She blinks in the luminous night. She doesn't follow. "Try?"

"To be made whole again. To become one."

"One..."

"Double-person," Lister says.

"Oh."

"We should take off our clothes."

Eliza swallows hard. But yes, she can see that all this fabric is in the way. So she sits up and wriggles her night shift off over her head, then pulls off her cap, for good measure. Now it's come to this, she sheds everything as easily as a chestnut its shell.

Lister's gleaming, her bare torso like one of those old Greek marbles; the small breasts of a huntress. Eliza's dazzled.

Very low: "Let me look at you, Raine."

Eliza shakes under this hard gaze. She straightens her back.

"We're not the same," Lister says. "But close enough to fit."

"Let's be closer." Eliza barely voices the words.

"Do you think?"

Thinking is not what this is.

"Closer still?"

"Closer and closer," Eliza breathes.

"As close as possible."

"Closer," she insists.

They draw closer. The shock of skin. Cold, with heat under.

"Together." Lister's whisper is a butterfly spreading its wings in Eliza's ear.

They press together hard, harder.

Still whispering. "Four legs."

"Four arms."

"Can't tell whose."

"All parts—"

"Hold tight."

"Tighter."

"We're one. Whole."

"Stay."

"Like this."

Mouths too. Lips warm and cool at once. Snake-tongued. Tangled inextricably. The embrace unbreakable.

In the morning, everything is different. At breakfast, the two of them sit among the Middles, sip milk, and rub dust out of their eyes when no one's looking.

The day drags by with an air of unreality, as if they're merely playing the parts of young ladies in a poorly written play. All Eliza can think of is the coming night.

At dinner, the Head reads aloud from an advice manual for young ladies; Eliza tries to close her ears to the droning. *"Endeavour to derive some instruction from everything you see or hear. There are lying looks as well as lying words, and even a lying silence. Friendship opens the gates, and she who enters, if not an ally, is a treacherous foe."*

In the Slope at last. They get undressed in awkward silence, backs turned.

Mrs. Tate's soft footsteps. Eliza rushes to meet her at the door with the lantern.

"Ready, Miss Raine, Miss Lister?"

"Ready, madam," she assures Mrs. Tate.

"Good night, then."

"Good night."

In pitch-black now, without the lantern, Eliza waits for the passage to be quiet. Dreads the qualms that might slip in. Waits the space of a long breath.

Silence.

She and Lister leap at each other.

They can't see, can only feel their way through a maze of sensations. The astonishment of nakedness. The tendrils of napes, the hang and swing of flesh, the startling to life of breasts, the tender backs of knees, the varieties of fragrant stickiness, the hard push of velveted bone. The lifting and dipping and opening. Howls quite stifled in pillows of flesh. With fingers and thumbs and heels of hands, with lips and tongues and teeth, with wrists and thighs and the very hinges of themselves, the things they find to do...

A great wave flings Eliza to shore. Lips salty, battered, blinded.

And again. Gasping silently; holding breath.

No need to ask. Something like a dance of their own devising, something like a storm; it requires every drop of them and leaves them wrecked, then forces them to rise and begin from the start. They're so tired now, they slip and slide in and out of sleep. Seizing each other over and over as the first light of tomorrow cuts in between the curtains. Maddened and oblivious until the rising bell clangs.

Stuffing her hair into her cap, at the mirror, Eliza watches herself in the dawn twilight. Does this—

Would this count as—

Is this the face of a girl who's been debauched?

She's never felt so clean.

In Accounts, Lister rapidly chalks the long division on her slate and Eliza copies it. Lister slips her worn copy of Virgil from the pocket under her frock, and tucks it into the shadow of *Arithmetick Made Plain and Simple.* She puts a casual finger to a line so no one but Eliza will notice: *"Nunc scio quid sit Amor."*

Eliza reads the words three times. All she can guess is, something about love?

With a lead pencil, moving so lightly it barely leaves a trace, Lister glosses it underneath: *Now I know what love is.*

The days go by like wisps of fog. Only the nights are real. As soon as Mrs. Tate walks away down the passage, a flint is struck within Eliza and Lister, and joy flares up, illuminating and filling the garret. Without a word, without any sound that could betray them: the loosening, heating, holding still, pulsing, lingering, hurrying, rising. Gripping and squeezing and pressing and parting and probing and piercing and mashing and crushing their bodies together till they're bruised. All in a silence that sings with deafening sweetness inside them.

If Eliza and Lister sleep late and only the bell wakes them, they pull away as if they're tearing their own skin, and try to keep their hands off each other while they splash at the washbowl and throw on their clothes, but sometimes they're drawn back together despite themselves, so close, frocks yanked up in haste, with nothing dividing their tangled legs. Then the second bell rips them apart again. The room has such a curious fug, Eliza has to prop the window open to the March breezes before the two rush down to breakfast still throbbing, muffling their scented fingers in their skirts.

Each has been told she looks tired. Lister blames bedbugs; Eliza, bad dreams.

In the daytime she's groggy and distracted, preoccupied by Lister's wiry body, which seems to radiate through its incongruous girl-costume. The sleek kidskin of Lister's jaw; those two muscular dimples in the small of her back; the smooth, leathery skin of her heels. And Eliza is even more unsettled by a ticklish, new awareness of parts of herself. That dip inside her elbow that Lister sucked so hard she marked it; the place on Eliza's right shoulder blade that leaps at the slightest touch; the nook below her left ear that Lister describes as the softest silk ever spun. Her slippery wet that comes for Lister every time, the nectar that Eliza gives her, or she gives Eliza, and either way it won't stop spilling. Her breasts that tighten and pang when Lister plays at being an infant that nothing else can soothe. And the nameless, perhaps unnameable, betweens and unders and ups and deeps inside, parts Eliza is half-convinced she didn't have until Lister bared and brought them to life with a spark from her godlike finger.

A whole week passes before they broach the subject. (Eliza's been afraid to break the spell by speaking—burst the bubble of their bliss. And whenever they're alone together, it seems as if their lips are used most eloquently for kissing.) Finally, one mild afternoon, strolling along the Manor Shore and eyeing the pair of swans, she demands, "Who taught you?"

A half-laugh. "Nature, I suppose. Who taught *you*?"

"But Lister." Eliza stops short. "You seem to know how—" Hot in the face. "To know everything. Surely you've understood this..." This what? "...all along?"

Lister shakes her head. "Only a vague, violent longing, since the cradle."

"Really?"

"I had the impression I was one of those new forms that spring up without rhyme or reason, as when one bud on a bush blooms in a different colour. One of Creation's little jokes."

"You're not a joke," Eliza tells her.

"Not now that I've found you." She takes Eliza's gloved hand and tucks it through her arm, squeezing it tight.

"I've earned three inattention marks this week," Eliza complains, "whereas you do your work as well as ever."

Lister shrugs that off. "It's just a knack for getting things by heart. My waking thoughts and my dreams are all occupied by you. When you walk into the room, I shake, and I ache here." She rubs the bone in the middle of her chest. "I'm over head and ears in love with you."

"Oh. Lister."

"Raine, Raine."

What can it mean, for the two of them to be in love? Nothing that needs explaining to them; nothing they could explain to anyone else.

Eliza wakes with a heavy, luxurious feeling. Slick, so much so that she fears for a moment that she's wet the bed. But when she pulls up her night shift, it's bull's-eyed with red. She bursts into tears. "I'm damaged."

Lister chuckles. "It's only your French cousin."

"Oh." Eliza claps her thighs together. *Her time,* as girls say, come at last.

"Mine visits every fourth Wednesday, like clockwork. *The Red-coats have landed*—there's another phrase for it," Lister says merrily.

Eliza stares at the scarlet swath across the sheet.

"Don't fret—cold water will take out the blood." Lister digs a length of cloth out of her dresser. "Now, if your cousin comes on very gently, a folded napkin should do, but if it's a soaker, you can add sheets of paper."

Eliza watches Lister line the cloth with scrap pages covered in her own writing, as neatly as if she's making up a parcel for the post. She puts out her hand: "I can manage."

"I like seeing to you. Lie down and let me."

So Eliza does.

At night, the small light of their cheap taper expands, making a glittering pool of Eliza's Indian goods. "And this is the muslin called woven wind." She drapes it over Lister's lean limbs. "One sari takes months to spin—so fine it can be pulled through a ring."

"I can't feel a thing, and I can see right through it!"

She thinks of a story to please Lister. "There was this princess Zeb-un-Nissa, a poetess who memorised the whole Koran and never married—the Emperor's favourite daughter. She was taking the air in the garden one day when her father stormed up and rebuked her for being stark naked, and she assured him that she was wearing seven suits of woven wind muslin."

Lister laughs, stroking the fabric with the back of her hand. "I'm too plain for such finery."

You, with all your other gifts, Eliza thinks, *what need have you of beauty?* "There's nothing plain about you."

"Oh, come now..."

"Yours isn't a feminine loveliness," Eliza protests, "but you're well made. Beautifully made."

Lister's smile is rueful.

"Like a well-forged machine, fit for purpose." She puts her hands on Lister's hard shoulders.

Then she retrieves William Raine's birdcage from her bottom drawer, and takes out the little gold locket. "I believe my eye should just fit in this."

"Your eye?"

"The paper one that you stole."

Sheepish at being found out, Lister corrects her: "Salvaged." She goes to find the scrap in her volume of Ovid.

Eliza gets out her nail scissors and trims it to an oval before pressing it into the locket. She fastens the delicate chain at the back of Lister's neck.

"I'll keep it under my shift where no one will see," Lister promises. She sets one palm between Eliza's legs, over the cloth, and says, "You're growing warm," and Eliza's dissolving already and rising to her touch, and it's starting all over again.

The Juniors bring Miss Robinson cowslips and anemones by the fistful. Miss Lewin sniffs at the jars left on the desk with appreciation. "Spring at last! My friend Mrs. Morrice has already heard from our quondam neighbours that the banks of the Thames are quite purpled with bluebells."

Lister hoists her eyebrows obscurely at Eliza.

"Did you catch that?" Lister asks in the empty classroom, after the others have rushed off. "*Our* quondam neighbours."

"What does *quondam*—"

"*Former,* but my point is, in Hammersmith, Miss Lewin wasn't living with her parents but with this Mrs. Morrice, and it sounds like they're together in York too. Which means..."

Eliza belatedly gets it. "Oh, Lister, no."

"What else can it mean?"

"Spinsters sometimes share lodgings to halve the expense."

"But does one of them up and move two hundred miles north with her friend, when the friend takes a new job? That's a very dear friend indeed, I say."

Eliza forces herself to consider it: Miss Lewin living with this Mrs. Morrice—a widow, or is that a courtesy title for a woman of mature years?—something along the lines of husband and wife. The two of them in private, in the night. She covers her mouth with her hand.

Stiffly: "Does the notion disgust you, Raine?"

"Not that." Eliza rushes to correct the misunderstanding. "I only mean, picturing them, at their age—any persons at their time of life."

"Ah," Lister says in amusement.

"Besides, I'd rather—" Eliza drops her voice to the smallest whisper. "I want it to be just us."

"The only two in the world?"

She nods, obstinate. "Doesn't it feel like our invention?"

A very fine day; Gymnastics is held on the grass among the ruins. "Dumbbells *up*," Miss Robinson orders.

The Middles heave the weights aloft as they carry

on discussing Boney's character. "A tyrant may have a few sound ideas," Lister argues. "He's decreed the Jews should be treated as equal citizens, for instance."

"Hear that, Margaret?" Nan asks.

Eliza cringes.

"I did." Margaret reverses her twist, panting as she maintains her grip. "Was there some special reason I should?"

"Well." A giggle.

"Go on, Nan." Margaret speaks with a dangerous coolness. Her dumbbells clang overhead.

"With grace and control, young ladies," Miss Robinson urges.

Nan raises her eyebrows at Fanny, asking for help.

"Well, but Margaret, aren't you . . . you know?" Fanny asks.

"Am I not what?"

"A Jewess? Or half, or so?" Fanny's voice is a squeak.

"Fanny!" Frances scolds.

"Don't take offence," Fanny tells Margaret. "It's just what we—what I thought I heard."

Nan clears her throat. "Or that your mother might have been a convert. Secretly Jewish, you know—a Murano."

"Murano is an island of Venice," Mercy informs her. "You mean Marrano."

Margaret lets out a sardonic laugh. "Sorry to disappoint, but to the best of my knowledge my mother was plain Christian English."

"So you know her?" That's Lister, asking the unaskable.

Margaret's going to tell them to hold their blasted tongues, Eliza thinks.

Instead she sets her dumbbells down and scans the Middles as if weighing up whether she can trust them. "In confidence..."

"Yes."

"Of course!"

Margaret speaks low. "I believe she was the nursemaid who raised me until I was sent to school. In my father's will, he left her sixty pounds a year for as long as she'd stay single and childless. If he was just her master, why would he have cared whether she ever married?"

The Middles all nod at that.

Eliza is impressed. Margaret could have kept up the mystery, could have said, *My mother was a very great lady.* It's risky to admit to what some will always call base blood.

"Sixty pounds doesn't seem very much," Frances says sympathetically.

Margaret only purses her lips.

* * *

That night, Myrtle Grove; Mother's ankle bracelets make their musical clinking. Eliza (very small in the dream, no bigger than a mouse) runs after her and tries to speak, but the words come out in English, a shrill, piping English that makes Mother frown in confusion.

Eliza wakes, puzzled, with such a heaviness on her chest. Mother understood English perfectly well, but in the dream she seemed to have forgotten every word of it. Why didn't Eliza or Jane think to ask her to write to them, when they boarded the *King George*? (A misgiving now: could their mother write? Eliza can't remember whether she ever saw her with a pen.) Why didn't Eliza beg for a lock of that shimmering black hair, at least? Because she was only six, she supposes. Because although there'd never been a time when the girls hadn't known they'd be going on the great ship to England, it had never been spelled out that the trip was to be for ever.

"What's the matter?" Lister kisses the tears away as if sipping nectar.

"I just wish I knew whether Mother protested, when Father took us onto the boat."

"I'd have wept, if I'd been her," Lister says.

"You would?"

"Shrieked and fought for one last embrace."

This is some comfort. Eliza slides her arms around Lister and holds her so close it hurts.

"Not that family are always kindred spirits, though," Lister murmurs. "My mother bore and reared me, but you'd hardly guess it from the way we jar each other."

Eliza nods. "Like Jane and me." Sisters in name and face, aliens under the skin.

"Love comes not when it's contracted for but when it will."

"And just think, seven months ago, you and I were strangers!"

"I was never a stranger," Lister tells her solemnly, "only your true match in disguise."

They press their faces together till they stick.

Eliza seems to slumber through the days—doing just enough, in each lesson, to avoid punishment—and live only at night.

One morning very early she's woken by Lister's whisper like a moth in her ear: "Come down!"

She's groggy, bewildered. "What is it?"

"A surprise."

So Eliza scrambles into her frock, stockings, and nankeen half-boots galoshed with leather. The Manor's still quiet—it can't be much later than half-past six—so the only people they pass are the housemaids toting laundry. Eliza smiles at the tiny one, who's staggering under a basket as big as herself.

Outside the grass is sparkling with dew. "Hurry," Lister says, "or we won't have time to try it."

"What is it?" Eliza demands.

"This way." Lister leads her to the abbey ruins, where the massive alders are dressed in their spring green already. Under the thickest tree, she and Eliza are curtained from view by the leafy branches. Eliza spots something new: a rope dangling from a point so high she can't see where it attaches.

"I happened to find a length discarded, hanging on the wall of the Ropewalk," Lister tells her, "so I coiled it up and dragged it around the back of the Manor, just before bed the other night. Then I tied a pebble to the end of a ball of string, and threw that over the branch..." Lister mimes it. "I almost blinded myself a few times when the stone fell back too close."

That horrifies Eliza.

"In the end it went over, so I secured the rope to it and pulled that up..."

"But what's it for?"

"A swing. I know it's not a proper one with a seat like you had in India," Lister apologises. "But I made knots at the bottom for your feet."

Eliza laughs with delight.

The lowest knot is two feet off the ground. She's not sure she'll be able to manage this, after all these years, but she can't say no. So she seizes the coarse rope above her head and jumps on, her legs flailing at first. Her heels find the knot and clamp on, even as her body's skimming across the dark circle under the alder. A tiny scream; Eliza finds she does remember this sensation after all.

"Want a push?"

"No!"

But as she swings by, Lister takes her by the hips and shoves her so hard she's flying. Her hands are burning on the rope, and her right foot's cramping, and her vision spins as she rotates and whirls across the—

"Ow!" Spiked, hooked.

"You're caught on something," Lister calls up.

"What is it?"

"A dead branch, looks like. Let me..."

But Eliza's weight is pulling her down, and as she wriggles her shoulders she hears an awful rip—

Flung to the ground. Last year's alder cones pressed into her hands and knees.

Lister, repentant: "My love, are you hurt?"

"Only my pride." Eliza's up, breathless, brushing herself off, trying to gather the tatters of her frock.

Lister bursts out laughing. "Give up. It's a rag now."

They hurry back to the school, Eliza holding the

remnants of cloth around her. They've almost made it up the back stairs when they run straight into Mrs. Tate.

The mistake Eliza makes is trying to make light of the incident. If she played up her sense of guilt and her bruises, she might have earned only a disobedience mark. But she's still so weak with merriment, she makes the error of assuring the mistress that the frock doesn't matter: "I have half a dozen just like it."

Mrs. Tate's face pulls tight, as if on a drawstring. "Your funds are not at issue, Miss Raine. Your guardian will be gravely disturbed to hear of your destruction of property and scorn for rules."

Eliza casts her eyes down. "I beg your—"

Mrs. Tate cuts her off. "In disgrace for a week, the pair of you."

Odd, how little disgrace stings, once it's begun. She and Lister both have to wear the blue belts of Juniors, but since everyone in the Manor knows they're Middles, the belts are really nothing more than a comical costume, like Pantalone's slippers. The two are obliged to spend all their meals together at the disgrace table; this is the opposite of hardship, especially as they're the only ones there this week. "Our private banquet," Lister murmurs.

"How considerate of them to lay it out for us back here, where we can be alone."

They have to stand, but they don't mind that either. So as not to spill their gruel they lean right over their bowls, and their faces almost touch. "It's taking all my reserves of self-control not to kiss you," Lister whispers.

Strolling through the grounds, forbidden to converse with the other pupils all week, Eliza and Lister are constantly on the edge of laughter. Eliza forgets her umbrella, and doesn't go back to fetch it; careless, she tilts her face up to the spring sun.

The rope has been cut down, they find when they visit the great alder. "But only as far as a man could reach on a stepladder," Lister points out. The remnant dangles above them, swaying snakishly in the breeze.

In Accounts, Eliza's entirely distracted, staring at Lister's right hand. Such a small, pale thing, lying quietly on the desk. No one would ever guess what it can do.

"The Great Hall of York Assembly Rooms have thirteen brilliant-cut lustres"—Miss Robinson writes *13* on the board—"each composed of eighteen branches. How many wax candles burn there at a time? Miss Raine?"

Eliza blinks. "Thirteen by eighteen. Ah...two hundred and four?"

"Two hundred and thirty-four," Mercy corrects her.

"That must cost the proprietors a fortune in lights," Frances remarks.

"Miss Smith the candlemaker would know!" Nan snickers as if she's said something very witty.

Later that day, Miss Lewin beckons Eliza into an empty classroom, to spout platitudes. "Friendship is of course the jewel of youth, Miss Raine."

Eliza looks blank.

"It's often said that the amity among girls should remain general rather than particular. *Be friendly to all but worship none,* the proverb has it. Affection ought to cement together the whole community, much like the mortar between these stones." She pats the classroom wall.

"Bricks," Eliza mutters.

Miss Lewin's eroded eyebrows go up. "Quite right, Miss Raine, this oldest part of our ancient Manor is redbrick. Though correcting one's elders would seem more characteristic of Miss Lister than yourself."

Eliza flushes. Can it be true that Lister's character is rubbing off on hers? It's a fact that Eliza used to tremble for an hour if someone gave her a cross word. But mostly it feels to her as if the opposite is true: once you've found your mate, you can be all the more yourself, glad to take the opposite part in the dance.

"But my point is that I'm all in favour of particular friendships, in principle," Miss Lewin goes on in a flustered way. "The soul recognises something in another, doesn't it—reaches out, chooses, knits to that one and no other. I remember my own schooldays... Past the age of twenty, I must warn you, nothing's felt with quite the same vividness."

Suddenly Eliza's dreading that the ageing spinster is going to confess something about Mrs. Morrice.

"Friendship can cheer, soften, strengthen, uplift..." The mistress seems to be arguing with an invisible opponent.

"Yes," Eliza says, in case her long silence seems sullen.

Miss Lewin's slightly liver-spotted hand flies up as if to hush her. "However, not every pairing quite fits. A mismatched bond can do as much harm as good, or more, even. Miss Lister has a remarkable quality of magnetism, but you mustn't set her up to worship as the Golden Calf."

Eliza's stomach curdles. Is that how it looks, from the outside?

"Her harum-scarum tomfoolery will lead her into trouble sooner or later, and I don't believe you're comfortable wandering in such marshy ways, are you?"

Why not, because Eliza's a timid mouse? Or because she's a foreigner, only at the Manor on sufferance, so she's risking more severe consequences than Lister?

What the woman says is true: Eliza's never felt less *comfortable.* Nor ever more alive. She bares her teeth in a monkey smile. "Thank you, madam," and she turns on her heel.

Right through the week of their disgrace, Eliza and Lister move in a magic circle, floating through the day. At night they barely sleep. Every wave of pleasure that crashes leaves a detritus of foam among the rocks, and makes ripples that grow and gather and mount up to the next wave. There's no end to Eliza's joy. She and Lister writhe and delve till they're sticky and sore.

On Monday Eliza wakes with an oppression in her head, and her throat is scalding. She gets out of bed for a glass of water, but black fills her eyes; she almost falls. Tries to speak, but it burns as if her neck's been slashed.

"My love." Lister puts the back of her hand to Eliza's forehead, and pulls it away. "You're sizzling. Get back to bed."

"Not allowed."

"Nonsense. I'll fetch Mrs. Tate."

Eliza drops down on the mattress and feels as if she'll never get up again.

Mrs. Tate recoils from a glimpse of Eliza's tongue.

"Whites on red, like a strawberry," she says with a grim nod.

"Scarlet fever?" Lister asks almost excitedly.

She nods. "You mustn't come near Miss Raine. Move your things to, ah, the Yellow Room—the bed that was Miss Betty Foster's."

Lister shakes her head. "Too late. I feel it coming in my throat already."

"Open wide?"

She sticks out her tongue.

"No spots yet," Mrs. Tate says doubtfully. "Well, I'll send for Dr. Mather."

Once the girls are alone, Eliza drags her head off the pillow. "My love, I'm so sorry I've passed it to you!"

"Oh, I'm perfectly well," Lister tells her. "I've no intention of being banished from your side, that's all."

"Lister! You mustn't catch it."

"I'm as strong as an ox. Lie still and I'll put a wet cloth on your forehead."

Dr. Mather arrives and tuts over Eliza. There have been cases of scarlet fever from contaminated dairies in town. As for Miss Lister, he can't be sure; she has no fever nor reddening of the tongue, but he's seen some patients come right through it with nothing but a painful throat.

"Since my case is so mild, I can nurse my friend," Lister tells him.

"Hm. I'll send up draughts for you both."

"Draughts of what?"

"Henbane, white poppy...Also some light nourishment. And no reading or writing, Miss Raine—just rest."

"Tell them to leave everything outside the door, won't you?" Lister asks in a gravelly voice. "As it's so very catching."

She goes out into the passage with him. Eliza hears Dr. Mather mutter: "Have them send for me if she vomits, wheezes, faints, or grows cold. Asiatics are often dangerously weakened by our Northern winters."

The week that follows is the strangest Eliza can remember. Her tongue swells in her mouth like a rotten fruit. A rash, rough as sandpaper, spreads from her cheeks down to her belly, and Lister has to pare Eliza's fingernails to stop her scratching it. Eliza should be miserable, but this is a reprieve from all regulations and routines. The real invalid and the pretender both live on bowls of broth, minced veal, chocolate, boiled blubbery, rice pudding. The raspberry throat syrups, and medicines heavily nutmegged to cover the bitter laudanum, leave them groggy and hilarious. The Slope is their hidden refuge in the clouds, and they never want to leave it.

Lister goes on at length about a pair of Irish cousins she's read about in a magazine. Refusing to be married off or put in a convent, the ladies ran away together twenty-seven years ago, and have been sharing a cottage in Wales ever since.

Eliza's surprised to hear they didn't get dragged back and locked up; instead, their escapade made them famous.

She and Lister lie in one bed and gaze up at the murky stain from where the roof leaked after three days of rain back in February. Lister nestles into Eliza's collarbone. "We really must have the ceiling raised."

Eliza laughs feebly. "But first we'll put in new windows. Gigantic ones."

Lister nods. "Now, if we have the floors taken up—"

"What, quite up?"

"Every board."

"Won't we fall through to the rooms below?"

"My gravitational studies suggest so. But after the initial shock, we'll find the prospect so much airier."

Eliza points downwards. "Not with the entire Tate family cluttering up the floor."

"Perhaps we'll send them elsewhere. Find them a cupboard in the cellars to live in."

"On further reflection, my love, perhaps we shouldn't change a thing. I'm so fond of the funny old Slope where first we met."

"You're right." And they start kissing again.

* * *

Eliza's first day back on her feet, the mistresses treat her like a china saucer; no one so much as asks her to recite anything.

After French, she seeks out Lister and finds her in the courtyard, studying the wisteria that hangs heavy from a diagonal drainpipe. "Why did the Head call you out of class?"

Lister makes a little face.

"You're not in disgrace again already?"

"Not exactly. It's a quarter day. When rents are paid," she adds reluctantly, "and school fees and such."

"Oh."

"Our smallholding is mortgaged to the hilt," Lister says, low and gruff. "Nobody's ever told me exactly where the money was found to send Sam and John and me to school at the same time, but..."

Clearly her bill is past due. "I'm sure it will be sorted, sooner or later," Eliza says weakly.

Lister nods. "Care despised, say I!" But she doesn't sound carefree, only defiant.

By the time of the Spring Fair, in the meadows north of Gillygate, Eliza's strong enough to join the Middles on the walk there. It's the second day of the Fair—less rough, rather more genteel. Lister would like to inspect the cattle on sale, but Eliza keeps hold of her elbow and says absolutely not, on account of the stink. The same goes for some cruel game in which a sparrow with clipped wings, in a hat, is put eye-to-eye with a man with hands tied behind his back, who has to bite the bird's head off before it can peck him.

The Middles see rope dancers, a juggler with seven plates spinning on poles, and a dozen women racing barefoot to win a linen smock covered in poppy-red bows. Nan's tempted by a gurning show, but Margaret won't let her waste sixpence just to see someone pull faces. "Here's one for you for free." Margaret contorts her features horribly, till her nose appears to be growing out of the side of her mouth.

Frances assures Margaret she could make a living as a gurner if she ever loses her ten thousand pounds.

The Middles stroll past fortune-tellers, a Punch and Judy booth, and something called a Spectral Phantasmagoria, which Frances says looks much too horrifying.

"It'll just be a magic-lantern show," Margaret tells her.

"Still."

There's a woman cutting people's profiles out of black paper, sixpence each. "That's how painting was invented," Lister comments as they watch over the artist's shoulder.

"With a scissors?" Margaret asks, sceptical.

Lister shakes her head. "By tracing a profile. Pliny tells us a Corinthian girl's lover was about to go off to war, so she drew around his shadow on the wall."

That sounds likely enough to Eliza. Wouldn't you do anything you could to keep your beloved's likeness, in case the memory faded?

The Middles finally agree on paying to go into Tussaud's Waxworks, because the sign guarantees that the huge tent holds SIXTY-NINE PUBLIC CHARACTERS MODELLED FROM LIFE. "Or death, in some cases," Lister says. "They have a head of Marie Antoinette."

Eliza finds all the figures inside unnervingly lifelike, but the one that moves her most is LORD NELSON BEFORE HIS DEATH AT TRAFALGAR, 21 OCTOBER 1805. It was only last November that the news of his victory reached York and made all the bells ring. She remembers whirling in the street with Lister, outside the gates of the Manor. And now, just four months later, touring the country, here's the poor admiral in waxen form as he looked the night before he was gunned down. Emaciated, his right sleeve sewn shut below the shoulder, his head scarred and missing half an eyebrow from previous battles.

"What a fright." That's Nan.

Lister turns on her. "Lord Nelson gave himself to his nation piece by piece, and saved us from Boney, so show some respect, missy."

Fanny reaches out with her little arm to touch his cuff, and the attendant barks, "Hands off!"

Four months is long enough to change everything, Eliza's thinking; in four months, the landscape of her life has been transformed as if by a volcano.

Outside the tent in the sunshine, the Middles eat Bath buns with sugared caraway seeds that get stuck in their teeth.

They're on the way home, almost at the edge of the Fair, when Eliza spots three words over a small booth: THE LIVING CURIOSITY. She hangs back to examine the signboard. The faded picture shows a hugely fat female, half-nude, skin mud-brown and...furry, could it be? An elaborate jewel pierces one side of her nose. DO YOU DARE TO SET EYES ON THE SAVAGE? 2D LECTURE AND TABLEAUX.

Lister's by her side. "Probably just a Yorkshire-woman daubed in shoe-blacking," she says awkwardly.

Eliza can't swallow this stone.

Lister tugs her away.

When Eliza catches sight of the other Middles, she slows, not wanting to talk to them, dragging like an anchor on Lister's arm. "Tuppence to view a human oddity." It comes out more furiously than she expected. "That's me, no?"

Lister turns and meets her eyes.

"Is that what—was that what drew you to me," Eliza demands, "that I'm..." Which word, of all the words? "...an exotic?" She's counting on an outraged, or at least reassuringly firm, denial.

But Lister says, "I've never cared for the commonplace. Perhaps it was your singularity that first attracted me."

Eliza's so angry, her vision swims. "You mean you saw my colour—"

"I saw *you,* Raine. All of you. I fell in love with you, in all particulars." Lister's gripping Eliza's hands, the heat surging through two layers of kidskin.

"But *why* me?"

She's expecting *Who knows,* or *Blame Dame Destiny.*

Lister shrugs. "Because I'm a great oddity myself? Don't let's waste time fretting. Who wants to be ordinary, anyway?"

"Almost everyone!"

Lister leans in close, as if to kiss her, right here in the middle of the dirty path, in front of the whole world. "Let's be a pair of originals instead."

And Eliza's courage flares up once more.

RAINE TO LISTER, 1815

MISS MISTER LISTER, Your Majestickness, or whatever you dub yourself these days in your vastly voluble vanity, ha! Still diarising *sans cesse,* are you, picking up every twig of fact to cram into this year—every stile you climb and book you devour and tea table you command, every raindrop that dares to land on you, every female you flirt with, every turd you drop?

For all your claims of candour, these days you wear a false face as comfortably as any mummer, zany, Merry Andrew, or Punch. A counterfeit PRICK through and through, I call you, from that lofty way of cocking your head, to your booming voice, to your gentlemannish stride, so damn your eyes, you may go to the bloody devil, say I. Oh ho, you don't answer me, but your silence speaks volumes, and remember I know who you are, you bloody backbiting shabbaroon shit-sack—

The crack-brains shout me down. All here grumble I talk too much and fast and frenziedly, my *babble,* they call it, well higgle huggle to them, if I dip my nib in a deep dark well, how can I help what truth spills out?

And furthermore I tell you I'm in sound mind, unjustly detained, and mean to emancipate myself and get the licence taken away from this madhouse for KIDNAPPING. I'm locked up here on the falsest of pretexts by my ENEMIES, chief among them hypocrite Duffin, who never was a father to me, only a stiff actor stumbling through that part and mumbling his lines. Also his feeble wife, who made not even a pretence of playing the mother. How the eels lurk under the rock. Better if those coldhearts had put me on the parish at seven years old than let me believe I'd have a home with them. And even more so, Mary Jane Marsh, their pal or rather puppet-mistress, who poured slanderous bile and foul calumny in their ears about "poor Dr. Raine's dirty *black progeny*." No sooner did I reach the age of majority and begin to dare to speak my mind a little than she dropped her pleasant mask and told me she'd always known I'd prove more trouble than I was worth, like my harlot sister—that my *black ingratitude* revealed my proud *black heart.* I was almost relieved the maggot-pie said it to my face, what in the seventeen years since I washed up on these shores I've suspected so many English of thinking about the little Nabobina, the stranger that dwelleth with them, the tawny, swarthy, dusky, dingy Eliza Raine. *You must be mistaken,* Frances used to tell me in sweet reproach, but no, Frances, lovely, foolish, dead Frances, you were mistaken, because you couldn't bear to think ill of your pale kind.

Well, all the fallacious forgeries written against me,

my tormentors may roll up to scatter to the winds or wipe their arses with them. CARE DESPISED, say I—at last I succeed in laughing to scorn the goggling quizzers. Farewell and a fig to punctiliousness, prudery, propriety, primmery, and all. I speak the language of my foes at the top of my voice, having forgotten any other. I roar like a tigress and wallop when and whom I like.

As for you, Lister, my onetime all-in-all, I'll worship no longer. You're a ninny, or no, a Judas, for letting my enemies convince you to take their side. Hadn't you sworn to cleave to me through thick and thin? *Falser than vows made in wine.* Didn't I grapple you to my soul with hooks of steel, and don't I bear the seeping marks still? *One pillow, one purse;* the purse was mine, but you spent from it lavishly. I obeyed and served and honoured and kept, and forsook all others. At first I was your only one, but in the end I was only one of them. The lovely ladies of Yorkshire's better-bred circles, whom you might never have met without me. *Fortune favours the audacious,* and you were that, all right, a panting, rutting dog, leaping from one to the next—Maria Alexander, Isabella Norcliffe, Mariana Belcombe. You might as well have killed me instead of abandoning me so.

And these long years since, how you kept boasting of still and always being my most faithful friend; how you inveigled me into living on mere crumbs of love. The priggish preachments I've endured from you, urging me to rise early and eat little and spend less, when my greatest expense has been gifts showered on you thirty pounds at a time, you treacherous bloodsucker. *Rich and rare were the gems she wore,* and I wonder now whether you only prized me for my diamonds.

I've shaken the scales from my eyes. Once upon a time I set you up as a golden idol, but now I take a great hammer and smash you to pieces. My curse on you, Lister. If you were to knock at the door, I'll say, *No no no, I know no such person as yourself,* which is true enough—did I ever know you truly?

Well, I hereby cancel any tie between us. The will I made in your favour when I turned twenty-one—I've put it in the fire. If you still have our letters, burn them too.

Matron Clarkson's come in, she's making a grab for my pen, but I'll

OVER THE WALL, MAY 1806

OVER THE HOLIDAYS, from the Duffins' country house in Nun Monkton and the Listers' smallholding in the Wolds, Eliza and Lister have written every day, using bland words to mask their meanings in case others open their post. At Easter, when Mrs. Lister has a girl born still, who is buried with her infant brothers, what Lister sends is, *All I pray for is to be back in York.* Eliza tells her, *I think of our happy times last term with the most vivid and perfect recollection.* Lister turns fifteen, and even though Eliza is miserable about missing her birthday, her spirits are lifted by Lister's letter, which hints heavily, *May the next year bring me more of that new species of happiness I discovered for the first time in the last.*

May, now, at the Manor School, and the lovers are never more than an arm's length apart; each knows, without turning her head, exactly what the other's doing, and what expression is on her face.

With the new season, the pupils change back into lighter frocks and cotton stockings. The warmer weather seems to bring sniffles, red eyes, mild fevers. The youngest Percival girl has an irritating little cough that starts up as soon as lights are out, and keeps everyone in Mid Hall and its adjoining rooms awake; Eliza's glad their Slope is on the other side of the Manor.

The grounds are fragrant with blossom and musical with birdsong that has an urgency Eliza's never noticed before; feathered pairs fly back and forwards, shaping their nests. The inseparable swans have settled down in the reeds on the Manor Shore and harass anyone who comes near. Beetles cluster on clumps of tansy, which some call golden buttons. Sometimes Mr. Halfpenny can be persuaded to hold Drawing class al fresco among the ruins; he likes to point out where Henry the Eighth pulled down the medieval church, chapter house, and cloisters, keeping only the Abbot's house but renaming it the King's Manor to erase all trace of the poor monks.

With three shillings of Eliza's, Lister bribes the woodcarver's apprentice to make her a broadsword in rough pine, which she hides in a crook of a tree, and as "Captain Lister" she gives fencing lessons to the Middles, who are armed only with branches.

Nan, who was left at school for these last holidays, goes on so much about being *homesick* that Lister finally throws down her wooden sword. It stabs the long grass and stands upright, quivering. "This *home* for which you long—I take it you're thinking of your

Scarborough house as it was when your mother was alive, two years ago?"

Tears quiver in Nan's eye. "A year and a half."

Fanny rushes over to comfort her.

"Don't quibble about Nan's choice of words, as if you're setting up for a schoolmistress," Margaret tells Lister.

"Face facts, Nan," Lister says, merciless. "You've been supplanted by your father's young bride."

The tears plummet.

"What you miss is the past. *Inreparabile tempus,* Virgil calls it—*irretrievable time.* You're not homesick but past-sick, except there's no such word."

"Because if it's not in Anne Lister's lexicon," Margaret says with scorn, "it must not exist in any language."

Fanny slides her shorter arm around her friend. "Motherless. Won't that word do? Just like Frances and Eliza and me, and Margaret too. You're not alone, pet."

Nan lays her head on Fanny's shoulder and sobs.

On such days, when Lister's high-handedness irritates the other Middles, Eliza's aware of a strange gratification. She doesn't want her beloved to be too popular; she can't bear it when Lister chats confidingly with any other girl. This jealousy is new, for her. She's ashamed to find such depths of possessiveness in herself. Perhaps Eliza's always been like this but never had anything to fight for till now.

Passing outside Prinny's sty, she and Lister always steal a minute to greet the boar. Lister makes a sling of her hands, and Eliza wipes her shoe on the grass before stepping up. Clinging to the stone sill, she leans in. Then reports worriedly, "He's eating his straw."

Lister tuts. "A noisome habit."

"Or perhaps he's just moving it about with his mouth. He seems distressed."

"Distressed? He's a pig."

"Still."

Lister leaves Eliza's feet to dangle and leaps up unaided to hang from her elbows beside her. Prinny roams his dim chamber with a weird restlessness, nosing his bedding into a pile. He flops his bulk down.

"There you go, Your Royal Highness. Have a rest," Eliza croons.

But he's up and circling again. His curly tail twitches madly.

"We should tell the farmer he's ill," Lister's saying, when something drops to the floor behind the boar. Not dung, a pinkish thing on a string…

"Oh!" A piglet: hairless, thin, stunned.

"Not Prinny at all. Princess!" cries Eliza.

(Though the real Princess of Wales, she remembers belatedly, is a strumpet who's not allowed to see her only child.)

The sow rotates and sniffs her piglet. Eliza's staring straight at her rear, its pink glistening. Another furious lash of the tail. The rude hole opens like the pupil of an eye and a *face* surges out, small snout, shut eyes. Plop, a second new creature falls on the straw. Staggering away already, trailing its wet cord, the piglet trips, circles back on tiny, confused trotters. "Oh, Lister, it's entangled..."

But the flesh-string snaps and releases the newborn.

The sow shoves straw aside with her great head. "Look," Lister says, pointing, "one more she must have dropped before we came."

Eliza squints into the room. "No, two."

"Three!"

They're laughing. "And you, who reads whole books on farming."

"The authors never said how to tell a boar from a sow."

Both of them are going to get marks for being late, but Eliza feels she's never paid such close attention to anything in her life.

Some mornings before sunrise she wakes in a languorous haze, still almost paralysed by sleep, to find herself already halfway to bliss—Lister urgent, on top of her in a sweat, her soaked fur on Eliza's fur, riding and pestling...

Afterwards, catching her breath, Eliza treasures the sensation of her whole person having been taken, used, had hard. As the two of them get dressed, Lister begs pardon for not having so much as stopped to ask; not having had the decency to wake her beloved first; having been as greedy as a wild beast.

Eliza smiles lazily. "I'm yours," she reminds Lister, "waking or sleeping."

What she relishes most of all is the knowledge that this highly rational Solomon of the School turns cracked with desire at the first dawn glimpse (or murmur, aroma, stroke) of *the most beautiful girl I've ever seen.*

Their walks take them farther afield, now that summer's begun. The fields seem all at once full of livestock and herders—dogs driving red-marked sheep into streams for washing, and cattle released from their barns to graze.

Princess has a litter of nine, or at least that's how many Lister and Eliza have been able to spot in the straw; it's hard to count creatures that keep wriggling past their brothers and sisters to fight for a go on one of her teats. The next time the girls have a chance to visit Her Royal Highness, the pigherd is there, dosing the sow. Eliza tries to slip away, but Lister peppers him with questions.

Princess has an infection—yes, farrowing is a perilous business.

"I count only eight today," Lister says.

The man nods abstractedly. "Bit the runt, didn't she? It must have strayed too near her head. First-time sows scare easy."

"Will she die?" Lister wants to know.

"Nah, she's mending—should live to have many more litters."

"But this litter? What'll become of them?" Eliza asks.

"Master will sell them in July, except for a pair Miss Hargrave wants fattened for Christmas."

"We should go now." Eliza drops to the ground.

Running's forbidden, as much as being late, so they glide-scuttle along the path. "Did he really mean Princess killed her own piglet?"

Lister nods, frowning. "In her fever, in a panic. Like that girl hanged at the Castle for smothering her baby, I suppose."

But the cases are not so very alike, Eliza thinks, because the sow can't have been driven by shame. Human beings have invented so many new sources of pain.

* * *

Another day, she and Lister are walking along Coney Street, past the beggar Eliza thinks of as Mad Margery, who sits on the flagstone crooning a waltz:

Rich and rare were the gems she wore,
And a bright gold ring on her wand she bore,
But oh her beauty was far beyond
Her sparkling gems or snow-white wand.

Head down, Lister nearly walks into a donkey-cart; Eliza has to haul her out of the way. "What are you reading that engrosses you so?"

Lister puffs out her breath and taps the tiny print. "In Cheshire... the arrest of some two dozen members of a secret club."

Eliza waits.

"They seem a motley lot—a few gentlemen, some waiters, everything in between—a youth of seventeen and a greybeard of eighty-four. One is charged with *committing an unnatural crime on another,* and a third with *having suffered it to be committed upon him.*"

But how can you allow a crime to be committed against you? "I must confess I don't—"

"Buggery," Lister hisses.

Eliza gives a little shudder. She thought that was only sailors.

"It says here they all addressed each other as *brother*."

"Why is this agitating you so?"

"They'll all be executed," Lister mutters.

"I'm very sorry for it, but— "

"You're being rather stupid."

Eliza takes a step back.

"*Acts contrary to decency and good morals,*" Lister reads. "Might that not be said of us too?"

She's flabbergasted. To associate their beautiful nocturnal invention with what those men get up to in their sordid den— "It's not the same!"

"I know. We're only following our natures. I've never swerved from my earliest bent," Lister insists. "Whereas the other act... for one thing, it's specifically forbidden in Scripture."

"Well, then."

"But I doubt the world would see the distinction."

Eliza's dizzied by a sensation of being looked at from the outside, as if by an angry archangel in the clouds.

"If it were merely a selfish taking of pleasure... but between us, it's more a matter of giving." Lister sounds as if she's arguing with herself. "Love surely justifies it."

"Love justifies everything." (But Eliza's troubled by

the thought that those men, those *brothers* in Cheshire, might make the same claim.)

Lister seizes her hand and holds it as they walk.

Eliza feels an irrational impulse to pull it away before anyone notices.

"You're the chosen tenant of my heart," Lister tells her.

"Just the tenant?" Flippant, to lighten the moment. "That sounds temporary. As if I could be evicted."

"The occupier, then," Lister says. "No, the owner."

Eliza manages a smile.

"What's between us is a private marriage."

That does excite her. To be a wife... but to Lister. She tries out the word: "Husband."

Lister quivers. "You'd take me as your husband?"

Eliza doesn't have to pause to think. "Out of all the people in the world."

A sort of wedding, then? A private one, like Juliet and Romeo's. To make good on all Lister and Eliza have said in the dark; to make their union settled, and right, in the eyes of heaven.

The next Saturday the two of them ask permission to take a walk on their own. They hover on the porch of St. Olave's until they're quite sure it's empty. In they venture, down the nave that's so chilly all year round, with its grubby hangings. They kneel together in a pew, gripping each other's icy fingers. They're not wearing any special clothes, and of course there's no music, nor any minister or witnesses. But the church feels so old and holy, Eliza's almost sick with excitement.

What would Dr. Duffin think of her (not yet fifteen) taking such a solemn step as this marriage—vowing herself, for life, without his permission, without even his knowledge? Which is absurd, Eliza tells herself, because how could he give permission? This is something beyond the reach of her guardian's comprehension. He'd call it playacting, absurd, sacrilegious. Little he knows.

Lister picks up a worn copy of the Bible and whispers, "I wish I had a ring to give you in return for your diamond."

"It doesn't matter," Eliza says. "You've given me so much."

"But if I'm the husband, as it were..."

Eliza looks around in a sort of desperation. Here's a bit of straw on the flagstone. She snatches that up and coils it around her fingertip three times, twists it till the circle holds. "Will this do?"

"Yes." Lister has the diamond ring out, and swaps it for the straw, so each has one ready to put on the other's finger. *To bestow,* Eliza tells herself solemnly, *to endow.* Along with all their worldly goods, and their hearts, for ever and ever.

"Are we ready?"

She nods. They kneel face-to-face on the worn canvas hassock, their thighs almost touching, their hands clasped the way capsized sailors might cling to a spar. On Lister's mouth, Eliza smells the preserved apricots they had at lunch, and feels the awful irrevocability of what she's doing. Signing herself over, trusting Lister with her one life.

"For mutual help and comfort," Lister intones like a minister, "we two persons present now come to be joined and coupled together. Not unadvisedly, lightly, or wantonly, like brute beasts, but in the fear of God."

The fear of God. Eliza wonders whether they might be struck by lightning for adapting the marriage service to make it fit.

"Eliza Raine, wilt thou have me to be thy wedded husband, to live together, to obey and serve me, love, honour, and keep me, and forsaking all others, keep thee only unto me?"

The words rise in her throat. "I will." After a moment, she remembers to say: "Anne Lister, wilt thou have me to be thy wedded wife, to live together . . ." She loses the thread.

Lister takes it up fluently. "To love, honour, comfort, and keep in sickness and in health, and forsaking all others, keep only unto thee?" Then answers, in her own voice: "I will." She holds up the little loop of straw. "For better, for worse, for richer, for poorer, in sickness and in health, as long as we both shall live." She slides it onto the ring finger of Eliza's left hand. The straw catches at the knuckle, then locks into place.

Eliza repeats the line as she sets the diamond on Lister's finger.

"With this ring I thee wed."

"With this ring I thee wed."

"With my body I thee worship."

"With my body I thee worship."

Lister drops the formality and whispers in her ear like a kiss. "You're mine now, Raine."

"Yours, entirely."

"We're sealed."

"We're one."

That night they lie in a sweaty tangle, long after their taper's fizzled out. "I'm too happy. I may burst," Eliza whispers. "My pulse is going like a bell."

Lister puts her ear to Eliza's bosom, listens and chuckles under her breath. "I'm just as bad. I've never known such happiness in my life."

Now they're married, they're starting to build elaborate castles in the air. From this extraordinary present moment, they plot possible futures. "No one will be able to bar our way, once we're twenty-one," Lister insists. "The minute we're of age, we can join forces and sail off to the banks of the Arno."

Eliza feels like a leaf, sucked up by a breeze and whirling into the unknown. "Remind me, which one is the Arno?"

"In Italy, silly! It runs through Florence."

"But Boney?"

"Oh, the time we're speaking of is still more than six years off. The Enemy will be long defeated by then, and all roads will be open."

Six years: a yawning gulf. One of their Sunday lessons floats up in Eliza's mind: *So Jacob served seven years for Rachel: and they seemed but a few days, because of the greatness of his love.* If Eliza gives way to despair at the length of time she'll have to wait to live with Lister, it means she's doubting the *greatness* of their love. So instead, she asks, "What kind of house will we take, in Florence?"

"One with a study and a garden. We'll keep a horse and a light carriage. Partners for life," Lister murmurs.

"Beloved companions," Eliza adds.

"Sharing one pillow."

"And one purse." That gratifies Eliza, that her four thousand pounds, shared with her friend and lover and husband, will be the magic wand to work these wonders.

* * *

In class, Frances asks, "Monsieur, when the war ends—"

"Isn't it over yet?" Nan sounds querulous. "We don't seem to hear much about it."

"That's because we're losing," Margaret mutters. "Boney's just seized the throne of Italy."

Eliza gives Lister a worried glance.

"Only the northern Kingdom," Lister corrects Margaret, "and our Navy has the upper hand at sea."

"But when peace does come, sir, will you go home?" Frances asks the master.

His laugh is dry. "Unlikely, mademoiselle. My France... *elle n'existe plus.*"

Eliza's sorry for the man. Not just exiled from his mother country but alienated; unwilling to go back even if he were allowed, because his France is no more.

Fanny asks, "Oh, but why?"

Monsieur looks out the window at the azure sky over York. "A wise Greek once said, *On ne se baigne jamais deux fois dans le même fleuve.*"

"One doesn't bathe twice in the same river?" Nan puzzles over that. "I'm sure I've waded into the shallows of the Derwent a dozen times."

"It's a figure of speech," Mercy snaps.

"Every time you get in," Lister tells Nan, "it's different drops of water."

Nan shakes her head. "It's still the same river, though, just as I remember it. Same place, same cold, same wet, same smell..."

"*Allons, mesdemoiselles*. Back to our lesson."

One of the Seniors, Miss Simpson, is leaving early to be married, because her mother says a May wedding is *much the charmingest*. When Miss Hargrave expresses doubt about the wisdom of curtailing a young lady's education even by a few months, Miss Simpson goes around school sneering at the unmarried teachers as *a gaggle of pathetic Misses Teach'em,* obliged to support themselves because no man would have them.

Eliza knows what it's like to be transformed from schoolgirl to wife overnight, the beautiful shock of this metamorphosis. But she struggles to imagine also taking on the public duties of that role and running a household. Would it feel like ageing ten years in a blink?

The eldest Miss Parker, too, won't be returning after the summer, having turned nineteen. She's dreading the prospect of being the first of her family to have to leave the Manor.

"My aunt tells me your sister's not coming back either," the little Tate girl remarks to Eliza.

Who's about to contradict it—then has a qualm.

"Is it true?" she asks Jane, catching her in the passage before lunch.

An impatient shrug. "I'm almost seventeen."

"Not for months yet, you're not."

"Well, Duffin's given permission."

Given in to Jane's daily carping and wheedling, that must mean. "Do you really believe your education's complete?" Eliza doubts Jane's ability to reckon change from half a crown.

Her sister laughs in her face. "Child— "

Eliza's standing up for herself in a way that's new, since the secret wedding: "Don't call me that."

"Don't talk like a naif, then," Jane tells her. "Duffin had to stash us somewhere, didn't he? We were hardly sent to the Manor to be *educated*."

Eliza falters: "Finished, then."

Jane shakes her head: "To learn the rules of the game."

"So... do you mean to stay at home now?"

Her sister's eyebrows tilt. "Micklegate—do you call it that, *home*?"

Eliza can't say she does.

"I mean to try my luck in Pontefract."

"What's in Pontefract?"

Jane raises her eyes to heaven for patience. "Lady Crawfurd?"

Eliza's heard nothing of their cousin recently. "She's back in Yorkshire? You're going to pay her a visit?" She remembers the hippopotamus teeth.

A grimace. "Live with her and look about me, till I find something better."

"Find a husband, you mean."

It's a tease, but Jane doesn't deny it.

This seems a miserable plan to Eliza. "Pontefract—that's just a small town. It can't have more to offer than York, surely."

"But a baronet's wife will be able to introduce me in circles that a doctor can't."

"Even if she lives apart from her husband?"

Jane growls it: "I admit it, I'm scraping the barrel." Despite the warmth of the May day, she pulls her shawl so tight that her shoulders hunch. "I wouldn't mind a Company man who'd take me back to India."

Eliza stares. "Are you so fond of our mother country?"

"Perhaps I've just had enough of this bloody one."

The vulgarity makes Eliza blink. Somehow her stomach is tight at the thought of Jane going so very far away, repeating their endless voyage in reverse, putting oceans between the two of them, leaving her little sister behind (a doll-like figure on a small island, shrinking fast). "We speak of going to Italy someday," she blurts out. "Miss Lister and I."

Jane snorts. "That brat's all talk. Italy, forsooth! It might as well be Xanadu."

"It's as real a plan as yours," Eliza says between her teeth.

"No, it's not. As long as you're single you won't be able to lay hands on a penny of your inheritance for another six years." Then, with an impatient sort of kindness, "Get yourself a husband, I say. Then life can begin."

Eliza's madly tempted to say, *I have a husband. My life has begun.*

She goes looking for Lister, and finally discovers her in the courtyard under the wisteria, crooning to a pigeon.

O fare thee well, my little turtle dove,
And fare thee well for a while.

Lister's amused to hear of Jane's decision. "So your sister means to hand self and fortune on a plate to the first Company man passing through Pontefract?"

"It would seem so," Eliza says.

"But won't Dr. Duffin send any such fortune-hunter packing?"

"How can he, if Jane insists on offering herself as prey? She's never had much of a soul," Eliza adds, feeling less disloyal than regretful.

"Then she's no true sister of yours, my love."

Eliza doesn't repeat what Jane said about *get yourself a husband*. "Why couldn't nature have made you a boy?" She speaks flippantly so as not to hurt Lister's feelings. "Wouldn't that have been easier, all round?"

Lister surprises her by saying in a thoughtful tone, "I doubt it."

"But the freedoms you'd have had, as Sam and John's elder brother..." *Shibden Hall, very likely,* she thinks.

"I'd have gone to school with them, rather than to the Manor. I'd never have known you."

Eliza's mouth is dry at the very idea. "I suppose we might still have met, in society?" *Married, even—lawfully, openly?*

Lister shakes her head. "Met, perhaps, but only in passing. Men and women live so divided. No, all in all, I'd rather be with you as I am."

Standing at the mirror the next morning, Eliza's been trying to fix her curls, but Lister has her from behind and is pulling up her skirts. There's no time, they'll be late for breakfast, but it doesn't matter because pleasure makes its own time, a little bubble that floats in time, above time. Eliza's hands drop; her head sways and rolls back onto Lister's shoulder; her back arches.

Lister moves harder.

Eliza's legs heave and jolt and buckle. Glimpsing herself in the glass doubles the thrill. The peak of bliss comes closer, faster, like a thunderstorm…

But Lister stops moving.

Eliza can't bear delay. She seizes Lister's wet hand, presses and grinds on.

White, in the glass behind Eliza's own image, not the white of her frock or cap or Lister's, but farther back, in the gap of the slightly open door, the briefest flash of another white cap, dress, face—

Eliza freezes. A stone blocks her tongue.

The door shivers on its hinge. Steps hurrying away.

Lister whispers, "Was that—"

"Mercy." It sounds like a plea. "Mercy saw us."

Lister pulls away, spins around. Hauls up her hem to wipe her hand on her petticoat. "Are you sure?"

"I saw her face," Eliza groans.

"Hell! I trusted we were alone up here, with Cook and the servants gone down hours ago. I thought I heard steps, but—"

"I heard nothing," Eliza admits. "No warning, till I saw her, in the mirror."

Lister takes a long breath and gathers her forces. (Even through her terror, Eliza loves to watch her beloved's mind at work: a great complex machine, clicking and whirring.) "Listen, Mercy won't have the nous to understand what she saw. She may suspect, but—"

"We're ruined," Eliza contradicts her flatly.

"Shh," Lister orders. "Let's not be seen to miss breakfast."

In the refectory the two sit several places apart, absurdly, as if they've had a tiff. They keep up stilted conversation with their neighbours.

Sitting at the end of the table, Mercy seems to chew her roll with her usual stolidity.

Eliza's aware of Lister launching into a story from the *Herald* about a butcher who's to be hanged for having forged notes from the Swann bank. On Eliza's other side, Margaret and Frances are discussing the rules of mourning dress. Eliza tells herself to make some show of taking part in the conversation. "Are we talking about a particular deceased?"

"A particular deceased?" Margaret echoes.

Only then does Eliza notice that the atmosphere is peculiar; that the Juniors' tables are gappy and several girls have their heads down, whimpering. "Do excuse me, I don't know—"

"Didn't Mrs. Tate send Mercy around first thing this morning, with the news?" Frances asks.

Mercy the Merciless. Eliza's heart is banging like a gong. "What news?"

Margaret whispers, "The littlest Percival."

The cough that wouldn't mend. "No!"

"It happened in the night." Frances's eyes are brimming.

"The poor child." Eliza tries to remember whether she ever exchanged a word with the youngest Percival. To think of your life ending at school, before you ever emerged into the wider world; snuffed out in the chrysalis.

"She's to be buried at St. Cuthbert's, where their father's the minister."

The four other Percivals are missing, Eliza can see now, rushed off to be measured for their black crepe. "Will the sisters go to the funeral?"

Frances shakes her head. "Only their menfolk. The *delicate sensibilities of girls,* and so forth." She sounds unlike herself, almost sardonic.

"Did Mercy not go up to your garret, then?" Head tilted to one side, Margaret seems to be considering Eliza with more than her usual sharpness.

Mercy, sitting there a few feet away, would be the type to loudly insist on having done her duty and gone to every bedroom in the Manor. Maybe now is when she'll denounce the lovers, this very moment.

All Eliza can muster is a stagey yawn. "I did hear someone gabble something at the door, but I was half-asleep." She keeps her eyes away from Mercy and prays the girl will let this pass.

Mrs. Tate orders the rows of pupils to be quiet, and the Head stands and begins to preach in a low, shaking voice: "From the vicissitudes of the world, my children, we learn the uncertainty of life and the certainty of death."

All morning Eliza finds herself avoiding Lister's gaze, and Mercy's too. Which is absurd, because if Lister's right and their classmate's not sure what she glimpsed, having no way of fitting it into her strictly ordered mind, then their best hope for carrying it off is to behave quite as usual.

At lunch, the lovers meet under the alders. "Perhaps Mercy ran straight back to Mrs. Tate this morning. Or Miss Hargrave." Eliza writhes at the thought.

"But we haven't been summoned to the parlour," Lister argues.

"They might be considering what to do." It's no ordinary offence. "Or the Head could be writing to your parents right now, and the Duffins."

"To the devil with them all."

"Lister!"

"If we're to be accused, we should at least have the chance to defend ourselves." She speaks as if they're innocent.

"Defend ourselves how?"

Lister flails, which is a rare sight. "There's no proof."

"But Mercy *saw*—"

Lister attempts a haughty speech: "Miss Smith may imagine she glimpsed something in a mirror, which only testifies to her own impurity of mind. A girl of such low origins, growing up in the foulest alleys—no doubt she's seen filthy things."

This takes Eliza's breath away. A new side of Lister: the hunter, the warrior, no holds barred. "That won't work. The Smiths are known to be the most upright—"

Lister cuts in: "Religious zealots. Delusional, fancying exotic vice where none exists."

Unable to speak, Eliza shakes her head.

In Lister's own honest voice again: "I love you, Raine. I will *not* be the means of your destruction."

"You're prepared to look the Head in the eye and lie?"

"Gladly."

"Then I'll do the same." Though Eliza doubts her own powers of deception.

All week, the two of them don't touch. By day, dread binds their arms to their sides, in case they're seen, heard, suspected. Even at night, they lie as still as marble Crusaders in their separate narrow cots, in case one of these mornings they have to stand in Miss Hargrave's parlour and say, *No, never, how could, I don't, what could you possibly mean?*

The sun pries their eyes open before four. They lie listening to each other's ragged breath. Lister whispers, "Are you ashamed?"

Eliza, too shrill: "What?"

"Be frank with me. Is yours a coward love?"

"How dare you?" Eliza says, instead of yes or no.

"Come here, then."

Eliza does, of course she does, hurries to Lister's bed. Two steps, and the border's crossed.

Their touching's not the same now. How could it be? So fraught with a deep-down shuddering at the thought of being exposed, misunderstood, laid bare. From now on, will the two of them always be looking over their shoulders, listening out for footsteps?

When they go to Italy together, Eliza decides, they will have a room that locks from the inside.

It's not the same, no; she finds it's sharper than ever, fiercer, more precious. Eliza knows what they're risking and why they're risking it. How far they'd go to keep this. They touch each other as if they have no skin.

"It's been a whole week," Lister murmurs into Eliza's neck, after. "I don't believe Mercy's told. We'd have heard something. Has she spoken to you? Any hinting looks?"

"No."

"Nor to me. Perhaps she's not sure of what she saw."

Eliza doesn't believe that. She remembers all too well

how her own body was lashing about in the mirror, signs surely unmistakeable even to a strictly raised girl who's never seen or read or heard about such things. "She must have decided to hold her tongue."

"But why? To keep such a secret—to forgo the chance to inform the proprietors—"

Eliza shakes her head. "Nobody rewards a messenger who brings such news." She sees now that the sisters would be appalled if such a story landed at their feet, like a sack of stinking innards from the Shambles. The shame of having to acknowledge what they'd have to call *vice* in their school, like mould in a basket of shining fruit. The awful necessity of expelling two girls at thirty guineas a year plus extras each, and on such grounds.

"Mercy the Merciful," Lister breathes, like a prayer.

They'll never be able to ask their classmate her reasons, Eliza realises. All they can do is accept the unexpected grace of Mercy's silence.

On Saturday, the whole school crowds into the refectory for Judgement and Consequences. Who'll be barred out this time, debelted, or disgraced? The pupils' current besetting faults, as observed by Miss Hargrave and her sister, are *tale-bearing, lassitude,* and *wool-gathering*. The Vanity Mask, Fool's Hat, Liar's

Tongue, Ass's Ears, and Quarreller's Sash lie on the mistresses' table in case they'll be needed. The line forms: Seniors, Middles, then Juniors.

But Jane and Hetty are lingering at the back of the refectory, Eliza notices. Surely they can't be refusing to queue up?

"Any marks?" Mrs. Tate asks the eldest Miss Parker, the one who's drifting around the Manor in a haze of valedictory fondness.

"No, madam."

"Any merits?"

"One, for courtesy."

Eliza throws another glance over her shoulder. Hetty's bent over, clutching her back as if she's been kicked by a horse. Jane's tugging her pal's elbow, trying to pull her towards the door.

"The treat this week will be gravy," Mrs. Tate announces.

A terrible, guttural groan escapes from Hetty. She's quite doubled over now. Jane has her under the arms, to keep her from collapsing.

"Miss Marr! Are you not well?"

As Hetty straightens up and arches with a roar of pain, the bulge of her belly stands out against the thin white cloth.

Eliza blinks, unable to make sense of it.

Miss Hargrave's saintly expression turns aghast. Whispers are filling the refectory; gasps, even titters.

It's Jane's face that breaks the news about what's happening to Hetty: Jane's appalled but unsurprised face.

After Hetty's been taken away—moaning and thrashing in some kind of invalid chair on wheels—the school can talk of nothing else.

Over the next few days, information (or, put another way, speculation) trickles in: it's said that the infant has been born alive, perhaps very scrawny, perhaps of a wonderful size; that the Marrs are keeping their fallen daughter shut up, on bread and water; that, on the contrary, they've barred the door to Hetty and she's had to beg for refuge at the County Hospital on Monkgate; that she's named her debaucher as an army officer, an eminent merchant, a tailor, a carpenter's apprentice, or has refused to name any father at all.

The first day Eliza catches sight of Jane, crossing the courtyard, she hurries up to her and begins a question with "Your friend..."

Jane turns on her. "I knew nothing."

Eliza supposes Jane has been interrogated over and

over by Miss Hargrave and Mrs. Tate. Isn't it the very definition of friendship, to keep such a secret?

Her sister steps closer and says, iron-cold, "It's none of my affair."

Left alone in the courtyard, Eliza finds herself thinking again that school is not a rehearsal for life's play. Not for Hetty, nor for Eliza and Lister, nor any of them. It's the first act of the piece, performed once only. It comes to Eliza that she'll be reliving these brief days for the rest of her life.

The following week, posters are nailed up all over town for the Race Ball, which is to be—doubling the glamour—a masquerade.

"I've been racking my brains to come up with a scheme," Lister tells Eliza one night in the dark.

"What sort of scheme?"

"You *shall* go to the ball, Cinderella."

"Don't talk nonsense."

Having so narrowly escaped disaster, these days since Mercy glimpsed them, Lister is more hectic and daring than ever. "I mean that you and I will watch it through a window."

"What window?" Eliza wants to know. "Even from the Manor's east range, we'd barely be able to glimpse the carriages drawing up."

"No, I mean a window of the Assembly Rooms," Lister says. "You and I will be in the lane, peeping in, seeing everything."

"How on earth—"

"Trust me, Raine."

What other choice has Eliza? At this late stage, the only answer is *yes*.

So on the Saturday evening, the two of them ready themselves for bed as usual, as far as appearances go. "*Audentis fortuna iuvat,*" Lister teaches Eliza out of her Virgil. "*Fortune favours the audacious.*"

"Say it again?"

"*Audentis fortuna iuvat.*"

The third time, Eliza pronounces it with her, correctly enough.

But after Mrs. Tate takes their lantern at nine on the dot, Lister brings out their hidden taper and they strip off their night shifts. Underneath they have on their Sunday best. Eliza's insisted on lending Lister one of her snow-white muslin frocks, and an unstained pair of sharp-pointed, stencilled silk pumps, only slightly too big for her.

"Follow me," Lister breathes in the passage. "If we happen on a maid or a teacher, freeze. Should anyone call out . . . well, we'll flee back up here, I suppose, and throw ourselves under the covers."

Eliza trembles at the thought. She picks her way after Lister through the maze of the Manor.

The door into the courtyard is locked, so Lister turns aside and leads her through two of the tenants' deserted workshops, testing every window on the outside of the building. After a couple of rooms in a semi-derelict condition—what little furniture's left is draped in dust sheets—she finds one window a little ajar and whispers, "Victory!"

Eliza clambers through after her. Down onto the rough grass.

It's so lovely out there in the dark that Eliza's dread lifts. They canter across the turf, careful to avoid any cowpats that catch the starlight. Lister loses one of her loose shoes and has to hop back for it. Never mind the Race Ball; Eliza would be happy to stay out here, playing Hide and Go Seek among the mossy ruins. "The front gate's sure to be bolted," she hisses.

"But they never bother locking the back one, even at night." Lister leads her the other way, towards the river, where the door in the wall does in fact swing open, letting them through to the Manor Shore.

From there it's an easy run around the massive bulwark of Lendal Tower and St. Maurice's Church, then a quick right on Blake Street. The Assembly Rooms hum with noise, and are lit up so blazingly, the alley beside seems plunged in blackness. Lister dips into it, and Eliza rushes after.

Lister's up on her toes with her chin on a sill, trying to see into the ball. She moves down to the next.

Eliza objects, "Won't the dancing be at the front?"

At a third window, Lister says, "Aha—the room where they leave their coats and cloaks."

Eliza jumps as a door scrapes open and a pair explode out—a liveried youth and a red-faced parlourmaid. She pulls back, but the couple don't look the girls' way; already kissing, they break off to scuttle farther down the alley, away from the street and the light. They've left the door hanging ajar. Staring after them, it comes to Eliza that the footman and the maid are going to do—*it,* something like what she and Lister have invented in the privacy of their attic. The couple are following an urge equally desperate, so urgent that they'll make do with a noisome wall in an alley.

But now Lister has Eliza by the hand and is tugging her towards the open door.

"What are you—"

Lister whoops it: *"Audentis fortuna iuvat!"*

"Are you mad?"

"My darling girl, the worst they can do is throw us out."

Eliza goes hot in the face. To be ejected as mannerless schoolchildren from the Assembly Rooms—

But Lister's hand is hard, relentless, tugging her

through the door, into a narrow passage. Lister turns sharply left and they're in an empty room hung with outer garments on pegs, scarves and shawls draped everywhere. Pieces of costumery too, cumbersome headdresses and feathered masks that their overheated owners must have already shed. Paper labels hang from some items, but there are also quaking piles on two tables, several stylish silk top hats and flattened bicornes with cockades spilling onto the floor, as well as canes, a few swords on belts, even... How do any guests find their own things again?

Lister's snatching up an armful of crumpled cloth that proves to be two black cloaks with white domino masks sewn in. She throws one over Eliza before Eliza can say a word. Blindness, then light, askew; Eliza straightens the cloth and blinks out the little holes. Is that herself she's glimpsing in a mirror? No, Lister, unrecognizably identical now, Eliza's wicked twin. The two of them cackle and hoot.

A footman marches in, laden with cloaks, and recoils—

The girls stand like statues.

"Beg your pardon, madam—misses—"

Somehow the trick's worked.

Lister sweeps past the footman without a word, her masked face tilted away. Eliza hurries after and nearly trips over the hem of her frock.

Down the passage, which is hazed with smoke from men's pipes. Eliza's turning her head, trying to take it all in. A Harlequin, several dairymaids, sailors, some kind of witch or hag, a great muscled nun with a beard, a woman in baggy trousers under a glittering smock. An extraordinary mask turns out to be half Belle, half Beast.

Lister pulls up, and Eliza bumps into her sharp shoulder blades. "Thirsty?"

Eliza's afraid they'll be found out as interlopers if anyone looks at them up close, but she is dry-mouthed, from the running and the fear and excitement. And if they're risking so much for this adventure, she supposes they should enjoy it. "Vastly."

So Lister plunges into the Refreshments Room, her narrow frame ducking between the real guests. Eliza hovers in the passage, then decides it only draws more attention to her, so she forces herself into the room, which is round, with curved niches and a bulging frieze, a dome rising to an octagonal lantern. She tries to move, if not with Lister's confidence then at least with the air of possessing a ticket and having every right to be here. A boar's head in brawn, grimacing. A swan swimming on jelly, already half-eaten, its alarming ribs laid bare. As Eliza approaches the laden tables, a domino costume to her left holds out a cup with no saucer, making her jerk.

"It's me!" the domino says in Lister's deep voice.

Eliza accepts the drink and puts it to the slit in her mask. It dribbles and burns sweetly and lemonly as it goes down. "Punch?" she gasps.

"I'm on my second."

Dutch courage: her whole insides feel the glow.

"Can I help you to a biscuit?" Lister asks genteelly, striking a pose. "An ice? Syllabub, soup?"

Eliza laughs and shakes her head at the thought of trying to drink soup through her mask.

"Then come on."

"Where?"

"It's time to dance."

"Lister, no!"

"We've come this far..."

Eliza stumbles after. They only have to follow the music through an assembly room where people sit playing cards, then a narrow vestibule, and finally the Great Hall.

It's long and massive, with dozens of marble columns in Egyptian style that go up so high, Eliza can barely make out the ceiling's elaborate cornices. Dark staining in one corner, from a fire. She looks up at the dazzling candelabra and remembers the figure of two hundred and thirty-four wax candles. What if one fell into somebody's hat—would it start a conflagration? Such a crowd! Hundreds of masked revellers. A false beard that looks as if it's made of a cat. A tartaned Highlander, a robed Mandarin, a chimney sweep. Turbans, gold veils; one woman's embroidered gauzes, sashes, and bangles remind Eliza of her mother.

At the far end, musicians are tucked behind potted shrubs: Eliza recognises a pianoforte, a cornet, a harp, and a violin, or is it a cello? The fellow at the end is playing a whistle with one hand and slapping a little dangling drum with the other. Flags decorate the walls: England, Scotland, Ireland, and other possessions of the King's. The Great Hall smells honeyed, like a hive; wax from the floor, probably polished that morning, and now warmed by all the soles and heels rubbing and spinning.

The minuet ends and a more raucous country-dance begins. Lister pulls her into the set. Eliza's already sweating behind her mask. Men promenade with partners on their arms, some barely masked, little bejewelled half-masks held up on long sticks. Breathless, hot, she wants to rip off this domino and yet she never wants to take it off because the musicians are playing a reel now, wild and raucous. Snapped fingers, the odd yowl. Hop, jump, skip, clap. A tall, spurred boot catches on a gauzy drape and rips it. A woman crashes into Eliza and her bracelet scratches Eliza's arm. There's molten wax spattered on Lister's black-clothed head—from the crystal candelabra overhead, Eliza realises.

A bare face, in Eliza's. A footman, who rattles off, "The Master of Ceremonies' compliments, and might he have the honour of making your acquaintance, ladies."

Eliza's speechless. She and Lister have been smoked out.

"At your *earliest* convenience."

"We're just leaving," Lister tells him winningly.

The footman frowns. "If you'd like to come this way, the Master— "

Instead Lister grabs Eliza's arm and dives through the dancing couples, and Eliza lets herself be pulled along as if she's floating downriver, through the rapids. At the mouth of the passage she glances over her shoulder and sees the dancers have closed up after them like the waters.

At the door into the alley, the two of them throw down their dominos and run.

Out on Blake Street, bare to the cooling night air, Lister nearly crashes into a watchman with his staff and lantern; only the clatter of his rattle alerts her in time to swerve. They nip into Lop Lane and come out at the precinct of the glorious Minster. Left is Bootham Bar, and once past that they can see the ancient chimneys of King's Manor emblazoned by the light of the risen moon.

"It seems absurd to go all the way down to the Shore

in the dark," Lister says, panting. "Don't you think we might manage the front wall?"

Eliza would much rather not. But why should she be the pricker of bubbles? "I'll go first, if you'll give me a hand up."

Lister drops to one knee by the wall to make a step.

Eliza does her best to wipe her silk shoes on the grass before she climbs onto Lister's thigh. She fits her other foot into a hole between the stones and pushes up on them. She's not willing to fail in front of her fearless beloved. She reaches for the rounded top of the wall and grasps it. "Push?"

Lister's hands under her, shoving so hard Eliza manages to throw one leg over the top of the wall.

"All right?"

She's scraped her thigh a little, but she's straddling the wall now. "All right."

"Can you see a soft spot to land?"

"First let's get you up."

Lister waves away her offered hand. "Drop down. I'll be right behind you."

"Just let me pull you up before I— "

"No, then we might both topple."

Deep voices going by; a top hat and a bicorne. Horrified at the prospect of being seen, Eliza swings her legs to the Manor side and peers down into the soft darkness. It looks like grass, at least. She takes a breath and launches herself.

She's crashed into a bush, a little prickly, but she's all right. She brushes leaves off her skirts and peers up.

Lister's head pops up over the edge. Teeth catching the moonlight. "Ahoy!"

Eliza waves back.

Lister pushes herself up on her hands and gets her feet under her.

"Come down."

But she crouches on the rounded stonework like a merry frog or a gargoyle. "I've never seen the Manor from such a vantage point." She twists to look over her shoulder. "Nor the city."

"Come."

"Oh, my lovely Raine, what a night."

"Hurry!"

"Look at me. I'm the Emperor of Eboracum, Chieftain of Eoforwic, Commander of Jorvik, Lord Mayor of York!"

Eliza's still laughing when Lister rears up cock-a-hoop to her full height, striking a heroic pose, but the flounce of Lister's frock is caught under her borrowed shoe and skews her sideways so she falls, flailing through the air. She hits the grass with a sickening crunch.

Eliza tries to get her up at once, but finds Lister can't put any weight on her leg. Lister crumples, she yelps, making sounds Eliza's never heard from her. "Leave me. Find that window at the back where we got out," she orders in gasps. "Run upstairs and get into bed. In the morning—"

"I'm not leaving you here all night!"

Lister subsides. "Well, once you're in nightclothes, then go and rouse Mrs. Tate. Say you woke and I was missing—you looked out a window and glimpsed me down on the lawn."

"Don't be ridiculous. Which window in our north wing could I possibly have seen—"

"Say you ran around the school looking out all the windows."

"That sounds quite mad."

"Do it! Now!"

Almost afraid of Lister, Eliza backs away. She tiptoes around the irregular perimeter of the Manor, half sobbing with frustration. She finds the open window and gets in somehow.

Upstairs. In the Slope, she strips off and throws on a night shift. Pulls on a nightcap and shoves her front curls into it. She dashes past the box room to the door behind which the four maids sleep, and hammers on the door to wake them.

A night of chaos and recriminations. Lister's carried upstairs, face crinkled with pain, spouting her absurd tale about sleepwalking and tripping over a rock. She's dosed with laudanum. Eliza lies on her own bed, insomniac, listening out for Lister's ragged breaths.

When Dr. Mather comes into the Slope, before dawn, Eliza begs to stay while he examines Lister's awful calf, purple and swollen like a giant plum. As he presses and probes, Lister grips Eliza's hand very hard. The drug's made her pupils tiny.

"A very nasty break indeed, though none of the bone pieces has pierced the skin, thank heaven." The doctor unrolls a sticky bandage from a jar and wraps the shin tightly.

Lister hisses with pain. She speaks in the detached tone of an interested observer. "What's that stuff in the jar?"

"White of egg, vinegar, and wheat flour," Dr. Mather says as he daubs it on with his fingers, thickly covering the whole bandaged area. "It stiffens as it dries, and keeps the limb in good posture, without the dangers of tight binding."

She winks at Eliza grotesquely: "The heat of my leg should bake it into a Shrewsbury cake."

Eliza can't smile.

On top, Dr. Mather adds a curious device, a cylindrical cage of wood and leather that he adjusts and straps just below the knee and above the ankle. "You'll need to stay off this leg for three months, Miss Lister, and rest as much as possible."

Outraged: "Three *months*?"

"And rest as much as possible, to improve your chances of healing fully."

Her *chances*—so it's not a sure thing, Eliza deduces. And in the meantime, how on earth will Lister be able to get up and down all these stairs to lessons?

Whispers of girls in the passage outside; giggles, even.

"You're a popular young person," Dr. Mather murmurs as he packs up his bag.

Lister manages a grin.

"Your mishap seems to have put your schoolmates in a tizzy."

Does it count as a *mishap,* then, Eliza asks herself—pure bad luck? She and Lister are the only ones who know it was the kind of not-quite-accident that happens to a daredevil cavorting about on top of a wall. Then again, it could be argued that being born a daredevil was the first mishap in Lister's life.

"This is a very small world," Lister tells Dr. Mather. "Even the slightest stir makes a storm in a teacup."

When the doctor's out in the passage talking to Mrs. Tate, Eliza hovers by the door to eavesdrop.

"If there are any fragments floating about in there," he's saying, "there's a risk of a putrid infection, gangrene, amputation, or worse."

It only strikes Eliza now that a person could die of a broken leg.

Mrs. Tate's whispery voice is harder to make out. After a few minutes, she comes in, funereal, and addresses Lister: "My sister's writing to your parents."

"Don't send me away." Not a plea but a refusal.

"Our maids are too few, and have far too much to do already."

"I'll look after her," Eliza wails.

"Calm yourself, Miss Raine. Your education would not be well served by playing nurse to— "

"I don't care about my education."

A cold look from Mrs. Tate. "We each have duties proper to our station. Running up and down stairs with trays is not yours."

"Put me in that little storeroom by the kitchen," Lister proposes.

"Oh, you cause enough disruption already, Miss Lister. Besides, your people will want you home."

"I assure you, they won't," she growls. "Let me stay."

"I wouldn't have it on my conscience," Mrs. Tate says. "I've already hired a hack to take you all the way to Market Weighton, with your leg up on cushions to lessen the jolting."

Eliza feels her ribs cave in. Her sobs mount.

Mrs. Tate sighs. "Really, Miss Raine, considering you were fast asleep and suffered no injury—"

"It's the shock," Lister says.

Eliza weeps on.

Once the two of them are alone, and she's dried her face, she tries to pack Lister's trunk, following instructions. She breaks off so they can hold hands, palms sweaty with dread.

"So the die is cast, my darling wife," Lister says. "Dame Destiny means to part us a while, for her obscure amusement."

"Don't be witty," Eliza snaps, "not now."

"I'm sorry. But we must bend to the dictates of fate."

"You told me we make our own."

Lister's face twists. "Up to a point."

"But you *said*—"

"It was a figure of speech, Raine. We must be practical now. Bide our time, and plot our reunion. *Non si male nunc et olim sic erit.*"

Eliza doesn't ask.

"That's Horace," Lister says. *"Things may be bad but they will get better."*

So often in her fourteen years Eliza's been told to reconcile herself to partings, as if life is one long schooling in separation. "Do you promise to write?"

"Every day. Remember it's not even twenty miles,

and I'm sure to be back after the holidays. By the end of July, for the start of term, if I mend as fast as I'm expecting, or August at the very latest."

But Eliza can't believe the Listers will send their prodigal back.

"I'll get better in leaps and bounds," Lister insists. "I'll be doing handstands by September."

Oh, Eliza doesn't doubt her beloved's firm intentions, or her tough and skilful bones. But Fanny was so young when she fell on the cliff, and her arm never really mended. And there's another problem. "How will your parents think it worth the expense?"

"Merely because I got into a scrape here? I've been getting into scrapes since I was born," Lister reminds her with a laugh.

"What if they decide that fifteen is old enough to leave school?" Still not exactly *polished*. The Manor tried to mould Lister, and the Manor failed. "They must have guessed that you can teach yourself more out of books than you'll ever learn here." The weight on Eliza's chest won't shift; she gulps for air.

"But you know how persuasive I can be. And once I'm up and about again, my energies will wear them out."

"Face it, Lister, they can't afford the fees as it is." Money, filthy money. Eliza wishes she could break open her account at the bank and shower her beloved in gold.

Lister sounds oddly calm; maybe it's the laudanum. "You seem to view our happiness through a concave mirror. What exactly do you fear?"

"Losing you!"

"Impossible. We're not two people anymore," she tells Eliza. "I'd know your thoughts, even a thousand miles away. How can we be separated when our two souls are one?"

But that's just a story, one of Lister's thrilling stories. Eliza's tears start falling again and she can't catch them.

The Head's parlour. Eliza stands alone, eyes on the Turkish carpet.

"Miss Lister seems too sturdy for, ah, somnambulism." Miss Hargrave's dry lips have a chewed look about them.

Eliza shrugs as if she's equally bewildered by the incident.

In a whisper: "It seems far more likely to my sister and me that your roommate climbed out a ground-floor window *on purpose* to cavort in the grounds."

Eliza tries to make her eyes flare in shock. No mention of the ball—ah, so the Head, despite her agitated state, has no notion of the full extent of their crime.

A strained sigh. "While eccentric, Miss Lister does

come from one of our oldest county lines, and will always be respected. Yours, Miss Raine, is a peculiar position."

Eliza's lids squeeze shut. She knows; since she first came to this country, has she spent a day free of the burden of this knowledge?

"Your birth from an irregular union is no fault of your own, my dear," Miss Hargrave assures her, "but a stain it remains."

You're a bastard, Eliza translates. It's almost a relief to have it stated baldly at last.

"Your complexion, too, should be no bar but may, alas, prove one."

A brown bastard.

Eliza's voice comes out hoarse. "Will you be asking Dr. Duffin to withdraw me?"

The Head throws up her bony hands like a fan. "Not at all. I pledge my protection as long as you deserve it. I'm merely emphasising how important it is for you to linger in the safe harbour of the Manor School for as long as possible."

This woman means to be kind, Eliza tells herself.

Miss Hargrave shakes her head as if it's all too much to bear. "The sad fact is, you've been raised to marry into a certain class... of which many members will judge you ineligible."

Eliza swallows hard. She's been studying the wrong

book all along, memorising passages that won't be on the test.

"However," brightening, "the more exemplary your character and accomplishments, the heavier they should weigh in the scales, surely. The more likely that a gentleman of good family will consider you worth the risk."

The risk of sneering looks and comments about his bride? Or the more substantial risk of bringing little dusky children into the world, under a cold Northern sky? How many generations until they'd be washed white enough?

Eliza wrestles with herself; she won't cry.

The Head's mouth droops. "Though I do wonder if in the end you might not be better off returning to your native land, where your face and funds would surely attract an officer of some sort."

Rage, surging. These people taught Eliza to be English, scolded any trace of India out of her, and now they tell her to go back to where she came from?

The lovers' last half-hour in the Slope, where Eliza realises—totting up the dates—they've been cocooned for nine months. Dreaming away their time, never anticipating this rough birth.

Lister's cot is stripped now, as blank as an envelope. She's quoting Virgil again: "*Durate, et vosmet rebus servate secundis.* Which means, *Endure, and keep yourselves for better days.*"

Eliza asks mutinously: "When should I expect them, the better days?"

"Our confidence in our mutual attachment will shorten the time."

"Our *marriage.*"

"Indeed. We must be philosophers for a while."

There's no more wishful thinking about getting Lister's parents to send her back to school, Eliza notices. "How can you be so damnably stoical?"

"With considerable difficulty. Come, let's plan. You'll visit me for the holidays, as soon as the Manor breaks up at the end of June—and for every holiday after that. Think what those longed-for nights will be."

Eliza makes herself nod.

"Our letters will bring such relief," Lister promises. "We'll use a secret code so nobody else can read a word of them."

"What secret code?"

"We'll make one up! Numbers, mathematical symbols, bits of Latin . . . It'll be child's play." Lister goes on: "We'll learn the same songs and sing them at the same time. You'll conjure me up in dreams so vivid that it'll be as if I'm waiting in your sheets every night."

A tear shoots down Eliza's cheek.

Her lover leans in and catches it with her lips, then licks them. "What is it? Do you doubt me?"

It would seem a betrayal to say so.

"As soon as Dr. Duffin lets you leave school, we'll be free to be together."

"Be together, where?"

"I'll make it my mission to charm him into inviting me to Micklegate, or Nun Monkton. Or we might stay with my family—my parents hope to move into Halifax one of these days, which would be a step up from the farm."

None of this sounds real to Eliza.

"And once we're twenty-one," Lister says, "and you come into your funds—"

"Yes!" But Eliza shrinks at the thought of those unbridgeable six years.

"Time speeds up after childhood—everyone says so. It'll fly by. What's a few years to a lifetime, my love?" Lister pleads. "Once we're of age and the war's over, how can they stop us from going off to the banks of the Arno?"

There's no time to quarrel and reconcile, barely enough time to say goodbye. Instead of answering, Eliza looks around for a present. She empties her writing things out of her father's red donkey-skin case, and hands it over. "Think of me when you use this."

"Oh! I will."

"And you have my eye, in the locket?"

Lister pulls it out of the neck of her frock on its little chain. "A lock of your hair too?"

Eliza grabs her nail scissors. She chooses a piece at the nape of her neck. And then changes her mind, and lifts her hem, embarrassed but resolute.

Lister's eyes are wide.

Eliza hands her the scissors. Lister cuts a tiny curl, and puts it to her lips, inhales its fragrance. Eliza shakes down her skirts, straightens them.

Lister pries the eye drawing out of the locket and tucks the hair in behind it so no one else will ever know it's there.

But they've missed their chance for a last kiss because, with no warning, here come the housemaids for the trunk and bag. Two unfamiliar men wheel in an invalid chair, and the maids help Lister into it.

The lovers stare at each other, horrified. Is there no more time at all? Neither of them speaks a word of goodbye.

Then Lister's pushed off down the passage. Gone.

It comes to Eliza that she'd rather die than resume her old life without Lister, the bareness and hollowness of it.

Her bed is still strewn with pens, papers, banknotes. Seized by an impulse she hardly understands, she opens the slit to the right of her waist and shoves the whole mass of money down into her pocket. Wrenching open her drawer, she pulls the fat jewel-roll out of the bottom of the birdcage and stuffs it into the other pocket. Her dress is distorted now; she grabs her summer cape to wrap around herself. She catches herself in the looking glass: her swollen eyes and wild expression.

Eliza thunders along the passage. Halfway down the second staircase she catches up with the men, who're sweating under the weight of the invalid chair. Lister's clutching the arms, but she rides with a swaying dignity, as if on the back of an elephant. Something so princely about this nobody from the Wolds. Eliza's about to call to them to wait. But there's no sign of the maids, and she seizes her chance to give this impression that she is in charge. She orders hoarsely, "Let me go in front."

The men wait for her to squeeze by.

"Dearest—" Lister's eyes are startled, shiny, almost as if she's about to weep, though Eliza's never seen her weep.

Eliza says nothing, only holds doors open for the men as they push Lister along the corridor. She's preparing her argument for when she's stopped: *Miss Lister's in pain and needs a companion on the journey.* If Eliza's firm enough, there's a chance she'll prevail.

But the school is quiet—all the pupils are in class, and it seems no one is coming to see Lister off, no mistress, neither of the proprietors. So no one challenges Eliza at all. The men tote the invalid chair out the door, over the gravel of the driveway, to the waiting hack with its step folded down.

Lister says, "I can manage— "

But the burlier one scoops her up without a word and deposits her inside the carriage, with her plaster-cast leg propped up on the seat opposite. Lister bites down on a groan. Eliza hurries up the two steps and lands on the seat beside the foot in its lone, half-off sock.

Lister stares.

Eliza puts a finger to her lips.

The other man folds up the step and shuts the door while the first drags the empty chair away. Eliza doesn't trust her voice to thank them, so she makes do with a civil nod out the window.

The crack of the whip, and the horses move off. Eliza doesn't give the Manor so much as a parting glance.

"My darling, you'll be put in disgrace for a month for this!"

So Lister doesn't understand; she still believes this is a schoolgirl escapade. They're in under the shadow of Bootham Bar now, pushing into the heart of the town.

Eliza leans over and puts her hand on Lister's other knee. "Husband."

Lister's eyes light up at the word.

"Let's go now."

"Go where?"

"Go off, run off, together," Eliza says, "as we've planned."

Lister frowns.

She rushes on: "Not to Italy, of course, not yet. But somewhere." She hears her vague, childish tone. More firmly: "There must be so many places in Britain we could hide." Not *hide*—that sounds furtive. "Where we could be alone, I mean. Together. Like those Welsh cousins."

"Irish," Lister corrects her.

"We'll take lodgings in some city—" Trying not to think of the practical difficulties of nursing Lister; three months of bedrest; the risks of infection.

"Unaccompanied females of fifteen—fourteen, in your case? We'd never be allowed, Raine."

Why must Lister be at her most practical right now? Where's the harum-scarum madcap from the night of the ball? (Last night. Was that really only last night?)

Eliza recognises the ancient timbered frame of the Merchant Adventurers' Hall. That means they're on Fossgate, about to rattle over the narrow wooden bridge with the fish stalls. "We'd—we'll pass ourselves off as older," she argues, fumbling back into the future tense. "Seventeen, eighteen? In London, say, where there are a million people..."

"And how on earth would we manage for money?"

"I have some." Patting her distorted skirt. "And my jewels."

"Oh, my generous love! If we tried to pay for lodgings in pearls, I expect we'd be had up for robbery."

Eliza bites the inside of her cheek, hot-faced.

"I cherish you for this gallant offer," Lister assures her. "It's like something out of a romance."

"No, it's not."

"But even if we could pull off this marvellous trick, what would we do when your cash ran out? Who can live on love alone?"

Eliza wants to say, *I'd live with you in a coal cellar,* and she also wants to smack Lister's head against the side of the carriage.

Walmgate Bar rears up ahead, with its twin-towered, crenellated barbican, the city walls' last and strongest defence. They must have come a mile in less than five minutes. How fast everything can change; how easily a life can be discarded.

Lister grips Eliza's hand hard. "For two young ladies to elope from school—you must see it would mean ruin."

All Eliza can do is keep shaking her head.

"We'd be throwing away our reputations, dragging our names into the mud. Ingratitude, rebellion, rash folly, fraud, impurity, madness, even—the things that would be said of us! There'd be no coming back from this, Raine."

"I wouldn't want to come back!"

Just one more minute and the hack will be plunged into darkness, through the iron-studded oak doors and under the rusty portcullis, then out the far side, beyond the thick and ancient walls of York, into the light. Into a wide-open country.

But all at once Eliza feels her confidence draining away, like blood leaking from a secret wound. Lister's right, no doubt; isn't she always right? Cleverer than Eliza, more knowledgeable about the world, more sure of herself, more sure of everything.

Eliza believes she could still win this fight; Lister loves her too much to refuse her, or to force her out of this carriage. But she finds she loves Lister too much to carry on, to drag her away into a future that seems all at once obscured by fog. (Ignominy, shame, filth, hunger, worse?) *I will not be the means of your destruction.*

"Stop," she says. Too low for the driver to hear. "Stop!" She reaches up, half standing, and thumps the roof.

She feels the horses reined in, the wheels slow. She leans across and kisses Lister once, their mouths bumping hard enough to bruise as the hack comes to a halt. Eliza staggers, almost falls. Then she pushes the door open and jumps down before the driver can come around.

She slams the door shut and walks away before she

can lose her nerve, or did she lose her nerve already and is that why she's walking away? Her skirts are thick with paper, heavy with jewels, silver and gold. She spins around and throws one hand up, whether to signal *goodbye* or *wait* she hardly knows, as the horses move on and the wheels turn and the carriage bears her beloved away.

RAINE TO LISTER, 1815

Lister—

The red mist has cleared. I would apologise for the last words I sent except that I know you've read none of them.

I couldn't write yesterday as I was in the strait-dress, my sleeves crossed in front and tied behind. But today I kept my voice very soft, and begged for the loop instead. (This is a merciful invention of Matron's; the leather belt keeps my elbows by my sides so I can't lash out, but can draw or write, at least, rather than having to sit stewing in my thoughts.)

Oh, what a spectacle I am. A crazed calf, roped. Like the Dane, I assure you *I am but mad north-north-west*. There are days like this when I find myself able to preserve an unruffled demeanour. Others, when I can't help but burst out in what Matron calls my wild fits or paroxysms. (But why is it that when a respected man such as Duffin loses his temper and roars, no one accuses him of being deranged?) There are even occasional days when I wake up suffused with happiness, but Matron Clarkson frowns in concern and calls that mania.

Through all moods, I keep my secret somehow, Lister; I don't breathe your name. I can't bear to hear how the doctors would rewrite the story. How small they'd make it, or how sordid. *Overattachment to a female friend,* perhaps; an *unhealthy state of dependency;* the *fantastical and indecent delusions of spinsterhood.*

In the privacy of my skull, I remember every minute. How I caught love like a cold, at fourteen; or you did, and passed it to me; how it flared up between us. How we slept, rose, learned, played, ate, inseparable. I couldn't tell my own pulse from yours. We spilled ourselves like ink.

So roll me in your arms, my love,
And blow the candle out...

If only I could merge my phantom lineaments with that young Eliza's; warn her; ask her whether our schooldays shaped us once and for all, or only revealed our true underlying forms.

I only regret that I didn't let you etch my name on the classroom window and immortalise me in hard glass, which might last longer than paper; I wish our love were recorded in the annals of the world. Though it does say for all to see, on that window, if only they've wit to read it—

With this
Diamond I cut
this glass with
this face I kissed
a lass

I wonder, the pupils who've spotted that, these last nine years, what do they make of it?

You and I bestowed ourselves on each other in a ceremony that, if it wasn't valid, was no less earnestly meant.

O fare thee well, my little turtle dove,
And fare thee well for a while.

I thought we were sealed and one for ever. Was I gullible? Did you mean it then, even if you don't now? What I give, I don't, I can't take back. Was yours a coward love? Did you tell me lies—or is love a story a lover tells in all sincerity, before time gives it the lie?

Fare thee well the love I bear thee,
Hopeless yet shall true remain,
Never one I loved before thee,
Ne'er thy like shall see again.

I'm an automaton that winds itself up to write the same message over and over. A botched, severed Child of the Earth. I bathe in the same river, and it's never the same, and it never changes. Invisible hands spinning me around and around. *Here I bake, here I brew, here I make my wedding cake,* but I can't break through.

Matron Clarkson coming for my pen now. Too soon—

Whenever I'm allowed to write, Lister, I mean to continue this same letter. That way I can tell myself I'm not being thwarted, quite, only delayed. I feel the rage bubbling up in me like a poisonous gas, but I breathe it out through my nostrils and try to smile.

No loop holding my arms to my ribs this morning; I'm trusted with the full use of my limbs. Dr. Mather comes in to take tea with me.

He speaks of the long gestation of disease in such a case as mine. "It disguises itself as mere moodiness or eccentricity, Miss Raine—grows under the surface for years till it bursts out."

Does he believe it was there, hidden in me, when I was first under his care, as a girl, at the Manor? I don't ask. I shudder at the notion that the year we spent in the Slope—all I felt, when my heart first opened like a bud—could have been nothing but an early symptom.

I try to read Dr. Mather's jottings upside down; I make out *lucid interval* before he shuts the notebook. *Lucid interval:* is it in the Venerable Bede that life is compared to a small bird flying into a feasting hall that's all ablaze with light and heat, then out the other end, back into the dark?

"But I don't believe this is a mere interval." My voice as low and ladylike as I can manage. "I've been perfectly calm for several days. What if I have recovered my senses?"

"A happy possibility, indeed." He says it gently, gamely, almost as if he believes it. "Time will tell."

"If I'm lucid for a whole week, will that convince you and Dr. Belcombe?"

"My dear lady, the disorder has its seasons, and we must not relax our vigilance too quickly. A physician of the name of Latham gave evidence to the House of Commons about two young patients; he'd discharged them both as *of sound mind,* whereupon one had hanged herself, and the other had thrown herself into the river."

The story makes me flinch. "If I have a month of calm, then? Two months?"

Dr. Mather shifts in his chair. "A patient who hopes to earn her liberty by comporting herself sedately for a set period might manage it, but only by an immense and harmful effort of will."

Oh, so he thinks me a cold-blooded plotter, waiting to be released to rampage shrieking along the ramparts of York?

He fiddles with his teaspoon. "I'm troubled that your tone suggests my co-proprietor and I are conspiring to keep you here. This is what we mind-doctors call a *paranoea*—a delusion that sees malice where there is none."

I press my lips together hard. So the only way to show that my confinement is unnecessary is not to object to it? If I protest against my confinement, I only prove that I need to be confined?

But if it's true what Dr. Mather says about the mad being capable of a sustained performance of sanity, then I wonder how many people going about their business out there in the world may only be keeping their wildest impulses in check by means of such an *immense and harmful effort of will*. Like actors pretending with all their might, trapped in a play on which the curtain never comes down. And if one of them does manage to keep on the mask of a sane woman for her whole life, can she not be said to be sane enough, more or less, for all intents and purposes?

In case he reads my silence as sullenness, I gesture to offer him more tea.

But he's reaching for his cane, murmuring about having tired me.

"Not at all." I find I can't keep silent. "I'd lay money I'm at least as well as the general mass of humanity," I say through my teeth. "So why may I not go..."

I trail off. Go where?

The apartments you and I might have rented, Lister, in the storied city of Florence. Our castles in the air, all blown away like tufts of cloud. My past lodgings: dear Myrtle Grove on the Choultry Plain, little rooms I took in Halifax, Bristol, York. To think that I managed to live on my own, with only a maid, for years on end. A grown woman with a wide acquaintance, who enjoyed most days and endured others; bore the *slings and arrows* about as well as anyone. How did I lose that knack?

"Miss Raine?"

I blink at Dr. Mather.

His tone is respectful: "Where would you propose to go? Do you know of any situation in which you could be placed more safely and comfortably than here at Clifton House?"

If only I did.

Is that what it comes down to, then—a matter of accommo-dation? If I had a home, people to take me in, would Dr. Mather let me out this very day? Is it my single, solitary state that keeps me prisoner here? If I only had a family asking, begging for my release, my return, swearing they'd bear with me through all weathers. If I had someone, anyone in this wide world to love me.

A soft horror creeps over me now at the thought that the good doctors will never let me out. My protectors, my captors. They'll keep me here month after month with the best of intentions, year after year, for my own good, as my black hair starts to ashen; perhaps for the rest of my days.

Still calm, today.

I think back to the Manor, and those you and I knew. Since Miss Hargrave's death last year—of an apoplexy, I heard, brought on by shock when one of her pupils eloped—Eliza Ann Tate is now ruling over the School in her aunt's place. And of course our poor old dancing master, Mr. Tate, sank deeper and deeper into his melancholy, and came to his end in York Asylum. (Questions were asked in Parliament recently about the way the late Dr. Hunter treated his mad paupers, and how fast many of them died. I shake at the thought; I'm aware how much worse my conditions could be.)

As far as I know, Betty Foster and Nan Moorsom are still living at home. Including you and me, that's four of the eight Middles who are old maids still, though marriage was the sole profession for which we were raised. Only two wives: sensible Mercy Smith, and

Margaret Burn (now Mrs. Holmes), who's somehow ended up in Naples, as if she stole our dream of Italy. Then there are the two of us who are gone already. Poor Fanny Peirson only made it to seventeen before her lungs gave out. Lovely Frances Selby married a vicar and was taken at twenty in her first childbed, just like the mother who bore her.

Why am I still alive?

At times, this past year, I've thanked Matron Clarkson and the doctors for preserving my life. But my future seems one long blank, an endless path through fog. I remember too much, yet can't trust my memory. It distorts things, as if I'm looking through water.

Sometimes I even…

A crime and mortal sin to do it, a scandal to say it, a weakness even to think it. That seduced maid in the song you taught us, *who hanged herself one morning in her garters*. That nurse Meg: could she really have dropped little Fanny's hand and let herself plummet off the cliff at Whitby?

Well, nobody will read this. So let me write down that I sometimes find myself wishing I'd had resolution enough to end it all before I ever came to this.

A knock at the front door, this morning. (I'm scribbling this down while it's fresh in my mind, as proof, so I won't have to wonder, when I wake in the night, whether I dreamed this extraordinary meeting.) Matron Clarkson asking if by any chance I feel able for a visitor.

"What visitor?"

"Miss Lister."

At first I say nothing, in case it's a cruel trick by the doctors to test whether I'll fall into a frenzy.

Then heat rises up my neck, my cheeks. I long, absurdly, for a mirror, so I can see what I look like, what you'll see, when you set eyes on me.

When I come into the small parlour, there you are, oddly all in black like a gentleman on his travels. The air of a doer, a darer, your own master. Turning about, inspecting the room—always loath to waste an idle second, always making mental notes for your diary. Mariana's gold band still on your right hand, I notice.

"Raine! Miss Raine," you correct yourself. Then, "Eliza, if I may?"

My throat's stopped up. I'd prefer *Raine.*

"It's a great relief to see you look so well." Less certainly: "Are you well? You've put on some flesh. I've called on several—well, at least one previous occasion, but you weren't receiving. And of course I've had regular reports of you from the good doctors. All in all"—eyes running from corner to corner like mice—"this place seems a very well-ordered . . ."

The advertisements call it a *retreat.*

"...house," you finish.

From a distant room, a sudden wail. Your eyes narrow with panic.

I almost laugh. I find I can't bear chitchat. (The one advantage of being a lunatic is release from the rules of decorum.) "Have you been abroad yet? Seen the world?"

A disconcerted chuckle. You shake your head. "I still have great plans."

"You've not won distinction by your pen?"

"Not yet."

"Where are you living?"

"At Shibden Hall," you say. "Since poor Sam— "

It occurs to me that since you lost your last brother, this past year, your uncle must consider you next thing to a nephew. I'm curious: "Will you inherit?"

You don't prevaricate; you nod.

I suppose at this point your uncle knows you better than to fear you'll take a husband and leave the estate out of the family.

I ask, "Have you come to stay with your friends on Micklegate?" Meaning the Duffins; their names stick in my craw.

"No, as it happens—the Belcombes on Petergate," you say. "Mariana's been with me all spring and summer, and now we're paying her family a visit."

Pain like the kick of a horse, and I realise I've been

foolish enough, in the flush of surprise, to imagine you've come to York expressly to see me. Was this stroll out to Clifton even your idea, or Dr. Belcombe's suggestion? Less than a quarter of an hour's walk; barely a leg-stretch to you. Is Mariana passing an hour shopping, or waiting for you in crumpled, aromatic sheets?

"Oh, my dear girl," you murmur, with what I can only assume is compassion. "Still harping on that string—harking back?"

I could go for your throat, and blame it on a passing derangement.

But I only stare at you—your unbeautiful face, tight with guilt. I wish I could explain that time moves differently for those inside these walls; that all the days are confused and confounded; that the present is a waiting-room with only one window, facing back, offering a fixed view of the past, like the inerasable lines of a woodcut. I change the subject: "So you have your double prize."

You don't seem to follow.

"Shibden," I spell out, "*and* a wife."

Your face falls, and your voice drops to a husky whisper. "Not quite. Mariana's to marry soon."

I blink, startled. "A man, you mean?"

"A gentleman of fortune." Your mouth like a knot in

tree bark. "Needs must. It seems to us the only sensible solution. We'll pay each other long visits."

That little *us;* I'm almost touched that you don't want me to know that you've lost the game. I can't prevent myself from quoting in a sardonic tone what you said to me, in the carriage: *"Who can live on love alone?"*

You hear the echo, and wince. "But you, Raine, tell me, are you…" The tiny aspiration of *happy*. But instead of saying the word, you ask, very low, "Do they care for you well here?"

I could tell you that they feed me before I'm hungry; they wash me when they want me clean; they let me play my piano until one of the other patients complains; they only bind my elbows to my sides if I lash out. This is life in an institution. A soldier, a prisoner, a workhouse inmate, a nun, a patient, a pupil, a lunatic—must they not all necessarily obey, living at such close quarters like books on a shelf?

I say none of that, because I know now that you won't, can't, save me.

Your eyes brim. I've never seen you cry.

"Have you burned my letters?" Half hoping the answer will be no.

"Most of them, as soon as you asked it," you say, nodding. Then add, "Not all."

Oh, the sweet hurt of that.

You take your leave, assuring me you'll call again, next time you're in York.

A rainy day. This evening Matron Clarkson is letting me keep my pen as long as I like, as long as I'm quiet.

I look down on my whole course of life from an eagle's height. It's a sad story; if it happened to another girl, I'd weep for her.

Eighteen years—three-quarters of my twenty-four—since I was shipped away, India an ever-receding gauzy horizon behind me. School was my England and England was my school. From the start, my position was a peculiar one. I was studying the wrong books all along; I never quite learned the rules no matter how hard I studied them.

Eleven years since you first glimpsed me, at a mad-doctor's party, of all places. Ten since we first spoke, in the refectory at the Manor. An orphan with the hungriest of hearts, how could I have resisted you? Nine years since the two of us first touched. Diamond and straw. *Love is merely a madness,* as Rosalind warns. Nine since we were parted at Walmgate Bar as I stepped down from the hack and it rolled away.

Like Ophelia, *I was the more deceived,* stupidly slow to grasp my gradual bereavement. We both held on, but I held harder, longer, more desperately. Six years since the pair of us, at eighteen, made our début, at York's Assembly Rooms. (It wasn't half such bliss as three years earlier, was it, when we'd sneaked in wearing borrowed disguises?) From then on I lived on dwindling rations of your company, your letters, your attention. Four years since I settled in lodgings in Halifax, to be near you and your family—but you stayed away on one pretext or another, mostly with your Isabella. Little by little over the years, I lost you, like coins dropping one by one through a hole in my pocket.

Was it my fault—was I too fretful and moody, seeing dangers everywhere, in fact inviting them in? Was I too greedy, did I cling too tightly, like a child who treasures a chick so fervently she crushes it? Or was the break between us your fault—did you cast me off callously, or merely let me slip through carelessness? *Never one I loved before thee, Ne'er thy like shall see again.*

Three years since we came of age, grown women of twenty-one. We were finally free to run off to Italy together...except that the dream had dissipated. Somehow I made myself accept that I was no longer (if I'd ever been) your wife. With painful effort, in the end, I convinced myself it was my duty to give you up to Isabella...whereupon you turned around and offered yourself to our friend Mariana instead. So the more fool me.

Perhaps it was simply our fate? A common one. *Love kills time, time kills love.*

At twenty-four, I fear my tale is told. I played at ducks and drakes until all my stones were gone. Little by little my nest was torn apart. I walked through the wrong door and went astray. Drop by drop, I've drunk the whole salt sea.

After you, Lister, what had I left? I came into my money, but that was not enough to set me free. I waited. This England, my only country now. Fatherless, motherless, no home but this.

The wonder is that it was only last year that I quite lost my mind. Love may be a kind of madness, but it was the losing of love that made that first hairline crack in me. Not that I accuse you, Lister. After all, breakage can be blamed on the brittleness of the china as much as the rough handling. Isabella must have been so much stronger than me, since she survived you casting her off.

The year you and I were fourteen, we invented love. Strange to think that it was the beginning of the breaking of me, and the making of you. We were a pair of originals, as long as we were a pair. Perhaps the difference is that you embraced your singularity, and I cringed at mine. I might have stepped more lightly without that burden; perhaps I could have made a better go of a more ordinary life.

I keep reading my bundle of old letters; I taste them

as a doe browses, a berry here, a tender leaf there. On so many pages in indelible ink, proof that you once loved me. It only takes one kindling phrase to blow my dim embers into flames again. You called me your *first and dearest love*. I've never used such terms, because superlatives imply comparison, and for me there's only ever been you. I must warn you, not your Mariana, nor any other woman, will ever attach herself to you as strongly. As scenes of youth are impressed on the senses for ever, so the shock of first love leaves a hot thumbprint that nothing can match.

I confess to being tormented by what-ifs. If only you hadn't broken your leg, and we'd managed to stay together in our Slope...

Or if I'd insisted on leaving the Manor the day you did, stayed in the carriage at your side; cleaved to you and let nothing sever us...

If I hadn't brooded and worried, in the long years of absence...

If you hadn't flirted and lied...

If you'd been less giddy and I less jealous; if I'd been firmer and you tenderer.

Perhaps if we'd been allowed to stand up together in church and say before everyone, *I do*—

Hypotheticals, impossibilities. The dreams of youth rarely come to pass, I remind myself. We were not the first young lovers to fail at love in the end.

And I ask myself why the present tense is the only one that matters. Can't the past be a sort of present too, if I plunge into memory and swim like a fish? Since every moment is fleeting, gone as soon as noted, so perhaps past, present, and future are all thin slices of reality, all flickering, all equally (in some sense) true. If Celia and her Rosalind, though two centuries old and made of nothing but words, will never be dead as long as there are readers to open the play and let the girls escape together into the forest, then could it be that our love can live on, too, in the blood-brown trail of ink, as long as there are eyes to decipher it?

So I keep writing. Making my mark, staining the paper. I stroke the hushed weave and wonder what white stockings, what old shifts, were sold off and torn small to form this page. Rags of frocks I might have worn myself, or smallclothes that once wrapped your lean thighs. Bengali calicos and muslins, the cotton that drinks in the Indian sun, the English linen from drizzle-grown flax—all fabrics marry in the vat, in the end. Stirred, pounded, battered, and bladed into pulp, laid in flat sheets and slowly magicked into this paper. And Indian ink, made of lampblack and water, what's left after burning. Love has charred me. I lay my trace here and it smoulders on.

Your visit has done one thing, Lister—has proved that you haven't forgotten. Only please, don't remember me like this; call me to mind as I once was. Let me shine on, like a magic-lantern slide in your head. *Rich and rare were the gems she wore.* All I ask is for the memory of me to haunt you as you haunt me. Let our spirits touch and go on touching always, the way one page presses itself against the next.

E. R.
Sealed with my mark
Pensez à moi

AUTHOR'S NOTE

The history of Eliza Raine (1791–1860) is full of gaps and puzzles. She was born in Madras—now Chennai—on the southeast coast of India. Her father, William Raine, was a Scarborough-born head surgeon for the East India Company. Nothing is known of the name, age, family, ethnicity, or religion of the woman who lived with him for at least a dozen years (1788–1800). Both times he took a daughter to be baptised (Eliza on 14 July 1792), he put down "mother unknown," a customary euphemism to draw a veil over a partnership theoretically taboo but accepted in practise.

I've found just one reference in Eliza Raine's surviving letters to her being familiar, as a child, with "one of those very singular dialects of the East" (23 September 1812); one to her having "sprung from an illicit connection" (30 August 1812); one to her being a "lady of colour" (5 July 1811).

In 1797, at six and eight respectively, Eliza and her

sister, Jane, were sent to England. Also on board were their father's friend Colonel Cuppage with his six children, whose French-speaking ayah, Louisa, may have looked after the Raines as well as the Cuppages on the long voyage. We don't know where in England the Raine girls were between 1798 and 1803. Their father took furlough and sailed for home in 1800, but died on the voyage. His estate recorded payments to "Dr. Raine's woman" of twenty-four pounds a year, but she only outlived him by two. Eliza and Jane were left four thousand pounds each, payable on marriage or at the age of majority (twenty-one); the trustees were London bankers Thomas Coutts and Coutts Trotter, Raine's sister's daughter Lady Mary Crawfurd, and his Irish colleague and friend William Duffin.

The first document I've seen in the hand of Eliza Raine is a timetable and list of pupils and teachers she drew up, at twelve, at Miss Cameron's school in Tottenham, West London. It has York as her hometown, which suggests that by now Duffin and his Indian-born wife, Elizabeth Rule Duffin, were acting as the Raines' guardians. The Duffins seem to have taken the biracial heiress of another of his dead colleagues under their wing too: Hugh Montgomery's daughter Anna Maria Montgomery (b. 1784) gave her address as their country house at Nun Monkton when she married a York man called William James, and the couple would remain loyal friends to Jane and Eliza. (This is just one of many interesting connections unearthed for me by the outstanding genealogist San Ní Ríocáin.)

At some point in the second half of 1805, Eliza Raine drew up another list at Miss Hargrave's Manor School in York, where she was now a boarder and Jane a day girl. In a later letter she recorded that she'd first met Anne Lister on 2 August 1804, but not where. (I've imagined a first encounter at Dr. Hunter's, since Lister's aunt Anne was a close friend of his wife's, all the York doctors were acquainted, and the Hunters entertained a lot.) Lister and Raine only seem to have overlapped at the Manor School for about a year, when they were fourteen and fifteen.

Lister left the Manor School in the summer of 1806. (I've seen no evidence for the story that she was expelled from this or any of her previous schools.) The first known surviving entry in her diary was prompted, on 11 August 1806, by the end of a long visit from Raine to the Listers: "Eliza left us."

Raine became particularly attached to Lister's mother, Rebecca Battle Lister, and corresponded with her in the fond tones of an adopted daughter. She stayed at the Manor School for one more year, after which she and Lister spent stretches of time together at Lister's parents' in Halifax, and at the Duffins' in York and Nun Monkton.

By 1808, the lovers were using the Latin for happy, *felix,* as a cover word for sex. Given that they used the same secret "crypt hand" in parts of the diaries that Lister kept from 1806 on and Raine more briefly (July 1809 to November 1810), Raine may possibly have contributed something to the code's development, though its use of Greek and algebraic elements make it much more likely to be Lister's invention; Lister would use it for roughly one-sixth of her massive journal for the rest of her life.

When apart, the lovers wrote to each other constantly, not only by the post but via intermediaries, including Lister's parents and aunt Anne, Miss Hargrave and her family at the Manor School, and other teachers and friends, such as the Priestleys. They planned to "go off together" as soon as they came of age—probably to Italy. (Unless that was, or gradually became, more of a metaphor? Later Lister sometimes used the phrase "going to Italy" to mean consummation or a settled partnership.)

As for Jane Raine, she married an army officer called Henry Boulton and returned to India in 1808. When she came back two years later—without her husband, drinking heavily, and pregnant—she was a source of shame to her sister. (That 1810 pregnancy doesn't seem to have produced a child, but San Ní Ríocáin has discovered that in 1815 Jane did give birth to a son, named

Raine Boulton, who died at twenty-two months, with a burial address of Brunswick Square, the location of the Foundling Hospital.)

While waiting to "go off" with Lister, Raine studied French, history, geography, geometry, and botany; she wrote poems and songs and did a lot of sketching. Her letters referred civilly to the Duffins and their friend Mary Jane Marsh, who was part of the household by about 1809 and would become the doctor's second wife. (The notion that Elizabeth Duffin was an invalid, and Marsh her companion or a sort of governess to the Raine girls, seems based on a mistranscribed phrase in a letter.) Sometimes Raine lived away from the Duffins for long stretches—with her irritable cousin Lady Mary Crawfurd in Doncaster, and on her own (except for a maid) in Halifax and York—but had no permanent home.

Slowly Raine came to terms with the fact that Lister was never going to settle down with her. As early as 1808, Lister's eye was caught by the first in what would be a series of other women, Maria Alexander. Next and more seriously, from about 1810, Lister became involved with a mutual friend of hers and Eliza's, six years older, with rank and money: Isabella Norcliffe.

On the back of a note of Raine's to Lister on 27 November 1811, written after the letter had been through the post, is a poem about memory that could be by either of them, though its aching nostalgia sounds more like Raine to me:

Good night my friend may sweetest slumbers close
Thy wearied eyes in undisturbed repose
May watchful angels guard thy hallowed bed
And heavenly visions float around thy head
Long dreams of blissful happiness be thine
Long thought of her whom I adore be mine
Now sleep away with all thy shadowy train
For retrospection's fairy queen shall reign
'Tis she alone can every joy restore
Bid flowers revive that dyed to bloom no more
Snatch from oblivion's stream dead pleasure's ghost
Teach hope to promise what we value most
'Tis she alone when sorrow's faded form
Sighs in the wind and rides upon the storm
Bids the fast starting tear forget to flow
Dries up the spring and stems the course of woe.

By the time they came of age—the deadline for all their great plans—Raine had forced herself to accept that Isabella would be "the partner of your future years" (6 September 1812). But she stayed single-mindedly devoted to Lister and hinted that she would be glad to share a house with the couple. She made a will leaving Lister almost everything, and in the meantime continued to give her large sums out of her income of four hundred pounds per annum.

Starting adult life on her own seems to have knocked Raine off-balance. She had a wide acquaintance in the north of England, but some of her friendships (e.g., with Miss Marsh's sister Mrs. Greenup) went sour, and there are hints that Lister's family began to resent her presence, perhaps suspecting her of trying to marry Sam. She ruffled feathers by how she spent her money, for instance when she had tables inlaid with her coat of arms. But she also panicked about debts and deferred to Lister and her former guardian Duffin on matters financial and practical.

Courted by a local navy captain, John Alexander (Maria's younger brother), Raine enraged him and his friends by pulling back on the grounds of her prior commitment to Lister. Likely in a vain attempt to spur her beloved to jealousy, Raine confessed to her that she was actually in love with his oblivious friend Lieutenant John William Montagu. John Alexander would seem to have been a viable suitor, but William Duffin (who assumed he'd sexually seduced Raine) sent him packing. After trying the experiment for her health of a milder winter in Hot Wells, Bristol—where she found herself miserably isolated—Raine concluded that she'd have to live in or around York, for lack of connections anywhere else.

Retrospective diagnosis is a fool's game, but in some of her surviving correspondence from as early as 1810, we can read hints of mental trouble: dramatic quarrels and reconciliations, self-denigration, delusions of grandeur, paranoia, mania, depression, and suicidal thoughts. Equally, as late as the second half of 1814, Raine often sounds rational, mature, independent, and cheerful.

When Lister fell for their and Isabella's friend Mariana Belcombe, by about 1813, Raine had trouble hiding her bitterness, since the new passion seemed to make a mockery of her having nobly given up Lister to Isabella. Of the constant flow of letters between Raine and Lister, starting in 1806, that came to an end in 1814, fewer than a hundred survive—mostly Raine's to her "darling husband," rather than vice versa, for the simple reason that the papers that ended up with Lister (apart from the "school letters" she burned at Raine's request) were carefully preserved for the next two centuries, whereas almost everything in Raine's possession would be lost.

Raine's life fell apart when she was twenty-three. The crisis was prompted by Jane turning up again in a helpless state, and Eliza—instead of turning to Duffin—taking the initiative in bringing her sister to their old friends Anna Maria and William James in the capital, and consulting a doctor about whether Jane should be committed to an asylum. The what-if moment I find most tantalising is in September 1814, when Eliza left Jane in lodgings in London, and got an invitation from the Jameses to come to the seaside with them… but instead she insisted on going back to York. There, partly prompted by the quarrel over her handling of Jane, and partly by her feelings of being neglected in the Micklegate household, she broke with the Duffins and Mary Jane Marsh, telling them that she'd stifled her resentment of them for years.

At this point a series of letters from Marsh to Lister denounced "black" Raine, a ruthless snob and social climber, for her "black heart" and "black blood." This vicious prejudice is revealed nowhere else in the writings of their circle, who shared Raine's unspoken policy of not mentioning her colour any more than her illegitimacy. Lister's diaries of the time are missing (probably burned at Mariana's wish), and she doesn't seem to have made any response to Duffin or Marsh about Marsh's racism; in fact, having heard their version of the breach first, she took their side and wrote to rebuke Raine for her "misunderstanding."

Raine fled to the Belcombes, whether for Mariana's support or her father's expertise as a mind-doctor. Around 31 October, apparently voluntarily, she entered Clifton House, the small private asylum outside York that Alexander Mather (known to Lister and Raine from the Manor School) and William Belcombe had opened the previous year. Raine now made a new will, dated 21 November, leaving almost everything to her former suitor John Alexander. (Duffin claimed she'd actually written it in late October, before going to Clifton, but had misdated it, rendering it invalid; later he burned this will, which I think may in fact have been a valid one.) Raine's last surviving letters to Lister at the end of 1814 were written with Mrs. Belcombe looking over her shoulder, so should be taken with a pinch of salt: they're full of apology for her rage, gratitude to the Belcombes for saving her life, and hopes of a rapid recovery from insanity.

To be strictly fair to Raine's relatives, friends, and medical staff: they didn't save her from the asylum, but I've seen no evidence that they forced or tricked her into it, or plotted to keep her there, whether out of hostility or with any view to stealing her money. For the first year or so, according to Duffin and Marsh (who now pitied Raine as mad rather than bad), her times of "wildness" alternated with stretches of lucid rationality. She often refused to see old friends, and never seems to have asked to leave Clifton House. Much of her behaviour around this time sounds merely unacceptable in a young lady—whims, obstinacy, cunning, verbal aggression—rather than proof of serious mental disturbance. Marsh was the only one who ever mentioned Raine's ethnicity, and only for a brief period in autumn 1814, but her virulence on the subject, for which no one seems to have taken her to task, suggests that racism at least contributed to the general interpretation of Raine's behaviour as pathological.

Lister was deeply shaken by Raine's condition and visited her on occasion when she came to York. Business-minded, she pushed for Raine to be declared a lunatic by an official commission so that once she was a Ward in Chancery, the Lord Chancellor could appoint guardians to manage her care and property. Lister proposed herself for this role, as the heir named in what she and Duffin assumed was Raine's only valid will. But after Raine's Commission of Lunacy was held in 1816, it was Lady Crawfurd who was made her personal guardian, with Duffin and Robert Swann the banker (father to her schoolmate Mary Swann) entrusted with her financial affairs.

It is tantalising to wonder whether Raine's worsening symptoms, as the years went by, were the result, rather than the cause, of her being locked up. And whether, if she'd been less of an oddity (as a rich biracial spinster in love with a woman) in Regency England, or had a loyal family or partner demanding and working for her release, she might—like many other asylum patients—have managed to rejoin society.

The year Jane Raine died of consumption, 1819, Lady

Crawfurd moved Eliza to live under the round-the-clock supervision of a Mrs. E. Barker and her daughters in Grove Cottage on Lord Mayor's Walk in York, in the vain hope that she might improve when away from "the insanes." In 1823, Lister describes Raine as frequently playing the piano there. But by her early forties—Marsh (now Duffin's second wife) blamed Raine's "change of life"—she was up so much at night, and spitting and lashing out so often, that the distressed Barkers put her in a straitjacket. In July 1835, the Duffins and Lister brought Raine back to Clifton House Asylum so she could be kept under "stronger control," which Lister was convinced saved Raine's life.

In 1839, Lister instructed the solicitor Jonathan Grey that in the event of Raine's death while Lister was abroad, he should make a claim to her estate on Lister's behalf. But it was Lister who died the following year, at forty-nine, on her travels with her partner Ann Walker (the last of some dozen lovers) in what is now Georgia.

John Swann (Mary's brother) replaced his father as Raine's property guardian, and Mrs. Marsh Duffin was the new personal guardian; she reported that Raine seemed happier. By 1840, Raine was in a new asylum, Terrace House in Osbaldwick outside York, but the 1841 Census recorded her as back in Clifton House; when it closed down in 1853, she was returned to Osbaldwick. Raine died of a stomach haemorrhage at sixty-nine, on the last day of 1860. In the absence of any heir, the estate of this "bastard and lunatic" (grown to some eight thousand pounds) went to the Crown.

Anne Lister changed my life. Back in 1990, ducking out of the rain into a Cambridge bookshop, I spotted one of those unmistakable Virago green spines, which turned out to be Helena Whitbread's groundbreaking first collection of decoded excerpts from Lister's journals, *I Know My Own Heart* (1988). This kick-started my career in three different ways. A paper I gave about Lister led to the commissioning of my first book, *Passions Between Women: British Lesbian Culture 1668–1801* (1993), an attempt to satisfy my curiosity about what this unique Regency Yorkshirewoman could have read that shaped her confident sense of her own "oddity." I loosely adapted Helena's collection into my first play, also called *I Know My Own Heart,* about Lister in her twenties. It was staged in 1991 as a graduate-student production, with me stepping in at the last minute to replace the actor due to play Isabella Norcliffe; Helena Whitbread not only came to see it, but introduced me to her agent, Caroline Davidson, who's guided my career ever since. The play got its professional premiere with Glasshouse Productions in Dublin in 1993; published in 2001, it can be found in my *Selected Plays.*

Then, in 1998, I was Writer in Residence at the University of York for two months, and my partner, Chris Roulston, was a Fellow of the Centre for Eighteenth Century Studies, with an office in King's Manor. When we realised that this was the building where Lister and Raine had shared a bedroom known as the Slope in 1805–6, I felt a sharp nudge and began to jot down my first ideas for this novel. So in a sense, *Learned by Heart* has been two and a half decades in the making, and I've been fascinated by Lister and her dozen or so lovers for more than three.

What's changed over that time is not just our culture's belated readiness for the extraordinary Anne Lister, but an exponential opening up of the primary and secondary sources. Mostly thanks to Sally Wainwright's brilliant BBC/HBO drama series *Gentleman Jack* (2019–22)—as unconventional as its subject, and all based on her own words—Lister is finally famous for her five-million-word diary, which UNESCO has named a National Treasure. Wainwright devoted the proceeds of a screenwriting award to digitising the journals and has funded a PhD scholarship for ongoing study of Lister; I know of no other showrunner who grasps so well how history and entertainment can work hand in hand, or who's done half as much for the archive on which she draws.

I want to thank Helena Whitbread for taking the time

to show Chris and me Shibden Hall and the Lister diaries at West Yorkshire Archive Service in Halifax in 2015, as well as answering my endless queries since then. Our friends Fiona Shaw (the writer) and Karen Charlesworth showed us around King's Manor, Holy Trinity Church, and other Lister haunts, and Professor Christopher Norton kindly gave me a painstaking architectural tour of King's Manor in 2022.

These days, those curious about Lister can turn to Whitbread's two volumes of selections from the 1817–26 diaries, Jill Liddington's three about 1833–38 (the basis for *Gentleman Jack*), and biographies by Anne Choma and Angela Steidele. The Lister fandom is exceptional in doing participatory research, so readers can now immerse themselves in her complete, unedited diaries online, transcribed by an international network of more than a hundred volunteer "Code Breakers" under the aegis of West Yorkshire Archive Service.

By comparison, Eliza Raine is still appallingly neglected. Some of her correspondence with Lister first saw the light in Muriel Green's 1939 thesis " 'A Spirited Yorkshirewoman': The Letters of Anne Lister of Shibden Hall, Halifax, 1791–1840," though Green did all she could to hide the fact that they were lovers. Many more letters were usefully transcribed by the late Patricia Hughes in a self-published 2010 study (*The Early Life of Miss Anne Lister and the Curious Tale of Miss*

Eliza Raine), which is unfortunately full of confusions and guesses presented as fact. There remain scores of crucial unpublished letters and other writings by, to, and about Raine, mostly from 1803 to 1815, which I've been able to study only thanks to the generous help of archivists and Code Breakers, including Jude Dobson, Steph Gallaway, Kerstin Holzgräbe, Jane Kendall, Livia Labate, Chloe Nacci, Marlene Oliveira, Jessica Payne, Alex Pryce, Amanda Pryce, Francesca Raia, Lynn Shouls, Shantel Smith, and Kat Williams. This is the first time in my career I've owed a debt to crowdsourced research, and I'm deeply grateful to Steph Gallaway of PackedWithPotential.org (a hub for all things Lister) for making it happen.

Diane Halford brought key material to my attention, and when I reached out to David Hughes on Twitter, he decoded and transcribed a journal passage for me overnight. Anne Choma let me pick her brains; Frances Singh—the scholar who discovered that Raine was sent to England at the age of six rather than eleven—showed me scans of passenger lists; Helena Whitbread, Christina Grass, and Carol Adlam (whose biography of Raine I anticipate with great excitement) shared with me invaluable unpublished material. But above all, I need to thank San Ní Ríocáin—@SRiocain on Twitter—who responded to my relentless questions over the course of a pandemic year and has somehow managed to establish accurate histories for everyone from William Raine and his Yorkshire family, to the Duffins, to Eliza's schoolmates, friends, and teachers.

As a biracial child of the Subcontinent, sent "home" to a Britain she'd never seen, Raine was isolated in York, but she was not unique. What some called "country marriage" or "concubinage" between a Company man and an Indian girl or woman (often known as his bibi) declined from extremely common to rare and stigmatised over her lifetime. (One in three Company men's wills from 1780 to 1785 included bequests to native companions, one in four in 1805–10, one in six by 1830, and very few by midcentury.) In this novel I've tried to fill gaps in the personal history that Raine kept under such tight wraps, and to do so, I've drawn on the widely varied fates of several hundred other eighteenth- and early-nineteenth-century children, including Sarah Rudd (sometimes called Redfield or Radfield) Thackeray Blechynden, half-sister to the novelist William Makepeace Thackeray; Margaret Stuart Tyndall-Bruce; Mir Glulum Ali, Sahib Allum, renamed William George Kirkpatrick, and Noor un-Nissa, Sahiba Begum, renamed Catherine/Kitty Aurora Kirkpatrick, later Phillips, as well as their cousins Cecilia and William Benjamin Kirkpatrick; Banu "Ann" de Boigne and Ali Baksh "Charles Alexander" de Boigne; the Indian children of Johan Joseph

Zoffany, the painter; the seven to ten children of Hercules Skinner; the eleven children (by two mothers) of Isaac Meyers; the seven children (by three mothers) of Henry Wray; the six or more children of Sir David Ochterlony by several of his thirteen concubines; the six children Gerard Gustavus Ducarel had with Sharaf-un-Nisa, renamed Elizabeth Ducarel, one of the handful of mothers who settled in England and had an Anglican wedding; and Jane Cumming Tulloch, witness in the Woods-Pirie trial of 1810 (inspiration for Lillian Hellman's 1934 play *The Children's Hour*). Very few of the bibis converted to Christianity; some of the children were raised Hindu or Muslim by their mothers, but most seem to have been baptised Anglican, with no mother named. Some fathers bequeathed part or all of their fortunes to their (a common phrase) "brown children"; others abandoned or denied any connection with them. J. A. Cock, Hugh Adams, and Samuel Kilpatrick left their companions money only on the cruel condition that they agree to hand over the children to be educated in England. For more on these mothers, sons, and daughters, I recommend Durba Ghosh's *Sex and the Family in Colonial India* (2006).

The many graffiti I quote can still be read on the windows of what's now called the Huntingdon Room at King's Manor, though the tiny panes seem to have been moved around. The dates range at least from the

1740s to the 1930s; they were first noted in print in *Yorkshire Notes and Queries* (1885–88) but are crying out for a complete transcription and analysis. The sole account I've found of being a pupil at the Manor School is by an Eliza Fletcher, who boarded there around 1781 (in the time of Ann Vaslet Hargrave, mother to Miss Ann Hargrave and Mrs. Mary Hargrave Tate, who were running the school in 1805). Among the forty or so pupils in 1805, contemporaries of Lister and Raine's age included Raine's first friend Frances Selby (later Thorpe), Margaret Burn (later Holmes), Elizabeth Foster, Ann Moorsom, and Frances Peirson, and I've drawn on what details San Ní Ríocáin and I could dig up about these real women. Mercy Smith, Hetty Marr, and Miss Dern are fictional, but one of the Percival sisters, Ann Georgina (aged seven), did die at the school in the spring of 1806.

On 10 January 1804, the teacher M. A. Lewin sent her friend Arthur Murphy (the Irish playwright) vivid details about the Manor, including its granary, its live-in pig, and several of her colleagues, as well as her and Mrs. Morrice's move north from Hammersmith; this sole surviving letter of hers was by great luck preserved in his 1811 biography, where San Ní Ríocáin found it. The music and drawing masters, Matthew Camidge and Joseph Halfpenny, had long and distinguished careers in York outside of their duties at the Manor. By 1823, Frances Vickers was running a boarding school on Coney Street, and Hannah Robinson was listed as a schoolmistress on St. Andrewgate. Mary Hargrave Tate's husband, the bankrupt dancing master, is very likely the same Thomas Tate who died in York Asylum (notoriously harsh under Dr. Hunter's rule) in 1808. I've borrowed other details of boarding-school life from the memoirs of Dora Wordsworth, Mary Botham Howitt, Samuel Taylor Coleridge, Mary Wright Sewell, Frances Power Cobbe, Elizabeth Missing Sewell, Eugénie Servant, and the Woods-Pirie trial of 1810.

In 1819, Lister mentioned in her diary that Alexander Mather had attended on Eliza at the Manor School and that Dr. Duffin thought him clever, but "in proof of the man's abilities I shammed Abraham for a week—he never found it out." (As surgeons by training, though working in general practise, Raine, Mather, and Duffin were properly addressed as Mr., whereas as a physician with a university medical degree, Belcombe was entitled to the superior title of Dr., but since Raine was sometimes called Dr. Raine in Indian sources, I have erased this confusing distinction and called them all Dr.)

There's no hard evidence of the lovers gate-crashing the Assembly Rooms, just a strong hint from Lister, who in 1831 recorded telling Vere Hobart about her maid Cameron going to a ball: "said what fun to go & dance with her in disguise—but I never did those things now... Spoke of going to a ball disguised (or at least insinuated more than said) when at the Manor. I meant that in the great old audience, there I was, in the room." Black's Rarities really were on show at the Sycamore Tree in York's Minster Yard at that time, and "first woman jockey" Alicia Thornton did lose due to a slipping sidesaddle at York Racecourse, though in 1804; in 1805, she came back and won.

My work converged with that of my beloved Chris Roulston in a joint obsession during the monotony of COVID-19, when I was drafting *Learned by Heart* and she was writing "Interpreting the Thin Archive: Anne Lister, Eliza Raine, and Telling School Tales" (*Eighteenth-Century Studies* 55, no. 2 [Winter 2022]) as well as editing (with Caroline Gonda) the first essay collection on Lister, *Decoding Anne Lister: From the Archive to* Gentleman Jack (Cambridge University Press, 2023). Chris is, as Lister said of books, "my spirit's oil without which its own friction against itself would wear it out"—and this one is dedicated to her.

ABOUT THE AUTHOR

Emma Donoghue is an Irish writer who lives in Canada. She spent eight years in Cambridge, England, completing a PhD, before moving to London, Ontario. Her international bestseller, *Room,* was a *New York Times* Best Book of 2010 and a finalist for the Man Booker, Commonwealth, and Orange Prizes, and its film adaptation received four Oscar nominations, including Best Picture and Best Adapted Screenplay. She co-wrote the Netflix film of *The Wonder,* starring Florence Pugh.